EYE OF STONE

MEGAN O'RUSSELL

Ink Worlds Press

DEDICATION

For those still learning to fight back

EYE OF STONE

CHAPTER ONE

Trapped. Caged in. Locked up.

I shook my arms out, trying to convince myself not to slip back into panic.

Watched. Helpless. Weak.

"Stop it, Lanni." I pushed myself off my bed and started pacing the length of the small room Mari and I shared. The walk from our kitchen to the closet wasn't far, but it only took three passes for the wound in my calf to start throbbing.

They'd pulled out the shrapnel from the bomb and patched me up, but I was still supposed to stay off my leg and give the ripped muscle time to heal.

I didn't care.

I would've sprinted around the domes if I could. I needed the pain. It gave me something to think about besides being locked in my room.

Trapped. Prisoner. Alone.

"Shit." I dug my fingers into my too-short hair as my breath started coming in shaky gasps. "Shit. Shit. Shit."

I sped up my steps. My calf seized, shooting pain into my ankle.

I needed to get to Mari. I needed to see Alec.

I needed to get out of my room.

But I couldn't. I'd been placed in lockdown. Confined to my room by the Domes Council.

All the teens who'd survived the atrium bombing had been placed in isolation. I didn't know why. The Council hadn't said if they were going to question us. Or kick us out of the domes. Or if being trapped in isolation for the past two days was our punishment for daring to question the Incorporation.

I gasped as the pain shot from my ankle to my hip.

"Shit." I sat back down on my bed, propping my bad leg up.

They'd taken Mari to stay with our guardian, Miranda. Mari was mine to protect, but they wouldn't let her stay with me. I had to be locked in alone. And I couldn't fight them. Not with the damage I'd already caused.

What if they decided to kick me out of the Arc Domes for creating too much trouble? What if they decided I was irresponsible and Mari should live with Miranda permanently? What if my fighting to keep Mari with me while I was locked up made them angry at Mari? What if the Council decided to punish her, too?

There was nothing I could do that wouldn't make things worse. So I'd just let them take my sister. Alec had promised he'd keep her safe. But there were monsters everywhere, and I'd just let her walk away.

Useless. Helpless. Alone.

"Fuck."

I pressed my fist to the wound on my calf. The blazing pain drowned out every other thought in my mind.

Two days. It had only been two days since the bomb went off in the atrium. I'd only been locked in my room alone for two days, and I was already losing it.

I got back off my bed and limped to the computer screen set into the wall. I tapped on the screen, but it stayed blank.

"Shit. Shit." I pressed my forehead against the wall. "PAM, can you still hear me? PAM?"

Silence.

"Isolation. The world's shittiest way to deal with traumatized people." I propped my foot up on Mari's bed and took a few deep breaths.

Gritting my teeth against the pain, I punched my calf four times. Stars zinged through my vision, and a scream dragged itself from my throat.

I closed my eyes, making sure I'd be steady enough to stay upright before taking my foot off Mari's bed. Hot agony sliced from my hip to my toes as soon as I put weight on my leg.

"PAM, call medical. I'm in need of a doctor's assistance."

A beep came from the wall. "Medical has been notified. Are you experiencing a medical emergency?"

"Not an emergency." I lowered myself to the floor. "Just urgent."

I closed my eyes and leaned back against Mari's bed.

Reckless. Impatient. Foolish.

"Stop it." I dug my knuckles into my temples.

Don't be so hard on yourself, a different voice spoke in my mind. Jaime's voice.

A pang tightened the knot in my chest.

You almost got blown up. You're allowed to not be okay.

"No, I'm not." Heat pressed against my eyelids. "I have to take care of Mari. I have to figure out how to protect her."

Jaime lifted my hands away from my head. *You have to heal. You have to wait and see what's coming next.*

"But the city through the tunnel was attacked," I whispered. "It was..."

I couldn't even whisper it to Jaime. If PAM was listening enough to hear I needed a doctor, she could still be listening. Or recording.

I know. Jaime kissed my forehead. *You are stronger than any monster, Lanni Sampson. Don't let them make you forget that.*

"Lanni Roberts." Someone knocked on the door. "Miss Roberts, are you conscious?"

"Yes." I opened my eyes, swallowing the grief that came with imaginary Jaime disappearing. "My leg hurts really bad. I think I need a doctor to look at it."

"We're coming in, Miss Roberts."

"Let me unlock—"

The regular deadbolt I'd turned from the inside twisted, and the new magnetic lock—the one the guards had added to the outside of the door so they could trap me—didn't make any sort of noise as they disengaged it before opening the door.

A guard stepped into my room. He looked around like he was searching for a threat, like forty-eight hours of isolation would have made me desperate enough to try and attack him with a kitchen knife, before stepping aside and letting a doctor come in.

"What happened?" The doctor set her med kit down and knelt beside me.

"I was walking, and my calf just really started to hurt." I pulled up the leg of my pants. The skin around my bandage was bright red. "I know I'm supposed to stay off it, and I have been trying."

"We need to get her down to the medical corridor." The doctor looked to the guard.

"You can't treat her here?" The guard narrowed his eyes at her.

"The wound could very well be infected," the doctor said. "Do you really want to risk the health of a young woman rather than let me take her downstairs to treat her properly?"

"I'll inform Captain Tate." The guard stepped out into the corridor. "Bring the gurney."

"Thanks." I kept my voice low. "I really appreciate you coming to help me."

"It's my duty to ensure a bountiful future for the domes." The doctor gave me a tight smile. "Keeping you healthy is in the Incorporation's best interest."

CHAPTER TWO

"Unfortunately, I'm going to need to go back in and do some more work on the muscles in your calf. The shrapnel penetrated deep enough to do some real damage, but you should be a lot further along in your healing by now." The second doctor I'd seen in the last hour tapped away on her computer screen. "Are you sure you didn't do anything to it?"

"I was locked in my room." I propped myself up on my elbows, which for some reason made being stuck on my stomach on a hospital bed seem less like I was begging for someone to come and attack me.

"Were you trying to exercise in your room?" The doctor looked at me, pursing her lips like she could taste my coming lie.

"I might have paced a little bit." I gave what I hoped looked like an apologetic smile. "I was going stir-crazy."

"Isolation will do that." She went to one of the three metal cabinets along the wall and started pulling out supplies. "We'll numb you up and do what we can to speed the muscles' regrowth. You're going to have to actually keep off of it this time."

"For how long? I want to go back into the guard training program as soon as I can."

The doctor froze, a syringe in one hand and a vial in the other. It looked like she made herself take a breath before turning to face me. "The guard training program is outside my purview. But I'd say at least four days keeping off of it entirely and another week before you can run."

"That's not too bad." I resisted the urge to jump off the bed and sprint from the room. "Hopefully, they'll let me out of isolation by then."

The doctor went back to pursing her lips as she filled the syringe.

"This might sound stupid"—I shifted my leg away from her—"but do you think you could ask my guardian to come sit with me while you work on my leg? The bomb in the atrium has me a little jumpy."

"The bombing's made everyone jumpy." The doctor set the vial down on the tray and went back to the cabinet. "You're not supposed to have contact with anyone."

I looked down at my hands. It had taken days for them to perfectly heal my skin after burns had covered most of my body. A ripped up muscle would be easier to fix than that. I'd be back in my room in an hour.

"I'd just really like to know if Gideon's alive, and I'd like my guardian to be here in case he isn't." I blinked, forcing the heat that pressed against my eyes to form tears. "He jumped on top of me to protect me from the bomb. When they locked me in my room, he was still in surgery. I don't even know if he's alive." Tears rolled down my cheeks.

The doctor set a tub of blue goo on the tray.

"He's my boyfriend." I waited until she was looking to swipe my tears away. "And if he's dead, it's my fault. Can you please just call my guardian?"

The doctor chewed her lips. "I'll ask Captain Tate to grant permission for your guardian to be present during your medical treatment. You are still a student. Traditionally, a parent would be allowed to be present."

"Thanks. Does..." I gripped the sheet below me as genuine fear prickled in my chest. "Does that mean Gideon didn't make it?"

The doctor clasped her hands together, staring at her thumbs. "As a doctor of the Arcadia Domes, I am not at liberty to discuss any *current patient's* medical condition without that patient's express permission. Even if that patient has also expressed an interest in your wellbeing."

A new stream of tears flooded down my cheeks. "Thank you."

"Hopefully, this will keep you from doing any more pacing." The doctor went out into the hall, letting the door swing shut behind her.

"He's alive." I lay down flat on the bed, letting my cheek press against the softness of the sheets. "You didn't get him killed."

One worry crossed off my list.

If I could see Miranda, I could make sure Mari was all right. If I could find a way to see Alec, I could find out if there had been any more news about the attack on the city, make sure the monsters weren't about to blast their way through the glass.

And then...I didn't know what the *and then* was.

I let out a long breath as my hands started to shake.

Bang. The sound echoed through my mind. I knew it wasn't real, but my heart still started to race.

I could smell it. The rancid, burning stench that had come from the bomb in the atrium. But blood had taken over the scent. Gideon's blood.

I hadn't smelled the actual blast at the depot. That bomb had been too well planted. It had blown up the underground fuel tanks. Everything was just fire.

Bang. I had been right next to the bomb before Gideon pulled me away. It was my fault the woman had dropped it.

A sob hitched in my throat.

It's my fault. All of it is my fault.

I made myself sit up.

I shook out my hands, trying to stop the panic from coming.

Fire. Blood. Fear.

I swiped the tears from my cheeks.

The woman had built the bomb, not me. She'd come to the atrium wanting to murder us all. It was her fault, not mine.

Victim. Casualty. Collateral damage.

"Shit." I pushed myself off the table. Pain shot up my leg as soon as I put pressure on it. "Shit." I paced along the side of the room, taking deep breaths, trying to stop the panic from growing.

"What do you think you're doing?"

I turned toward the door.

The doctor had a look of mixed shock and anger on her face as she hurried toward me. "Why are you off the bed?"

"Sorry." I pulled away from her, gasping as a fresh kind of pain came from stepping backward. "I just couldn't lie there. I'm sorry."

"Sit. Now." The doctor gripped my arm as she steered me toward the bed.

"Is my guardian coming?" I sat on the edge of the bed, pointing my foot to make the pain keep coming.

"No." The doctor helped me onto my stomach. "Captain Tate didn't agree."

"Okay." I lay face down on the bed. I didn't even know I'd been jiggling my leg until the doctor gripped my ankle.

"You have to relax," the doctor said. "If you can't do that for me, I'll have to give you a sedative."

"You can't." I pushed myself back up. "I have to be ready in case…"

"In case?" The doctor shifted my arms out from under me, laying me flat on my stomach.

"I don't know." My brain couldn't come up with a lie fast

enough. "So much has happened. I don't know what I'm supposed to be ready for next."

"Just take deep breaths. The only thing you have to worry about right now is letting your body heal." The doctor rolled my pant leg back up.

"Do you know how long they're going to keep us separated?" I asked as she swabbed my calf with something cold.

"That is not in my purview. Little pinch."

The jab of the needle barely registered over the throbbing in my leg.

"Are they deciding how to punish us?" I asked.

"Again, that is not in my purview."

"Right. Sorry."

I settled my head on top of my hands.

"Have you been sleeping well?" the doctor asked.

"What do you mean?" I winced at the unnatural feeling of the inside of my leg shifting.

"Have you been able to sleep since the bombing?"

"They took my little sister away." Tears burned in my eyes again. I hated myself for being so weak. "She's with our guardian, and I haven't been able to see her."

"Is that all?"

Something like pulling came from inside my leg.

"Does it matter?" I asked. "As soon as you're done with me, I'll go straight back to being locked in my room. I don't need sleep to stare at the wall."

"I'm not just trained to take care of my patients' bodies. I'm also here to look after your mental wellbeing." The doctor picked up a tiny tube of pink stuff. "Stress can do horrible things to a person."

"Being locked up away from my sister is making my stress worse. I can promise you that."

"The isolation—"

"Is outside your purview."

"Unfortunately, yes." She set the little tube down and picked up a tool that looked like pincers. "So, is missing your sister the only reason you can't sleep?"

"When I close my eyes, I see the woman's face, that guard. When the bomb fell out of her hand, her eyes got so wide. I think she was afraid. And then she was gone." The tugging inside my leg got worse. "I keep hearing the sound of the blast. Feeling Gideon's weight when he jumped on top of me. I survived the explosion at the depot, and the attack after. A lot more people died there, and it was awful. But for some reason, I can't shake this. Everything just cycles through my head over and over. And I can't stop hearing the bang. It's just a stupid sound, but I can't make it stop."

"There's nothing I can do about you being sent back to isolation." The doctor switched out the pincers for a fresh tube of pink. "However, as your doctor, I can recommend rigorous trauma counseling. Daily sessions would be in your best interest. I'll have you brought down here for our sessions *if* you agree to stick to my orders and stay off your leg."

"Okay, I'll do it." I agreed before I'd really thought it through.

Dumb move, Lanni. Talking to a kep doctor about being traumatized is a horrible and dangerous idea.

It'll be better than being locked up all alone.

"In that case, you're going to be issued a fancy pair of crutches to use for the next week." The doctor smeared blue goo on my calf. "Healing from a violent trauma, both physically and mentally, takes time. But you will make it to the other side of this."

"Thank you." I gnawed on the inside of my cheek.

"I'll go see about those crutches." The doctor set the goo back on her tray.

Someone knocked on the door. "Visitor to see Miss Roberts."

I pushed myself back up onto my elbows as the need to flee and the hope of seeing Mari smashed together in my chest.

"You can come in." The doctor pulled off her gloves.

I twisted around, trying to see if it was a horde of guards coming to haul me away, or Miranda with Mari in tow.

A woman with honey-blond hair came into the room instead.

"Director Holbeck." The doctor gave a nod almost like a bow.

"I hope I'm not interrupting." Director Holbeck breezed into the room like she wouldn't have cared if she'd been interrupting a major surgery. "I heard Lanni Roberts had been brought to medical and didn't want to miss this opportunity."

"We were actually just finishing up." The doctor gave another nod and a tight smile. "I was on my way to get my patient some crutches so she can protect her leg."

"You poor thing." Holbeck frowned at me before shooing the doctor toward the door. "I'll keep her company while you go find crutches."

"Of course." The doctor left the room, abandoning me with Holbeck without a backwards glance.

"I've only been on crutches once." Holbeck went to the corner to grab a rolling chair. She pulled it over and sat right beside me. The scent of flowers wafted off her, like she was wearing the kind of fancy oil the people in the lux district back home could afford. "They were horrible. I'd broken my ankle in training. I swear, my hands hurt worse than the bone break."

"I'm only on them for a week, and I'm not really going anywhere these days." I twisted around to sit, keeping my leg propped up.

"You aren't. And believe me, it wasn't an easy decision for me to make."

"You put us in lockdown?" My heart hitched, skipping a beat as panic shot through me. I didn't know who Director Holbeck was. She didn't have a shiny nametag on, or even a uniform. But the clothes she wore were subtly nicer than a normal kep's. The fabric looked softer somehow, and the cut less generic. But why would a woman in fancy clothes decide to trap a bunch of teens in isolation? "I thought the order came from Captain Tate, ma'am."

"Captain Tate has been enforcing the house arrest, but I'm the one who gave the order." Holbeck leaned toward me and spoke in a whisper. "She was none-too-pleased with my interference, but we all must do what's best for the Incorporation."

"Always." Sour rolled into my throat as I tried to sound earnest.

"Usually, we prefer to let the Domes Council of each location decide what's best for their people. The community the citizens have built in every site is unique in some small way. The Domes Councils know their homes better than we do."

Than we *do. Shit.*

Sweat beaded on my palms.

"But sometimes, when things go awry, we decide it's time to step in. Like I did with you and your peers. I had to send that order straight from the top." Holbeck pointed up, toward the literal Incorporation Headquarters built into the mountain above the Arc Domes. She gave a little laugh at her own joke.

I tried to laugh back, but I couldn't make the sound come out.

"Do you know why I had to order the house arrest, Lanni?" Holbeck asked.

"No, ma'am."

"I don't want a stock response from you. I want to know why you think you've been isolated."

"It was all of us who were in the atrium when the bomb went off. We had—"

Bang.

I shook my head as the sound of the explosion resonated through my mind again. "We were there to talk about Dr. Kain's work. I think we were sent into isolation as punishment, or to give you time to decide how to punish us."

"Punish you for what?" Holbeck furrowed her brow.

"For—" I pressed my palms to the bed, trying to hide their sweating and stop them from shaking.

I didn't know what answer I was supposed to give. I needed

Alec to tell me what to say. Or Walsh to come up with a plan. Or Harper...

I made my breath hitch in my throat and let my chin wobble. "For gathering to talk about Dr. Kain's work without going to the Council first. It's just...after the fire, I wanted to know who she'd been, and I read her work and I got so scared. And then Gideon..." I dissolved into hysterical tears, hoping crying about my boyfriend who'd risked his life to save me would be enough to make the questions stop.

"Oh, Lanni. You've been through too much. You poor thing." Holbeck reached into her pocket, pulling out a handkerchief and passing it to me.

I wiped my face. "Thanks."

"But you've got it all wrong." Holbeck patted my knee. "I don't want to punish any of you. Every one of the survivors of that horrible guard's attack needs to be protected and helped. What you don't see is the threat that could do far more damage to the domes, to the Incorporation and all of you, than that bomb managed."

"What?" I looked to the door before I could stop myself, tensing as I prepared for a pack of werewolves to come charging in, longing to spill my blood.

"Misinformation." Holbeck leaned sideways, placing herself in my line of sight. "I've already spoken to Gideon—"

"He's awake?" I looked back toward Holbeck.

"And terribly concerned for your wellbeing." Holbeck winked at me. "What Gideon wanted to do, making sure his peers were educated on the work of the late Dr. Kain, was a very admirable goal. But, as so often happens with the young, bright, and passionate, he didn't take the time to really understand the consequences of his actions."

"We didn't know there would be a bomb."

"Of course not. None of you can be blamed for the violence of that deranged woman."

I should be. I knew what we were risking. It's my fault. All of it's my fault.

"But not considering the consequences of speaking about Dr. Kain's propagation program without any context?" She patted my knee again. "That was a very foolish and damaging thing to do."

"I'm sorry."

"It's not your fault Gideon decided to rally his peers. But after the lies that woman spouted before she murdered innocent children—"

"Who died?" I twisted the handkerchief.

"Elliot and Casey didn't make it." Holbeck shook her head. "It's an unforgiveable tragedy."

Elliot, I knew. Casey, I didn't. At least not by name.

"That woman told you terrible lies about the events at the River Domes, and then she killed two of your peers," Holbeck said. "I had to make sure the spread of misinformation didn't infect the rest of the Arcadia Domes. Can you understand that?"

"I suppose. But how long do we have to stay isolated? We all heard what she said. We can't unhear it."

"Of course not." Holbeck stood and shifted to sit beside me on the bed. "Soon, you should all be able to go back to class just like before."

"Good." I let out a shaky breath. "That's good."

"I wish it could be sooner, but I'm starting a new program, and I want all the details in place before we give the announcement to everyone in the Arcadia Domes at the same time. That way, we can make sure there are no more nasty rumors confusing people."

She paused like she wanted me to say something.

"I look forward to hearing the announcement."

"It's better than that, Lanni." Holbeck put her arm around my shoulders, surrounding me with her fake scent. "I didn't come down here today just to check on you. I'm here because you're going to play a very exciting role in the new program."

"What sort of role?" I pressed a smile onto my face even as my hands started to go numb and the walls seemed to shift like they were closing in.

"You're going to be one of our two peer spokespeople, helping your age group step into their new roles with hope in their hearts and the good of the Incorporation at the very front of their minds. Dr. Kain's work will lead us into a prosperous and healthy future, Lanni. And the children this program helps to conceive will have you to thank for showing their parents the way."

CHAPTER THREE

The cold of the bathroom floor didn't make the dry heaving stop.

After a full night of vomiting, I had nothing left in my stomach. No tears left to cry, either. But I couldn't stop shaking and heaving. I couldn't make the sobs stop breaking in my throat. I couldn't get Director Holbeck's face out of my mind.

The way she'd smiled at me when she said she'd have the talking points and new clothes brought to my room so I'd be ready to stand in front of my peers. The way she winked when she said she knew she could count on me.

I should have stabbed her with one of the doctor's tools. Driven a scalpel right into Holbeck's neck and been done with it.

But I was a coward with too much to lose.

Helping Holbeck would get Mari home. And if I refused, if Holbeck looked as deeply into my files as the bomber had...

That guard knew. She knew I wasn't supposed to be in the domes. She was going to say it in front of the others. Tell them all I was an outsider.

I'd had to stop her from telling them. I didn't have a choice.

I'd just wanted to shut her up. I needed to get the gun away from her, but she dropped that stupid bomb.

Bang.

Elliot and Casey were dead. Two people had died because I needed to keep my secret.

Holbeck had come down from Incorporation Headquarters because the mess in the Arcadia Domes had gotten too bad for the people at the top to ignore.

It was my fault. I'd made the guard drop that bomb.

Because of me, Project Progeny was going to be announced today.

The heaving got worse. My head pounded like it was going to explode.

It should have. I wanted it to. I should have died in the atrium bombing. Not Elliot or Casey. If Gideon hadn't protected me, I *would* have died. Everything would still be my fault, but at least I wouldn't know about it if I was dead.

Mari. You have to protect Mari. Her life is worth more than anything else. Her safety is more important than your guilt.

The sobbing got worse. I thought my ribs would break.

My hands shook as I crawled into the shower. I managed to reach high enough to turn the tap on. I kept the water cold, trying to shock my system out of the mind-eating panic.

I should have been the one to die.

"Fuck." I dug my knuckles into my eyes.

You have to survive, Jaime whispered in my mind. *You're a prisoner, Lanni. Your cage is pretty, you can't see your chains, but you're still their prisoner. You can't blame yourself for doing whatever it takes to fight through another day. You're back in the cement box. Your only duty is to survive.*

"Then you should be here to save me." I tipped my face up into the water.

I wouldn't have made it this far. I have too bad a temper to think before I fight.

"You really do." I pushed my hair away from my face.

But you don't, Lanni. The kep are just another monster hiding in the shadows.

"The monsters we faced were never my fault."

Neither is this one. Jaime touched my cheek.

In that moment, I would have given everything just to feel his fingers trail along my skin. Just to know for one minute, one second, that Jaime was with me.

You got caught in the middle of this nightmare, Lanni. You aren't the one who started it.

"What am I supposed to do?" The words caught in my throat.

Whatever it takes to survive.

"I don't know if I can."

You don't have a choice.

"Jaime—"

Start with a shower. Get cleaned up. Get ready for Holbeck's people to arrive. That's easy, isn't it? You can shower.

"Yeah." I pushed myself to my feet. My legs shook. I gasped as pain stabbed through my calf. "I can shower."

I pulled off my sopping clothes, tossing them into a pile on the bathroom floor.

"I'm not sure if you would laugh at a shower or rip it apart." I scrubbed my arms, trying to make sure Holbeck hadn't left any of her scent on my skin. "The amount of water I'm wasting, you could have been rich from selling it in the trade hall."

I waited to hear Jaime laugh, but he stayed silent.

"Don't leave me." I leaned against the shower wall. "Jaime, please don't leave me. I need you to stay."

You should be careful about having too many conversations with the voice in your head. He didn't even try to hide his laughter. *I think the kep frown on delusions ruining their perfect citizens. I can't stay forever.*

"I know." I scrubbed the soap out of my hair. "But I really need you right now."

Okay. Jaime leaned against the shower wall. *I could've eaten for a month off selling the water you're sending down the drain.*

"We could've eaten real fruit, maybe even dried meat. They only eat fresh meat here. You'd love the fish we get."

Does it taste like anything other than salt?

We talked about the dome food while I towel-dried my hair. I knew Holbeck was sending clothes for me, but I got dressed anyway. I don't know if I was being defiant or just didn't want to sit in my room in a towel.

I made myself a breakfast of bland oats and sat staring at the bowl for a long time, trying to convince myself to eat.

Being hungry will only make you less prepared for whatever comes next. Jaime tapped the side of my bowl.

"I know what comes next." Nausea rolled through my empty stomach.

Do you really? I thought you only knew what Holbeck told you would happen.

"It's the same thing." I made myself swallow a bite of the now cold slop.

Keep going. No matter what, you have to keep going.

"Is that about the food, or becoming one of the monsters?" I pushed my bowl away. The tiny bit of food I'd eaten was already making me feel the need to puke again. "I'm not like them. I can't—"

A sharp knock came from the hall.

"I'm coming." I put my bowl in the sink.

Once again, the deadbolt turned before I reached for it.

I opened the door, expecting to find a guard, but instead, a plain-clothed woman with a cheerful smile and a beautiful face stood flanked by two guards in charcoal-gray uniforms.

"Lanni." The woman beamed as she peeked over my shoulder. "It's so nice to meet you. Is there someone in here with you? I heard you talking to—"

"Myself." I tried to smile, but my face couldn't manage it.

"They locked me in here alone with nothing to do except talk to myself. The doctor said she was going to take me for therapy, but—"

"I'm glad you've found a way to pass the time." The woman shooed me farther into my room. "It's unfortunate they had to cut off all communication. If you'd still had a tablet, or access to PAM, I could've gotten your script to you more quickly."

"Script?"

The woman snapped her fingers and one of the guards passed her a tablet. "Director Holbeck had planned on providing talking points, but given the format of the announcement, some scripted remarks ended up being the best choice."

"I'm sorry, I'm very confused."

"That's why the speech was chosen." She snapped over her shoulder again. "Hang the clothes in the closet."

Another gray-uniformed guard squeezed past us, carrying clothes that hung inside protective bags.

"Sit, sit." She pointed to one of the two chairs Mari and I had.

I was surprised she didn't snap.

"I'll get your hair done while you read over the script, and then we'll worry about your clothes and face." She pursed her lips as she studied my hair.

"Some of it got burned off in the fire that destroyed Dr. Kain's house." I touched the ends of my still-damp hair.

"I told you to sit." She said it cheerfully, but the brightness of her tone was almost worse than if she'd been screaming.

"Sorry." I sank into the chair.

"We'll get it trimmed up, and everything will be fine."

"Ma'am—"

"Miss Leigh." She patted my shoulder.

"Miss Leigh," I began again. "I don't mean to be rude, but everyone's already seen my hair the way it is. Does it really need to be trimmed?"

Miss Leigh gave a cheerful laugh. "Your peers in the Arcadia

Domes have seen your hair the way it is. But your speech today needs to be a shining beacon worthy of being preserved for posterity. And, while Project Progeny is beginning here, with any luck, the program will be implemented in all domes locations soon enough. The video we record today will be seen all over the world. You, little miss, are changing the lives of thousands. You are such a lucky girl."

I bolted to the bathroom as fast as my injured leg would allow, throwing up the little bit of breakfast I'd managed to eat.

"Let it out. Nerves are only natural," Leigh said. "Don't forget to brush your teeth. You need a sparkling smile for the cameras."

CHAPTER FOUR

W*hen I was young, my title was* orphan. *I was abandoned and alone. An expendable child.*

But I survived. I grew. And when I was finally strong enough to stand up for myself, I became formidable. *Then they called me* brave *or* dangerous. *Some used both titles at the same time.*

Then I heard the name Alliance *whispered on the wind.*

Warriors who would defy the monsters who wanted to slaughter us for the mere crime of existing. A group bound together by the simple, common goal of defending the people the world had deemed unworthy of survival.

The Alliance would stand against the Incorporation's butchers. They would fight against the beasts who slaughter children and mothers and fathers and lovers. They would offer me vengeance in the form of reshaping the world with a hope for a better tomorrow.

I found the Alliance, and I was called soldier. *I welcomed the changes they offered and joined the pack. Then I became* brother.

Now I am alone again. Isolated. Back to where I started at the boys' home.

The monsters call me worthy *for having obeyed their rules. They call me* promising *because they think I fight on their side. They call me* needed *because they want me to do an unthinkable thing to help them build a future I will burn.*

When the Alliance sent me into the monsters' den, they didn't know the worst horror I would be facing.

Defiler. Victim. Father. To fight against those words would be to destroy the mission my pack is depending on me to achieve.

I would ruin the things I want to be.

I am trapped and alone, and the words will not stop pounding through my head. I am willing to give my life, but I don't know if I can betray the person I have fought so long to become. I cannot become the monster I hate.

I am lost, and I am afraid.

I wish you were here to help me. I am not strong enough to stand against these shadows alone.

See you in the embers,

~C

Leigh kept pursing her lips and tsking as I followed her through the corridors of the Arc Domes. I wasn't sure if she was angrier about my slow pace or my crutches wrinkling my shirt. By the time we'd made it to the three flights of stairs I'd have to manage to climb to reach the atrium, she'd had enough.

"Just carry her." She snatched my crutches from me and glared at the guards. "I don't care which one, but someone pick her up and carry her. Now."

One of the gray-clad guards stepped forward. "Is it only your leg that's injured?"

"Basically." I shrank away from the guard without even meaning to.

"Good." He scooped me into his arms. "We're ready."

"If the Director is mad that we're running behind—"

I didn't listen to the rest of Leigh's angry muttering. I was too busy trying to convince myself not to fight my way out of the guard's arms.

He'd been careful when he picked me up, not even bumping my hurt leg. He kept my head well away from the wall as he climbed the stairs. But something about him holding me to his chest made me want to scream. Alec had carried me the same way. Alec had held me, and everything had gotten less terrifying.

I'd felt safe. Like I wasn't completely alone.

But with the guard, all I could feel was trapped and belittled.

Jaime. Jaime, I don't want to do this alone. Jaime!

Please.

I couldn't pull him back into my mind. Not with the guard cradling me.

I shut my eyes, running through what I could remember of the speech I had to give. Leigh had told me I would be able to read off of something but not where the words would be, or how many cameras there would be, or why anyone would care what a teenager had to say about the new torment the Incorporation had decided to unleash on its own fucking citizens.

"After I do this, I'll get to see my sister?" I asked as we reached the last flight of stairs leading up to the atrium.

"That's not my department," Leigh said.

"I'm getting a lot of that lately."

I smelled the atrium before I saw it. The scent of the trees and the stream filtered down into the stairwell. No hint of blood or smoke tainted the air.

Anger surged in my gut, making me wish I could puke again just to spatter the back of Leigh's hair with vomit. But my rage crumpled as the guard carried me into the atrium.

The trees were perfect. They'd already erased every trace of the bomb's blast. But the screams echoed in my ears, and the bang shook through my mind, forcing sense aside.

"Are you all right?" The guard looked down at me. "Miss Leigh, she's shaking."

Leigh spun toward me. "What's wrong with you?"

I bit the insides of my cheeks and dug my nails into my palms, trying to hide the fear I couldn't find a way to control.

There, on the ground, that's where Elliot had been shot. Had the dart been filled with poison? Was that what had killed him?

Or had he only been tranqued and shrapnel from the bomb had killed him?

I didn't know which face had belonged to Casey or where in the group she'd been standing. Had her body been torn apart by a swarm of deadly metal, or had one tiny piece of shrapnel hit her in just the right place to end her life?

I realized I was gasping as my lungs started throbbing.

There. That's where I'd fallen. Gideon had tackled me. His blood had been on my face. So much blood all over his back.

"Lanni!" Leigh patted my cheek. "Pull yourself together. You have a job to do."

"Why here?" My voice came out tight and small. "Why do we have to do this here?"

"Do you want to disappoint Director Holbeck?" Leigh narrowed her eyes at me. "After she came down from Incorporation Headquarters to give you the honor of helping your fellow—"

"I don't want to disappoint Director Holbeck." I reached for my crutches. "I just almost died right over there a few days ago, and I'm not really over it yet."

"Of course." Leigh's glower shifted into what I think she meant to be a sympathetic smile. "We'll get this done, and then you can go home and rest."

"Thanks."

The guard set me down, and Leigh let me have my crutches back. I followed behind her as we cut toward the far side of the dome away from the glass that looked out over the valley.

We passed the place where I'd been standing with Alec when I'd found out the Plains Domes had slaughtered most of the people back home.

Jaime. Mom. I still didn't know if they were alive or dead. I'd probably never know.

Panic pinched in my chest. The Incorporation destroyed everything in their path. And I'd agreed to help the demons.

Mari. Mari. Do this, and you can see Mari.

A horde had gathered at the far corner of the atrium, crowding around the entrance to Incorporation Headquarters.

Just get through until you can see Mari. You can face anything if it means protecting Mari.

They'd set up two rows of chairs in the front, but most of the people stood behind. All of them looked tense or afraid. A few people whispered to their neighbors, but there was no happy chatter or murmurs of intrigue.

A banner had been hung above a shiny, wooden podium. A picture of a man and a woman positioned on either side of a tree.

An older man stood next to Director Holbeck. They waited near the podium, both looking pleased with themselves as they spoke in low voices.

"Lanni!"

I looked toward the sound.

Gideon sat in a wheelchair tucked in the far corner. His face was pale, and they'd shaved off all his hair, but he smiled like he was relieved to see me.

I moved as fast as my crutches would allow, propelling myself toward him.

He winced like he was trying to hide his pain as he gripped the arms of his wheelchair and pushed himself to his feet.

"Careful, son." Captain Pace took Gideon's elbow.

"Gideon." A combination of guilt and relief dragged tears to my eyes as I finally made it to him.

He reached toward me, a smile lighting his face like I was an angel come to offer him redemption. "You're okay." He brushed his fingers along my cheek. "They told me you'd made it, but I couldn't"—his words caught in his throat—"you're okay?"

I leaned my crutches against the wall and took Gideon's face in my hands. "I'm so sorry." I touched the shiny patch of skin beside his right eye. "I never wanted you to get hurt. You shouldn't have protected me like that."

He pulled me into his arms, holding me close to his chest and burying his face in my hair.

"I don't want any of this," he whispered. "You have to believe me. I don't have any other choice."

I nestled my face against his neck. "Me neither."

He tightened his hold on me.

"How sweet." Director Holbeck spoke as though wanting to make sure at least the nearest section of the crowd could hear her. "Strength after tragedy. That spirit is what the Incorporation was built upon. Being tormented by the destruction of our planet and finding a way not only to endure, but to thrive."

Gideon kissed my temple. "I'm sorry." He held me for one more moment before pulling back.

"After the horrible violence I witnessed in this very atrium, I understand now more than ever how delicate and precious life within the domes really is." Gideon spoke even louder than Holbeck had. "As someone privileged enough to have been born in the Arcadia Domes, it is my duty and honor to offer every bit of myself to ensure the preservation of our home."

"Wonderful." Holbeck beckoned us forward.

I glanced toward the crowd. Hundreds of people were already staring at us.

"Can you walk?" I whispered to Gideon.

"Just let me hold onto you."

I gripped his hand, flexing my arm to support him like a cane, ignoring the pain in my leg that came with every other step.

Holbeck bowed us toward the podium.

It had only been set up with one microphone meant for Gideon and me to share. Two people with cameras stood in the center of the crowd, ready to record us so our message could be sent out to torture people around the world.

Just in front of the cameramen, a screen had been set up.

Gideon: Thank you all for gathering here today.

Gideon swayed as he read the screen.

"Can you get through this?" I whispered.

He looked at me, studying my face for a moment. "I have to."

He gave me a tight smile before shifting his weight forward to lean on the podium with his free hand. He didn't pull his other hand away from me. I don't know which of us was holding on tighter, only that I didn't think I'd be able to stay on my feet if he abandoned me.

Gideon looked at me one more time and let out a long breath before turning to the crowd.

"Thank you all for gathering here today. In the past week, the Arcadia Domes have suffered two terrible tragedies," Gideon said. "Our Outer Guard were brutally attacked by insurgents in the city they have sacrificed so much to protect. And right here, in this very atrium, one of our own turned against us."

He's alive. He didn't die to save me. I gripped Gideon's hand, needing to prove to myself that he was real.

"After plotting to destroy Incorporation resources and spread dangerous misinformation, a coward took her own life in the attack, slaughtering two of my peers in her own selfish act of violence," Gideon pressed on.

He didn't say her name. I'd never heard anyone say the guard's name. It was like they were trying to erase who she'd been. Part of me thought it was justice. Part of me knew the Incorporation was trying to hide the horrible things they'd done by wiping out the memory of the woman they'd driven to such awful desperation.

"The losses we have sur"—Gideon stumbled over the words—"The losses we have suffered over the past year have endangered all of the Incorporation's citizens. The losses the Arcadia Domes have suffered this week have forced us to reimagine our future within these domes. Every day, when I wake up breathing clean air, go downstairs to eat a breakfast of healthy food, and go to school where I am given the best education this world has to offer, I remind myself how lucky I am to be a citizen of the Incorporation.

"But the Arcadia Domes were not built for my comfort. All of us are living in a lifeboat, built by the founders of the Incorporation to give mankind a hope for survival. We are here so that years from now, a generation of healthy humans will be able to walk out into the world and begin to rebuild what was lost to greed, ignorance, and evil." He straightened up, speaking with conviction. "In all things, it is our duty to consider the generation that, years from now, will be the hope for a new world. That is why we are here. That is why the Arcadia Domes must survive.

"The tragedies we have endured will never be forgotten." His voice caught in his throat. "But we will press on, and we will succeed." My fingers throbbed as he doubled his grip on my hand. "Just as the Incorporation asked the original citizens to sacrifice their freedom to live inside the domes, we now ask our peers to give their all to provide what is necessary for our mission to succeed."

People started clapping. I didn't know why.

Gideon turned to me, shifting aside to place me closer to the microphone.

I looked to the screen.

Lanni: Dangerous rumors have been spreading through the Arcadia Domes.

Be excited, be determined, be present. That's what Director Holbeck wanted.

I just wanted to get Mari back.

"Dangerous rumors have been spreading through the Arcadia Domes," I began. "After witnessing firsthand the damage misinformation can cause, I am honored to have been asked to speak by Director Holbeck. I am here not only to tell you that all of us who were injured in the bombing in this very atrium will recover and be stronger than we were before, but also to have the honor of announcing Project Progeny."

A little gasp came from the crowd. I looked toward the sound but couldn't see who had made it. There were too many faces.

Most of them were adults, but there were other teens, too. The ones who hadn't been in the atrium and hadn't been put in lockdown.

A pack of guards stood in the middle.

My breath hitched in my chest as I found Alec in the horde of kep.

I met his gaze. There was pain in his eyes and fear. For one foolish moment, I thought he would run up to the podium and rescue me. But he just tightened his jaw and kept staring at me.

"Lanni," Gideon whispered.

I tried to take a breath to keep speaking, but the air got stuck in my throat.

A little movement in the crowd caught my eye.

Walsh. He shifted his weight. His hands were flexing in front of him almost like he was preparing to attack. He looked at me. There was a question in his eyes, but I didn't know what it was. I couldn't trust him enough to believe he wanted to help me anyway.

"Lanni," Gideon whispered again.

"I'm okay," I said it loud enough for my voice to carry through the microphone.

Walsh shook his head, wincing as he tucked his hands behind his back.

"Project Progeny is a way for my generation to help rebuild the population of the Arcadia Domes, allowing us to move forward as a healthy and thriving community." I kept my gaze fixed on the screen. "When I first heard of the program, I'll admit, I was scared. In looking at the concept of planned copulation from an uneducated point of view, the prospect seemed terrifying. But after speaking at length with Director Holbeck, I'm now certain there's nothing to be afraid of."

Gideon let go of my hand. For a horrible second, I thought he was abandoning me, but he wrapped his arm around my waist, holding me close to his side.

"Over the coming days, all Arcadia Domes citizens between the ages of seventeen and twenty-seven will be separated into groups. Each group will represent a different phase of Project Progeny," I said.

Gideon's name flashed on the screen.

"We have to make sure we stagger our new arrivals for the sake of our medical staff." Gideon kept his voice light, like he was telling a joke.

"Within each group," I read, "we'll all be assigned a partner. Think of it like any other project you've been given for the good of the domes."

I reached across Gideon, grasping his free hand.

Bang. The remembered sound pulsed through my mind. *Bang.*

"The assigned intercourse will take place in a safe and medically appropriate environment. The timing of the pairings will be carefully supervised to ensure maximum possibility of conception." My voice came from far away. I wasn't the one speaking. I had to believe it wasn't actually me saying those words. "Once one group achieves conception, the project will move on to the next group in line, and those who have completed their copulation cycle will be able to return to their normal partners."

Gideon pulled me back so my shoulder pressed against his. I wasn't sure if he was swaying or I was. I don't think either of us could have stayed standing on our own.

"A little time apart from each other," Gideon said. "A tiny sacrifice to ensure the future we're all here to protect. As someone who has spent his life striving to become an Outer Guard, I have long known that I may someday be asked to give my life for the good of the Incorporation. And now I have the honor of helping the Incorporation to create life. Project Progeny is an endeavor that will bring joy and prosperity to us all. And I, for one, am grateful for the privilege of being a part of this groundbreaking program."

CHAPTER SIX

They put Gideon back in his wheelchair as soon we were done speaking. They kept him on the other end of the line of people behind the podium, as far away from me as the guard who had taken my crutches could manage. My leg burned and my chest ached like someone had punched through my ribs and flattened my heart.

I tried to focus on what Director Holbeck was saying as she addressed the crowd. But a high-pitched buzzing filled my brain, and I couldn't hear past the sound. The noise of it dug down into my spine. I almost missed the bang that had haunted me for days.

A doctor spoke after Director Holbeck. I couldn't hear him either.

I watched Alec. He didn't flinch at whatever the Director and the doctor said. Not a single raised eyebrow or clenched jaw. He'd turned to stone. I wanted him to look at me. I wanted to scream to the crowd that I was sorry for all the things I'd read off that damn screen.

Alec never looked my way.

I caught Walsh watching me. He held my gaze for a moment, but then just shook his head and melted into the crowd.

After the doctor, Captain Tate stepped up to the microphone. When she'd finished speaking, the crowd dispersed. Some practically running, others lingering nearby, like they were hoping someone would announce the whole thing had been a joke.

I crutched toward Gideon. His two guards had already started pushing him away.

"Wait." I gave up on the crutches and limped after them. "Gideon, please wait!"

"Lanni." He twisted in his seat, gasping like even that small movement had hurt him. "Just give us a minute," he begged his guards. But they kept pushing him away.

"I just want to talk to him." I picked up my pace, ignoring the heat tearing through my calf.

"I did what you—"

"You're not supposed to be on that leg!" the doctor who'd treated me shouted, blocking out Gideon's words. "Someone carry this girl. She obviously can't be trusted on her own."

A guard I'd never seen before scooped me into his arms while another grabbed my crutches from me.

"Alec Quinn." I tried to wriggle out of the guard's arms. "Where's Guard Quinn? He can carry me."

"Let's just get you home." The guard tightened his grip on me.

"Let go of me." I pushed against his chest.

"Don't make this harder on anyone," the guard said.

I looked up at his face.

He was young, probably only twenty-three or twenty-four. Definitely under twenty-seven. He'd be placed in a group. If he had a girlfriend or a wife, she'd be placed in a group, too.

I stopped struggling. "I'm sorry," I whispered my apology.

"We all must do our duty to the domes." The guard carried me toward the stairs leading out of the atrium.

"Lanni." Leigh caught up to us before we could escape. "You did a fine job." She gave me a pinched smile, like she had another description she'd rather have used. "We're going to be using you for some posterity pictures later this week. PAM will let you know when the session is scheduled."

"Are they sending my sister home?" I asked.

"That's not really my decision," Leigh said.

"If you want me to smile in any of your fucking pictures, my sister will be home tonight." I turned away from Leigh, wishing I could walk away but still trapped in the guard's arms.

"I'll give Director Holbeck your request," Leigh said.

The guard carried me down the steps.

"Are you Dome Guard or Outer Guard?" I shifted, trying to see the badge on his chest.

"Dome," he said.

"Do you know when they're letting us out of lockdown?" I asked.

"You didn't listen to Captain Tate?" the guard carrying my crutches asked.

"I couldn't concentrate."

Crutch guard gave a single *ha* of a laugh.

"You'll be out of lockdown and back to school tomorrow," the guard carrying me said. "You're still grounded for tonight, and there are limits on gatherings. The Dome Guard will be actively patrolling as well."

"Patrolling." I tensed. "Where?"

"Everywhere," crutch guard said.

I didn't talk to them again except for a quick *thanks* as they locked me back in my room.

I sank onto the kitchen floor, just far enough from the door that it could swing open without hitting me.

The Dome Guard were going to be patrolling, keeping watch on their own people. They'd learned from the bomber. Push far enough and even kep will break.

I locked my fingers through my hair, pulling at the roots.

Bang.

I froze at the noise. It wasn't inside my head, but it didn't have the right resonance to be an explosion.

Footsteps pounded toward my door.

"Open it!" Mari shouted in the hall. "Open it. Open it!"

"Mar!" I was halfway to my feet when the door opened.

Mari launched herself at me, knocking me backward onto the ground.

"Careful. She's been injured," Miranda warned.

But Mari didn't hear her, and I didn't care.

I clung to my little sister as she lay sprawled on top of me, sobbing into my shoulder.

"You're okay, Mar." I kissed the top of her head. "You're okay."

"They took me away," Mari coughed through her tears. "I wanted to see you, and they said no. And they didn't tell me when I could come home or if I'd get to come home. And I never want to be where you're not. Not ever. And I tried to come home. I promise I tried. I snuck out and everything, but I got caught and they carried me back. I wanted to be here with you more than anything. And you were hurt and I needed to help you and they wouldn't let me. And..."

She kept talking, but I couldn't understand her words over her sobs. It didn't matter. I knew what all the words meant.

We were supposed to stay together. That was the deal we'd made when we'd left everything we'd known behind.

Mari and I were supposed to be able to cling to the one thing we had left. And the domes had taken her from me. They'd stolen my little sister, and there hadn't been anything I could do about it.

I rested my cheek on top of her head, my tears slipping into her hair as she gave up on words and just wept.

Miranda left a package of food on the counter and crept out so the guards could lock Mari and me in for the night.

Mari and I were still lying on the floor when she finally cried herself to sleep. I lifted her into bed and curled up behind her.

I lay there for hours, silently crying as I listened to Mari breathe.

When sleep finally swallowed me, the echo of the explosion and the image of Alec's stoic face chased me through my dreams.

CHAPTER SEVEN

It took me a long time to make myself leave Mari outside her classroom the next morning. I couldn't convince myself I'd actually be allowed to take her home at the end of the day.

That was the problem with living in the domes. If I fought them, demanded I be allowed to sit in the back of her class so I could make sure she was safe, the kep could lock me up again. Or decide Mari had to live with Miranda permanently. Or look into our past, trying to see what had made me so intent on protecting my sister from the Incorporation, and find out that I hadn't been transferred from the Ice Domes. That I wasn't supposed to be in the domes at all.

Push too hard. Say the wrong thing. Refuse to cooperate, and I could lose the right to protect my sister at best. Get us both thrown out of the domes to die in the wilderness, more likely.

The Incorporation had me cornered in an impossible-to-escape trap, and they didn't even know how screwed I was.

At least in the city I'd been able to run or fight. Helplessly letting monsters control my life was a level of bullshit fuckery city scum weren't equipped to handle.

I shoved my tablet into the waist of my pants as I crutched my way to my own classroom.

A few of my classmates passed me. None of them looked back at me.

"Lanni."

I heard the call from behind me and started crutching forward as fast as I could manage.

"Lanni." Walsh ran up next to me, slipping the tablet out of my waistband before I could slap him away. "Slow down. I've been waiting for a chance to talk."

"I haven't." I kept my eyes locked on the stairs to our classroom, keeping my pace quick.

"Do you need some help?" Walsh reached for my crutch.

"Don't touch me." I whispered as I rounded on him.

"What?" He actually took a step away from me, like I might stand a chance of hurting him.

"You fucking traitor." Tears burned in my eyes. I hated myself for being so weak.

"What are you talking about?" He glanced up and down the hall, giving a nod to one of our classmates as they passed.

"Don't lie to me."

"I've never—"

"Mari almost died because of you. I was actually starting to trust you." I limped a step closer to him. "But your"—I swallowed the word *pack*—"people attacked the depot. They tried to blow Mari up. You almost cost me my sister."

I turned away from him, racing toward class.

"Lanni, give me a chance to explain." He touched my arm.

I rounded on him, cracking my crutch against his knee hard enough to knock a normal human off their feet.

Walsh barely staggered a step.

"Don't bother." I focused on making the air go in and out of my lungs as I kept crutching toward class. It was stupid to snap like that in the hall. Stupid to even hint at what Walsh was where any passing kep might hear me.

Stupid. Temperamental. Weak.

Traitor.

"Welcome back, Lanni." Mrs. Hale gave me a smile that didn't reach her eyes as I made it to the top of the steps.

"Thank you." I tried to smile back but didn't manage much better than she had.

Elliot's seat was still at the front of the room. Someone had draped a little black cloth over his desk.

I hopped the last few feet to my spot, giving up on trying to move sideways with the crutches. The whole thing was stupid. If I'd been hurt back home in the city, no one would have made me use crutches.

But you would have risked dying of an infection, Jaime's voice whispered. *Or had a limp for the rest of your life. Or—*

Walsh slid my tablet onto my desk.

"Lanni you...you might need this."

I didn't look up at him as he walked to his seat. I wanted to chuck the tablet at his head. But I couldn't take the risk. Couldn't do anything but stay trapped in a kep-made Hell.

"Good morning, everyone," Mrs. Hale said.

I looked toward Gideon's seat. It was empty.

"I've been asked to go over some of the new guidelines with you again," Mrs. Hale said.

"Where's Gideon?" I raised my hand.

"Still in medical." Mrs. Hale sounded like she was trying to be comforting. "He'll be returning to class once the doctors clear him."

I opened my mouth to argue but caught myself in time, nodding and lowering my hand instead.

"All gatherings of more than three citizens not of the same family unit will have to be approved by the Domes Council in advance," Mrs. Hale recited. "All citizens not yet graduated from school must stay within their housing units between 8 p.m. and 6 a.m. All citizens must submit to searches of their person and dwellings by the Dome Guard upon request."

"All citizens between the ages of seventeen and twenty-seven must submit to sexual assault by order of the Incorporation," Tricia said. "All women must donate their bodies as incubators at the will of the Incorporation."

"Tricia." Mrs. Hale clasped her tablet to her chest.

"Sorry, Mrs. Hale," Tricia said. "I didn't mean to skip ahead in the list."

"That's not"—Mrs. Hale swallowed hard and looked to the ceiling—"that's not on the list I was ordered to repeat."

"We've already been told all about it." One of the girls at the front of the class looked toward me. "Lanni and Gideon's speech popped right up on the computer in my room. PAM wouldn't even let me turn it off."

I knew I deserved the hatred in her eyes, so I held her gaze, letting her pour her loathing into me.

"When are the group lists coming out?" Walsh said.

A flash of fear filled the girl's eyes before she turned back toward the front of the room.

"I'm not sure," Mrs. Hale said. "Soon. I've been told to...to prepare for students who will need to miss class when they're called for their...their appointments with their assigned partners."

I pressed my palms to the top of my desk, using every bit of willpower I possessed to keep from screaming.

A soft sob came from the front of the room.

You can't let them take Mari away again. Think of Mari. You can get through anything for Mari.

Mom made it through for us. I can be as strong as Mom. I can protect Mari.

"Let's get to work." Mrs. Hale tapped the screen that was the entire front wall of our classroom. An image showing a line of calculations appeared. "How can we best utilize the limited chemical resources to which we have access?"

I took notes on my tablet. I even raised my hand and answered a question. I have no fucking clue how.

I don't actually know how any of us managed it.

It was like we were all waiting, just holding our breath until the announcement came.

We moved to the Tropics Dome for the afternoon. Walsh tried to help me by taking my tablet. I shoved it into my waistband and pretended I hadn't seen him.

When the end-of-day bell finally rang, I considered tossing my crutches into the fancy grass beneath the trees and running for Mari as fast as my shit leg could manage.

But that would be too risky. Look too much like rebelling against orders.

So I crutched my way to get Mari, not breathing properly until I saw her waiting for me by the steps to her classroom.

She wasn't bouncing on her toes the way I'd gotten used to. She stood with both feet flat until she caught sight of me and then bolted toward me.

She almost knocked me over as she threw her arms around my waist.

Pain crept into my throat as I kissed the top of her head, trying to balance my crutches in one hand as I held her.

We didn't talk as we made our way back to our room.

I hated it. I wanted her to be the excited kid who rattled endlessly on about goats and what she wanted to be when she grew up.

What broke you? Did one of my failures steal your smile?

I wanted to ask, but I was too scared of the answer. Mari had survived so many traumas and horrors, I don't know if even she could have pinpointed which had left the deepest scar. I hoped she'd heal. I knew better than to count on it.

Mari opened the door for me when we got back to our room.

"I can make dinner," she grunted as she carried in the food box that had been left in the hall.

"You should do your schoolwork." I left my stupid crutches by the door, hiding my limp as I went to my chair to take off my boots.

"I'm not the one who's behind." Mari dragged her chair to the kitchen.

"Mar—"

"I'm also not supposed to be on crutches." Mari glared at me.

"Okay fine." I let out a big sigh and looked at my tablet.

Days' worth of work to catch up on. That should've been enough to keep me busy, but I couldn't concentrate.

I tapped the message icon at the top of the screen. No incoming messages.

I typed a message to Alec.

Come see me when you can. I stared at the six words for a full minute, making sure I'd put them all in the right order before hitting send.

"Miranda told me we'd be getting mangos soon," Mari said. "I pretended I like them. I hope I do."

"I'm sure you will." I scrolled over to my school assignments. "I don't think you've tried a fruit you haven't liked."

"Peaches are still my favorite."

"I'll ask when they're coming in season."

I opened up my botany homework.

The invention of aquaponics changed the future of humanity's protein sources. With the advent of—

PAM dinged.

"New dome-wide announcement," PAM's stilted computer voice spoke as the screen in the wall lit up. "Group listings for Project Progeny have been posted in the domes database. Individuals in group one will receive their appointment times and partner assignments within the week. All appointment times will also be forwarded to necessary supervisors and teachers."

My whole body went cold.

"All participants not in group one should continue their schedules as normal. Group two will be notified when their opportunity to serve arrives," PAM kept talking. "The Incorporation thanks you for your service."

The image on the screen shifted, turning into tabs for five different group charts.

Mari bolted to the computer, tapping to open the first group.

"Mari, no." I stood, grabbing her arm.

"I need to see." Mari wriggled away from me.

"You're way too young, Mar. You're not going to be in a group."

"But you are!" Mari tapped over to the second group. She ran her finger down the list before moving to group three. She was halfway through the names in group three before she squeaked a scream and shrank back toward me, finally letting me hold her.

My name was right in the middle of group three. Gideon was in the same group as me.

Alec wasn't.

Mari kept her arms wrapped around my waist as I flipped forward to group four, where I found Walsh's name, and all the way to five. I started shaking as I flipped back to two.

Alec had been assigned to group two.

I didn't bother fighting the tears that streamed down my cheeks.

I flipped back a group. There. The twelfth name on the list for group one. Harper Kemp.

Mari and I sank onto her bed, clinging to each other as the smoke from our burned dinner filled our room.

CHAPTER EIGHT

I slipped down the hall to Harper's room as soon as I'd finally gotten Mari to fall asleep.

I tapped on her door, glancing up and down the hall, just waiting for one of the four doors that wasn't Harper's or mine to swing open and have someone shout they were calling the Dome Guard.

Technically, I was out after the new curfew for students, but I hadn't left the building where I lived. I tried to promise myself I'd be able to plead ignorance if the Dome Guard came for me.

I tapped on Harper's door a little louder. "Harper, it's Lanni."

Seconds ticked past. I didn't hear any noise from inside her room.

Gritting my teeth, I tried a third time, wincing as the sound of my knocking carried down the hall. "It's Lanni. Open up." I spoke into the crack of Harper's door. "Come on, Harper. Let me in."

I held my breath, listening for the faintest hint of a jug being set down on a table.

Nothing.

Maybe she was out hiding in the shadows, trying to figure out how to murder me for betraying everything I should believe in.

Or she could be on duty in the vehicle bay. Or maybe the non-students who'd been shoved into Project Progeny were meeting and finding a way to stop the Incorporation from abusing us.

"I'm sorry, Harper." I limped back down the hall and crept into my dark room, trying not to wake Mari.

Our room still smelled like our burned dinner. I wasn't sure if the stench was making me nauseous or if the terror I was trying so hard not to feel had started infecting my intestines. I opened the window, letting in some of the perfectly filtered dome air.

We could never leave the windows open in our apartment in the city. Either there was too much smoke and ash in the air and we needed the windows shut to protect our lungs, or, on the precious days when it actually rained, we had to keep the apartment dry.

And all that was completely apart from keeping out desperate people who survived by breaking into other peoples' homes and stealing everything they could find. If a thief had gotten into our apartment, they would have made a killing off the treasures Amery had given us.

I stuck my face out the window, breathing in the scent of the flowers that grew around our building.

I am lucky. I am lucky.

You are trapped.

I sat on my bed, propping my bad leg up and staring at my tablet. I had more homework to do. I needed rest, but I knew I wouldn't be able to sleep.

I tapped on the message icon on my tablet and scrolled down to my message thread with Harper.

Harper,

I got that far before freezing up. I didn't know what to say. At least not in a way that wouldn't get me in trouble if the Incorporation decided to read Project Progeny's spokesgirl's messages.

I've been thinking about you since the attack in the city. I haven't seen you to make sure you're okay. I'm sorry for being a terrible friend.

I really need to talk to you, Harper. Please come by. Or tell me when I can come see you.

Mari misses you, too.

I'm sorry for everything,

Lanni

I read the words four times before hitting send.

The message to Harper closed, but I still just sat staring at my tablet, unable to convince myself I should do my homework.

Group three meant I had some time. Maybe the Incorporation would figure out what they were doing was completely unforgiveable before they even got to me.

That's sacrificing Harper.

I gripped my tablet. The only thing that kept me from throwing it across the room was not wanting to wake Mari.

I lay down, trying to convince myself to sleep. I don't know how long I stared at the ceiling, doing everything I could to stop myself from thinking.

Would they publicly announce the pairings? Who would Alec be partnered with? Whose child would he father?

Sour rose into my throat. I curled onto my side, trying to fixate on Walsh.

Walsh had lied to me. That, I could be angry about. The werewolves had attacked the city through the mountain. They'd followed us from the depot. I could be terrified of how they planned to attack the Arcadia Domes without risking panic or vomit.

"Lanni."

I bolted up in bed as someone whispered my name.

"Lanni." A shadow blocked the dim light filtering in through the window.

I stood, grabbing the shit kitchen knife that was my only weapon out from under my pillow.

"It's me," the voice whispered. "It's Alec."

"You scared the shit out of me." I slid the knife back under my pillow and crept toward him.

"I had to wait for people to go to sleep." He stepped over the flowerbed to stand right outside my window. "I just…I needed to see you."

He reached for me, grazing his fingers across my cheek like he wanted to make sure I was real.

I leaned through the window, resting my head against his chest. He wrapped his arms around me as best he could with the barrier of the wall between us, but it wasn't enough.

"I'm so sorry, Lanni." He spoke with his lips pressed to the top of my head. "I don't know what to do. I can't protect you."

"Shh." I took his face in my hands and kissed him. "I'll be okay."

Will she kiss him, too?

I tucked my chin and stepped away from him.

"Please." He trailed his hands down my arms. "I just need to hold you."

"Step back." I reached under my mattress, looking for the thin strip of metal I'd kept there before, but I hadn't used it since our room had been ransacked. I didn't know where it might have gotten lost, or if the Dome Guard who'd searched through the mess had taken it away.

I pulled the knife back out from under my pillow instead.

"Take this." I passed it to Alec.

"You can't be found with a weapon."

"It's a key, not a weapon." I pushed myself up onto the window ledge.

He didn't say anything about curfew or having to hide as I twisted and dropped to the ground outside. He wrapped an arm around my waist, steadying me as the pain in my leg drove the air from my lungs.

"Lan—"

I kissed him before he could finish saying my name.

The edges of my panic dulled as my body melted against his. The taste of his lips. His scent. The ridges of the muscles in his back. Things I hadn't even known I'd memorized were suddenly the comfort I craved.

I pulled my lips far enough away to whisper, "Not here."

I closed the window and slid the knife into the crack, pressing down the bar to click the lock into place.

"You're good at that." Alec wrapped his arms around my waist.

"Insomnia." I wriggled free to tuck the knife into the purple flowers, then took his hand, limping toward the back of our building.

"We can't." Alec pulled against me. "I want to, but if we get caught—"

"Then don't let us get caught."

He scooped me into his arms.

"I can walk." I didn't fight as he held me tighter.

"I'm faster." He brushed his lips against mine. "And can claim I was trying to carry you to medical. Where to?"

My thoughts flew to a willow tree where we could pretend the domes didn't exist.

I kissed the side of his neck and pointed in the opposite direction. "Cut through the trees here."

He carried me deep into the shadows, creeping past another housing unit and following my whispered directions to a place where dense trees grew close together, blocking all the paths from view.

He kept me in his arms as he sank to the ground, then shifted me to sit in his lap.

I leaned my head against his shoulder, letting him hold me tight as I tried to work out something to say.

"We're in separate groups." Alec's voice came out husky and raw.

I sat up straighter so I could properly look at him. His eyes were swollen like he'd been crying.

"I thought, when they announced the program, I thought they'd give us some choice. Let us at least have a say in who..." He shook his head. "I thought we'd at least have a chance of being paired. That if they made me go into that room, it could be you waiting for me."

"I know." I laid my hand on his cheek.

"But I won't be with you. I can't protect you. I can't keep some stranger from touching you. And they'll make me be with someone else. How can they ask us to just walk into a room and have sex with someone we don't want to be with?"

"You'll be okay." I twisted out of his lap to kneel in front of him.

"I don't want this. I want you."

"I know." I took his face in my hands and kissed his forehead.

"I want to choose you." He rested his forehead on my shoulder. "I want yours to be the body I know."

He took my waist. His hands were so big, it seemed like he should be able to fight against the whole world.

Alec had done so much to protect me, but we were locked in the Incorporation's cage, and none of us were strong enough to fight back.

I looked up through the glass.

Above the atrium, Incorporation Headquarters peeked out of the side of the mountain. Looming over us. Warning us all not to defy their power.

I let out a long breath.

I'm so sorry, Mom.

"It's just a body." I took Alec's chin, tipping his gaze up to meet mine. "It's a physical transaction."

"It's not."

"It can be." I traced the worried lines by his eye with my thumb. "There doesn't have to be any emotion or attachment. It's just two people using their bodies to give each other pleasure." I breathed through the tightness in my chest.

"It's more than that. I don't want some woman I don't know to carry my child. I don't want you to..." He shook his head, like even saying what the kep wanted to force my body to do was too awful to stand. He pressed his palm to my stomach like he knew right where the pain I refused to acknowledge had started to grow. "I should be able to protect you."

"You can't, but that doesn't mean we won't survive."

"I don't want to lose what we could have been because of this." The desperation in his eyes made breathing almost impossible.

"You won't." I kissed him, gently, just enough to make sure I wouldn't break him. "That room has nothing to do with us. This is completely different." I kissed him again. "*We* are different. Don't ever let yourself get confused."

I eased myself forward as I threaded my fingers through his hair. I held his gaze, inviting him, giving him the chance to make the choice.

His gaze shifted to my mouth. He touched my lips. "Completely different."

I kissed his fingertips.

He lifted me into his lap, shifting me so my chest pressed against his. He held my gaze as his hands found the bottom of my shirt. He trailed his fingers up my back.

I arched toward him, the tightness in my chest dissolving as the hum that raced through my body shouted I needed more than a grazing touch.

He kissed me. His mouth claiming mine as his hands found new places to explore, his thumb teasing the side of my breast.

I pulled away from his mouth, tasting his earlobe as I guided his kisses down the side of my neck. He paused, taking a breath like he wanted to memorize my scent and savor his yearning for me as he explored what we could be together.

But I needed more of him.

I tipped his chin up, kissing him as I backed away just enough to reach the buttons on the front of his uniform. The ridges of his muscles, the softness of his skin, I needed to memorize him, too.

I kissed down his neck and onto his bare chest, demanding a moment to discover the wonders of Alec as I tossed aside his shirt, before reaching down and beginning to lift mine.

"Let me." He took the hem from me, raising the fabric as though revealing a work of art. When he finally pulled off my shirt, he just stared at me for moment, studying my bare chest in the starlight.

He ran a hand up my back. I leaned into his palm, letting his strength support me. He laced his fingers through my hair, pulling me toward him as he kissed me.

The feel of his bare chest against mine made me want more of him. I needed him. I would burn up from the inside out if I didn't have all of him.

He lifted me off him, laying me down on the ground, twining his fingers through mine as he kissed me.

When the sun threatened to light the sky, he still hadn't let me have all of him. It didn't matter that I was ready. He wasn't. Even with the threat of being paired by the Incorporation, he didn't want to rush. Didn't want to hurt me. Didn't want to risk me having any regrets.

As he passed me my shirt, I told myself it was all right for us to savor exploring everything we could be together. Sex could mean more than profit or procreation. We should take the chance to discover what it could be for us. While he carried me back to my window, I actually believed my own lie.

We still have time.

CHAPTER NINE

I went to Harper's room three times a day that week. Once in the morning, once at night before curfew, and once after. She never answered her door. I could see on my tablet that she'd been reading my messages, but she didn't want to talk to me.

After everything Director Holbeck had made me say, I didn't blame her.

Gideon still wasn't out of the medical wing. The only person in class who wanted to speak to me was Walsh. Slipping away from him got a lot easier once the doctor let me stop using the crutches.

Alec hadn't been able to come back. All Outer Guard had been ordered to stay in the barracks. No one would tell me why.

Mari was the only thing that kept the panic from taking over again.

My little sister got me out of bed and made me eat breakfast. She counted while I did the exercises the doctor had prescribed. She checked in on my homework, making sure I wasn't just staring at the screen for hours. She made dinner. My seven-year-old sister made me shower.

But as much as Mari coddled me, I still couldn't get one word out of my head.

When?

Then, nine days after the announcement in the atrium, PAM dinged after we'd finished our dinner.

Mari and I both froze, waiting for PAM to start speaking in her falsely soothing, computerized voice. But a message for me popped up instead.

"No!" Mari leapt to her feet, shouting at the computer screen. "She's a group three. You can't have her."

"It's okay, Mar." I stood and pulled Mari into a hug, hiding her face against my side as I tapped to open the message.

Schedule Adjustment

Guard training program beginning 6:20 a.m. tomorrow.

Participant Lanni Roberts has been excused from cardio training. Report directly to the vehicle bay to continue with other participants.

"I'm going back into the guard training program." I loosened my hold on Mari.

"What?" Mari peeked up at the screen. "You just have to do training?"

"Yep." I kissed her on the head and guided her back to her seat.

"But you can't run." Mari wiped the tears from her cheeks with her sleeve.

"I'm skipping that part." My hands shook as I took two glasses down from the cupboard.

"Maybe this means it'll be a really long time before your group gets called."

"Maybe." I filled both glasses, fighting to keep my hands steady enough not to slosh the water as I set Mari's down on the table.

"We should have stayed at home." Mari dipped her finger into her glass.

"Mar—"

"Mom was wrong. It's not better here." She shoved her whole hand into her glass, making the water spill out over the sides. "She lied."

"She didn't lie."

"Did too."

"She just didn't know." I lifted Mari's hand out of her glass, giving it a squeeze as I nodded toward the computer screen set into the wall.

Mari knocked her glass from the table. "Then Amery should have told her." She yanked her hand out of mine and snatched a towel from the kitchen counter.

I hated not knowing if PAM was listening to us. I hated Amery for not telling our mom what life in the domes was really like. I hated myself for not telling Mari that, even if we could get all the way back to the city where we'd lived before, the domes had killed most of the people there.

"The guards are stupid." Mari mopped up the water on the floor. "If I were planning on hurting people, I wouldn't teach them how to fight."

CHAPTER TEN

Dome Guard lurked in the early morning shadows as I made my way through Bloom Dome the next morning. Curfew was over. I was allowed to be out of my housing unit and was supposed to be going down to the vehicle bay for training, but it still felt like they were going to pounce on me at any second.

I ignored the ache in my leg, walking with my chin up, trying to look like I was filled with purpose instead of fear. I nodded to the guards I passed, making eye contact with as many of them as I could. Not because I wanted to look the kep in the eye, just to prove I wasn't trying to slip by.

Most of them gave me a silent nod back, thoughtlessly returning my greeting. A few glared or looked away like they couldn't stand the sight of me.

My leg had started to throb by the time I made it down to the bay level.

The echoes of pounding feet carried through the corridor as the rest of the trainees ran.

I picked up my pace, wanting to beat the others to the vehicle bay. My gait was uneven. The ankle of my injured leg wouldn't work properly.

"Why the hell do they want me to train when I can't even walk quickly?" I hurried through the thick, metal vehicle bay doors, ready to wait for the rest of the group.

Three guards stood behind a table at the center of the space where we usually trained.

My heart rocketed up into my throat as my hand instinctively moved to reach for the weapon I didn't have.

But the guards didn't charge forward to arrest me, or yell at me for being somewhere I shouldn't. They all just silently glanced at me before going back to unpacking the cases on the table.

I scanned the massive concrete room as I went to the far end of where the line of trainees normally stood.

There were gaps in the line of trucks along the wall. I didn't know if that meant some of the Outer Guard had gone back out into the city or if the trucks had been destroyed when the guards had been ambushed.

Click.

I spun toward the table, not even knowing why fear had suddenly shot through my body until I saw the gun in the guard's hand.

He aimed the gun across the bay before turning it over in his hand to inspect it.

One of the other guards looked at me. He furrowed his brow like he could somehow sense my instinct to run. "Part of training today." He nodded toward the table where a row of guns had been laid out then pointed to the black-and-white targets on the far wall.

"Thanks." I tried to make my shoulders relax, but I couldn't.

The pounding of footsteps came through the door. A guard led the pack of trainees into the bay. Two boys who'd been in the group before the bombing ran right behind him, then six new boys, then Walsh.

Anger swallowed all my fear.

Walsh picked up his pace, cutting around the others to stand closest to me.

"Didn't think you'd be here," he puffed, like he was actually out of breath. Like the drugs that had changed him hadn't made him into a soulless monster who could sprint through the halls murdering us all without breaking a sweat. "How are you?"

"Don't." I took a step away from him and turned to face the guard in charge of our training.

The guard glared at us, waiting for the stragglers to make their way into the line. There were twenty-seven in the group now. Only three of us were girls.

"Welcome back to the program." The guard's gaze swept over our group. "And for the newcomers, welcome to the program that will train you to protect your home. I'm Guard Beck. Captain Pace has entrusted me with the duty of making sure you are prepared to join the Outer Guard.

"The dedication required to become an Outer Guard is something not many people understand. We risk our lives every time we leave the domes. We lost seven guards in the insurgents' attack on the city." Beck paused, taking a moment to let the number sink in, like seven kep lives lost should be horrifying to us all.

I chanced a glance at the other trainees. They all looked somewhere between horrified and determined. Even Walsh managed to look like he wanted nothing more than to rip out the throats of the people who'd attacked the precious Outer Guard.

"Seven guards in a day." Beck began to slowly pace the length of our line. "Seven domes citizens who devoted their lives to the protection of the Arcadia Domes, gone. Their knowledge, their training—"

Their DNA.

"—their lives, stolen from us by outsiders who don't understand the importance of the Incorporation's mission. You are here because you understand that loss, but none of you understand what it's like to be attacked by a horde of enemies. None of you understand what it's like to follow the order to hold your ground when you know those might be the last words you ever hear.

"But the Incorporation needs you to be strong enough to stand against the enemies that threaten our home. The Arcadia Domes needs you to have the determination and drive to become the guards we need to stand against the people who dare to endanger our mission."

Beck stopped and looked to the table where the other guards had unpacked the guns. "This training program was formed to help us fill the holes in the Outer Guard's ranks left by the abominable violence inflicted on our people. And now, after the bastards dared to come so close to our home, we have expanded the program, accepting more applicants to our ranks. I can promise you, not all of you will make it through this training. But for those that do, I can also promise you that becoming an Outer Guard will be the most meaningful thing you will ever achieve."

He stayed silent for a moment, like he was hoping his words would sink in and deeply impact our lives. I wondered if Captain Pace had written the speech for him or if it had come all the way down from Incorporation Headquarters. Either way, it was a hell of a lot different than the *get ready for pain* spiel we'd been given before.

"I'm going to take you through conditioning exercises, and hand-to-hand," Beck said. "Then you'll have the privilege of working with—"

One of the girls raised her hand. "Sir." She spoke before the guard had even acknowledged her. "If becoming an Outer Guard will be the most meaningful thing we do with our lives, will being in this program release us from participation in Project Progeny?"

For a moment, the entire bay was completely silent.

Beck stared the girl down. "Participation requirements for Project Progeny are not altered by guard status, either for Outer Guard or for participants in the guard training program."

"You're going to send pregnant women into the city to fight?" one of the boys said.

"Expectant guards will be restricted to in-domes duty for the duration of their pregnancy," Beck said.

"This is bullshit." The girl stepped out of our line. "You want us to risk our lives to protect the domes while the Incorporation wants to force us into a sterile room to—"

"Think very carefully before you continue to speak." Beck's tone was low. I couldn't tell if he was trying to warn her or threaten her.

"What are they going to do to me?" the girl shouted. "I'm already group one!"

The boy who'd been standing beside her reached forward and took her hand.

She yanked away from him. "No! I did not wake up early so I could train to defend a place that only cares about my womb. Besides, I need all the sleep I can get. Soon, I'll have a fucking baby keeping me up." She strode out of the bay.

The boy stared after her for a moment before squaring his shoulders and facing back toward Beck.

"If I can continue without any further outbursts," Beck said.

I raised my hand.

"I am here to train you to be an Outer Guard"—Beck turned his glare to me—"not to answer your questions like a school teacher."

"Sir." I stepped forward. "Can you tell us any more about what happened in the city? Who attacked us? Are they still in the area? If I'm here to train to defend the Arc Domes, I'd like to know who I'll be fighting against."

I'm not sure if the loathing that twisted my gut was for myself or for Beck as he stopped glaring and raised his chin like he was actually proud of me for asking.

"The origin of the insurgents is unknown," he said. "We lost good guards fighting against them, but as far as we can tell, they've either fled or gone to ground. Either way, we will protect the Arcadia Domes, no matter the threat."

"Sir," I said, "is it the same people who attacked the depot?"

"Not all information is meant for trainees," Beck said.

"If it was them, they all deserve to burn. They almost murdered my little sister at the depot. I'd kill them all with my bare hands if I could." I turned around to step back into the line, flicking my gaze over to Walsh.

He didn't look at me, but I could read everything in the tension of his jaw and thin line of his mouth.

I'd been right. It was Walsh's pack. I didn't know how they'd done it or what Walsh's role had been, but they'd destroyed the depot. They'd almost taken Mari from me.

Walsh, who I'd been stupid enough to trust. Walsh, who I'd helped cover up a murder.

A rumble pulsed in the back of my head like a roar of rage that couldn't escape. *Bang.* The remembered sound joined in with the furious screaming in my head. *Bang.*

I did the stupid exercises, and worked on pressure point strikes, and shot at a damn target with a guard's gun.

But none of it mattered. Even if I was foolish enough to try and fight a werewolf, Mari and I were digitally linked to Walsh. There was nothing I could do about the beast who'd tried to murder us. Our safety in the domes made me helpless.

CHAPTER ELEVEN

"In the days before the domes were built, preserving endangered species often fell on the shoulders of private philanthropists and zoos," Mr. Jackson said. "As society decayed, zoos closed, and some animals had to depend entirely upon the protection of wealthy individuals who dedicated their lives to stopping the extinction of species, both exotic and those once considered common."

"Lanni," Walsh whispered from behind me, "all I need from you is five minutes."

"The reliance on those outside the scientific community created its own set of problems." Mr. Jackson paced in front of our class. He always kept in constant motion when he gave his lectures in the Tropics Dome, like he wanted to make sure we didn't get distracted by the palm trees and the sounds of the monkeys hiding in the shadows.

I didn't really care about the monkeys, but Walsh leaning close to whisper to me made me mad enough to make concentrating almost impossible.

"I have to talk to you," Walsh said. "I've been trying to ask nicely for days. Don't make me get creative."

"Stay the hell away from me," I whispered back.

"Creative it is."

It had been three days since I'd started back with the Outer Guard program, and Walsh had been hounding me every chance he got. I wanted to rip out his eyeballs. Part of me wondered if that was how Harper felt about me banging on her door all the time. But I was Harper's friend who wanted to check on her. Walsh was a vicious beast who probably wanted me to help him murder another kep.

A cough, like someone fighting tears, dragged my mind back to the moment.

"—inbreeding destroyed many species," Mr. Jackson said like he hadn't heard the sound. "Though, in some cases, the swapping of genetic material by dedicated scientists helped to create enough breeding pairs to allow healthy offspring."

The sound of actual sobbing came from the front of our class.

The group shifted as one of the boys pushed his way forward.

Mr. Jackson stopped pacing as the boy wrapped his arm around a girl, holding her close to his side. She twisted, burying her face on his shoulder.

"If we could please focus on the class," Mr. Jackson said.

"She's group one," Tricia said.

"That has nothing to do with—"

"They're going to be pulling her out of classes starting tomorrow," the boy cut across Mr. Jackson. "I don't think it really matters if she focuses on your lecture about how endangered animals were treated better than us."

Tomorrow.

My hands started to tingle as every instinct I had told me to run. I hadn't known they were actually starting so soon. And with people who hadn't even finished school.

I managed to step away from the rest of the students just in time to puke in the fancy underbrush that didn't belong in the mountains.

"I'm sorry." I wiped my mouth with the back of my hand, swallowing the next round of sour that surged in my throat.

"No apologies needed." Mr. Jackson studied me like I was another one of his animals. "Just get yourself down to medical."

"I wasn't talking to you." I stepped around him to look at the girl. "I'm sorry. I'm sorry this is happening to you."

"Don't pretend to be sorry. We've already heard your speech about Project Progeny being the salvation of the domes." The boy held the girl tighter, like having her in his arms was the only thing keeping him from strangling me.

"It's..." I looked at my class. At the pack of kep I despised who had every right to hate me, too. "It was the only option they gave me."

"That's rich coming from a group three." The boy turned away from me, looking back toward Mr. Jackson.

"They wouldn't let me see my sister." My voice broke as pain pinched my throat.

The boy's shoulders tensed.

"I'm so sorry," I whispered.

A hand gripped my arm.

"Let me take Lanni down to medical, Mr. Jackson." Walsh stepped toward the back of the group, pulling me to follow him.

"I can fucking well walk on my own." I wrenched my arm out of his grip and strode away from the class, taking big enough steps for the pain in my leg to send spots dancing in my eyes. The stabbing in my leg tightened the muscles in my chest enough I could almost pretend that's what had caused the ache in my throat instead of the knowledge that that poor girl would be taken out of class tomorrow.

I stopped at the bottom of the stairs to puke again.

I pressed my forehead to the concrete wall.

It's my fault. They're going to take her away, and it's my fault.

Jaime, I need you. I'm trapped, and I need you.

"Lanni."

For one slim second, I thought it had been Jaime's voice, but a very real hand touched my shoulder.

I spun around, punching Walsh in the jaw before he could speak again. The impact streaked from my knuckles to my elbow, but Walsh barely even flinched.

"Great." He rubbed his thumb across the place I'd hit him. "Now I have an excuse to go to medical."

"You'd be healed before you even got there." I wiped my mouth with the back of my now aching hand. "Get back to class."

"I've been assigned to escort you to medical." Walsh bowed me down the corridor. "Do you want to walk, or should I carry you?"

"You even try to touch me and—"

"And what?" Walsh crossed his arms. "You'll scream? You'll tell the domes I don't belong?"

"You're a fucking monster."

"I never said I wasn't."

I bit my lips together as the anger in my chest threatened to overwhelm my reason and I almost lost the battle to not scream at him. I gripped my hands together until my fingers hurt. "Get back to class."

I forced air into my lungs as I started down the hall.

I wasn't the only one to blame for the girl being taken out of class tomorrow so she could be shoved into a sterile room so someone could force a child into her. It was Walsh's fault, too. His pack of monsters had destroyed the depot. His pack had attacked the city. They'd killed enough guards to make the Incorporation desperate. They'd done more damage than I had.

The sickness in my stomach was replaced by pure loathing. I managed to walk without wanting to hide from every kep I saw as I passed the classrooms where more doomed students were stuck learning all the reasons they should gratefully let the Incorporation abuse them.

The Incorporation was filled with monsters, too. I couldn't

decide who was worse—the wolves outside or the demons looming above our heads.

Something clenched around my stomach. For a moment, I thought I was going to be sick again. Then I realized my feet weren't on the ground anymore.

I started to scream, but a hand clamped over my mouth before I could make a sound.

"Don't make this worse," Walsh whispered in my ear as he carried me up a flight of steps.

I jabbed my elbow back, then reached behind and grabbed his hair.

He kicked the door closed. "Don't yank my hair out. It grows back more slowly than my skin."

I pulled harder.

Walsh let go of me, dropping me onto the ground.

I landed on my ass, but before I could scramble up, he'd grabbed me under the arms and lifted me to my feet.

"Don't touch me." I spun around and punched him in the ribs.

He gave a little cough but didn't stagger. "We need to talk, Lanni."

"So dragging me into a classroom is you *getting creative?*" I stepped back, eyeing my path to the door even though I knew I'd never outrun him.

"I was going to break into your room while Mari was sleeping—"

"Stay away from her."

"—but you wandered away from class, so I thought this would be easier."

"Easier? You don't deserve easy. You deserve to die in a fire like the one that almost killed my sister." I looked back to Walsh, ready for him to come up with some reason I was wrong or a threat to keep me silent. "Mari could have died because of you."

Walsh just stared at me, with wrinkles on his forehead and sadness in his eyes.

"Do you not even care enough to bother lying to me?" A weird laugh broke through the pain in my throat. "Your pack destroyed the depot. They followed us here, and they attacked the city."

He just kept staring.

"Say something, you coward. You almost murdered Mari."

He looked down at his hands, fixing his gaze on his palms. "I didn't know you. I didn't know Mari. I got my orders, and I did what I was told."

"You knew we'd be in the depot." I stepped forward, shoving him in the chest. He didn't budge.

"I knew my file had been tagged onto the transfer of Lanni and Mari Roberts, two Incorporation citizens who'd managed to hack their way into being sent to the Arcadia Domes. I still thought you were from the Ice Domes. Why should I have cared about two more dead dome dwellers?"

"We're not kep."

"I didn't know that." Walsh finally looked up at me. "I didn't even guess it until Mari started digging glass out of your side without flinching. Little girls who grow up inside the domes aren't supposed to be used to that sort of thing."

"You're right." I dug my knuckles into my temples and started pacing. "Mari is a little girl. A little girl who has survived so much, and you almost killed her."

"It wasn't me."

"So your pack didn't—"

"I didn't plant the bomb. I was waiting outside. After the blast, I sliced my head open and stumbled out onto the road to join the survivors."

"Great. So you were safe while Mari almost burned."

"Is it only Mari that matters to you?" Walsh stepped into my pacing path.

"She's my sister."

"There were other kids in that depot, Lanni." He didn't scream it, but it felt like he had. "Children died, and I hate that. I hate that the Incorporation has pushed us to do horrific, unthinkable things. But we are fighting for our survival, and when you weigh the thousands upon thousands of innocent lives the Incorporation has ended against what we did at that depot, are we really the monsters?"

"Yes. Because she's my sister." I made myself meet his gaze. "And I thought I could trust you."

"You can. I was supposed to make sure you and Mari never arrived at the Arcadia Domes. If you survived the blast, I was ordered to make sure Lanni and Mari Roberts died in the attack."

"It was your people who attacked us up on that cliff?" I backed away from him. "I killed one of them. You did, too. I saw you kill your own people!"

"I was ordered to fight with deadly force. They sacrificed their lives to make sure my arrival here was believable." Walsh held out his hand. "I should've shoved you and Mari into the attack team's path to make sure no one from the Ice Domes ever made it to the Arc Domes. But I didn't. I kept you alive because you're not the girls from the files I read. You don't belong here any more than I do. You and Mari are innocent in all this. I will do whatever I can to protect you."

"When your pack comes to attack the Arc Domes?" I wrapped my arms around my stomach, trying to convince myself not to run or vomit. "Because they're lurking in the city, ready to come kill all the kep."

"I—" He shuddered, almost like he could feel my fear and loathing. "I can't say anything about the pack's plans."

"Because ignorance will keep me safe?"

"Because the alpha of my pack ordered my silence." He shuddered again. "But I will keep you safe. I think I know how. I just need you to trust me."

"No." I backed farther away. "All I really know about you is that you're a werewolf who tried to kill my sister. I'm already tied up with the monsters of the Incorporation. I don't need to add trusting a demon to the list of ways I'm failing."

"You aren't failing. Project Progeny isn't your fault."

"Yeah, it is." I headed toward the door.

"I won't let them do that to you, Lanni."

"You've already told me enough lies."

I listened for his footsteps as I headed down the stairs and out into the corridor. I didn't bother trying to run, he could've caught me even if I'd been able to sprint, but he didn't come after me. I wasn't sure whether he'd given up on trying to convince me or just realized there was shit he could do to protect me from Director Holbeck and even less he could do to convince me to forgive him for his part in bombing the depot.

I'd made it down the first flight of stairs I needed to travel to reach the medical corridor before the overwhelming need to curl up in a corner and sleep sapped all the strength from my limbs. I didn't want to go to the medical corridor and pretend I wasn't sure that I'd puked in the Tropics Dome because I was so disgusted with myself my stomach was rebelling. I didn't want to try and sneak home to sleep in my bed, either. I just wanted to lie down in the hall and sink into the floor until there was nothing left of me.

Mari needs you, Jaime whispered in the back of my mind. *If you leave her alone with the kep, who will protect her from the Incorporation?*

I leaned against the wall, taking a few deep breaths to convince my lungs they really were supposed to keep me alive.

Ding.

The bright sound came from the speaker set into the ceiling.

"Lanni Roberts, report to the medical corridor," a female voice filled the hall. "Lanni Roberts, report to the medical corridor."

"All I did was puke." I dug my fingers into my hair and made myself head down the stairs to the medical corridor level.

I started planning what to say when the doctor asked why it had taken me so long to get from the Tropics Dome to the medical corridor. If Mr. Jackson thought my vomiting was a big enough problem to call down to warn the doctors I was on my way, then I could probably claim having gotten faint and needing to sit for a few minutes.

If the doctors wanted to know why Walsh hadn't called for them when I'd gotten faint, then I'd have to cover for him. I hated it. I hated him even if it was selfish of me to only care about Mari and not the kep kids who'd died at the depot.

I stopped at the bottom of the stairs to lean against the wall again as my leg got heavy enough I wanted to crumple to the ground.

"Mari needs me," I whispered. "Mari is all that matters, and Mari needs me."

"Lanni," a woman called from down the hall.

I pushed my shoulders back, trying to press a smile onto my face as I looked toward the voice.

Miss Leigh bustled toward me, tablet in hand. "When our guards missed you in the Tropics Dome, I was afraid we were going to be thrown off schedule."

"Schedule for what?" I asked.

"It's good to see you're walking again." Leigh took my arm, half-dragging me toward the medical corridor. "We'll get you an injection to calm your stomach while they're doing your makeup. Director Holbeck will be down in fifteen minutes, so we're really on a tight timeline. Honestly, I sent the memo to your teacher two hours ago, so he should've had you down here for preparation well before now."

"He was busy teaching." I pulled against Miss Leigh's grip as we turned the corner into the medical corridor.

The hall was clear until we reached Captain Tate's closed office door, but after that, guards in gray Incorporation uniforms were stationed along the walls, and plain-clothed people hurried from room to room. It was like there had been another attack and more wounded needed to be tended to, but the people darting around weren't doctors, and there weren't any screams of pain. Only tense voices and snapped orders.

A man carried a crisp, white robe across the corridor.

"I have Lanni," Leigh called to him.

"Wonderful." He looked to Leigh and me, only bothering to press a smile onto his face for a split second. "The room is ready. Completely pristine and sterile. We have the male already prepared and—"

"No." I yanked my arm out of Leigh's grip. "I'm group three." I staggered back. "I haven't been called yet. I haven't been scheduled."

I glanced down the hall toward my slim chance for freedom.

They could take Mari away! my own voice screamed in my head, but I couldn't make my body stop as I turned to bolt down the corridor.

"Catch her," Leigh said calmly, like she was only perturbed at my outburst.

I started to run but only made it ten feet before a guard grabbed me around the middle, lifting me into the air. I twisted sideways, biting him on the shoulder.

He screamed and dropped me.

Another gray-uniformed guard reached down to grab me, but I rolled out of his grasp as I pushed myself to my feet.

"Lanni, stop!"

Gideon's voice made me pause just long enough for two guards to grab me by the arms.

"It's for pictures." Gideon kept one hand on the wall as he walked toward me, like he still couldn't stand up on his own. But he had color in his cheeks, like he was healthy and healed. And he wore a white robe like the one the man had been carrying. He held out his hand, reaching for me. "They just want us here for pictures. We're in group three. We're still safe."

"Safe?" Leigh stepped between us. "The correct messaging is *have yet to be given the opportunity to serve the Incorporation.*"

Gideon nodded. "It's not our turn to serve the Incorporation yet." He came closer, still reaching for me. "We just have to pose for some pictures, and then we'll get to talk. They promised. Please, Lanni."

I stopped fighting the guards.

"The robe will cover any bruising." The man carrying the white robe frowned at me.

"It had better. Director Holbeck will be on her way any minute." Leigh took my wrist, yanking me out of the guards' grasp. She held on as tight as the guards had as she steered me into one of the medical rooms that should've been used by doctors. "One more outburst like that, and I'll have to tell Director Holbeck you're refusing to cooperate."

"What will she do to me?" I asked.

Leigh shoved me into a chair, and a woman with a makeup brush pounced on me.

"Quite frankly, Lanni, neither you nor I want to know the answer to that question."

CHAPTER TWELVE

It was a normal medical room, like the one they'd taken me to when the doctor had re-fixed my leg. Or at least, it *had* been a normal room before the Incorporation had gotten to it.

The gurney was gone, replaced by a bed with a white, fitted sheet. Curtains had been set up in both back corners of the room, creating little changing areas. A call button had been added beside the door like somehow that made up for the lock they'd placed on the outside to keep their victims trapped. Extra lights had been hung from the ceiling, and men with cameras crowded in by the bed, but I assumed they'd all be swept away as soon as the photo shoot from Hell ended.

"Both of you back into the changing areas," Director Holbeck ordered.

I stepped back into my corner, pulling the curtain to close me off from the rest of the room.

"Now when you step out this time, I want you to think joyful anticipation," Holbeck said. "You are here to do your duty to the Incorporation. On three. One, two, three."

I shoved the curtain aside and stepped forward, trying to

pretend I would find anything but Holbeck and her crew waiting for me.

Holbeck tapped the tablet in her lap, looking at the images the photographers had just captured. "Good, Gideon. Lanni, we need more joy. Go again."

"Yes, ma'am." I stepped back into my corner and pulled the curtain closed.

"May I, Director Holbeck?" Leigh said.

"Certainly," Holbeck said.

"Lanni, I want you to forget we're all here," Leigh said. "Close your eyes."

I gritted my teeth, keeping my eyes open.

"Now I want you to imagine you're stepping through that curtain ready to find the person you want to see more than anyone in the world. And when you come out here, you'll get to hold him. You'll get to feel safe in his arms and know that everything is right with the world," Leigh said.

Faint sounds of movement came from the other side of my curtain.

"Can you do that, Lanni?" Leigh said.

"Sure." I let out a breath and tried to focus.

Alec. If I could step through the curtain and find Alec. Armed and ready to fight against the people who were forcing me to make their fucking propaganda.

"On three," Director Holbeck said. "One, two, three."

I stepped through the curtain, trying as hard as I could to picture safety waiting for me instead of kep.

For a moment, I saw him. Standing there, reaching for me. A crooked smile curving his lips.

Jaime.

All the air flew out of my lungs.

I raised my hand. Ready to grab onto him and bury myself in his arms and make sure no one could steal him from me ever again.

"Good work, Lanni," Holbeck said.

Jaime vanished.

Gideon took his place. He stepped forward and grabbed my hand.

"I think we're ready to move on to the next shot," Holbeck said.

"We're going to need you on either side of the bed." Leigh tapped on her tablet. "You wanted them reaching across to hold hands, Director Holbeck?"

"I think it conveys the right feeling of unity." Holbeck nodded. "Get a few without the hands, too, just in case."

"Head of the bed?" Leigh asked.

Holbeck pursed her lips as she studied the bed like the white fitted sheet wasn't a symbol of doom. "I think it fits with the image of innocence."

Gideon gripped my hand. I didn't know who he was trying to keep from screaming—me or himself.

"Perfect." Leigh looked to Gideon and me. "Into position, you two."

Gideon kept hold of my hand as he cut around to the far side of the bed.

"Hold hands like you mean it," Leigh said.

"What?" I looked down at where Gideon and I were clinging to each other for dear life.

"Lock your fingers together. We want the world to know what a happy couple you are." Leigh pressed a smile onto her face.

I loosened my grip on Gideon's hand, trying to switch my hold.

"Is that really the message you want to send?" Gideon tightened his grasp, not letting me switch my grip.

"Of course," Leigh said. "You two are the spokescouple for Project Progeny."

"But do you want to portray us as a couple?" Gideon asked.

"You're going to be separating couples. Having us together seems like it sets false expectations."

"What do you know about messaging?" Leigh's smile tightened as her voice got brighter. "Do they have a unit about communicating with the masses in school now? Are you actually aware of the cultural differences that exist between different sets of domes?"

"I see Gideon's point." Holbeck stood and placed her tablet on her seat. "The romantic idea of the young couple in love doesn't fit with the true mission of Project Progeny. The project is about the greater good. The need to secure a future for the human race. Isn't that right, Gideon?"

"Yes, Director Holbeck." Gideon straightened up. I couldn't tell if he'd winced out of fear of Holbeck or residual pain from the injuries he'd gotten saving me.

"After all, *most* couples will be separated when they're given their assigned pairs." Holbeck placed both her hands on the foot of the white bed sheet.

"Most?" A jolt, like hope and horror blended together, shot through my chest.

Gideon gripped my hand so hard it hurt. "I'm happy to take whatever pictures you think best. I'm sorry for interrupting the shoot."

"Perfect." Holbeck patted the bed. "Lace your fingers together and look toward the camera with hope in your hearts. You are working for a cause that is so much larger than yourselves."

He loosened his hold on me just enough to lock his fingers through mine before clinging to me again.

"Now smile," Leigh said as Holbeck sat back down in her seat.

"What did you mean by most, Director Holbeck?" I kept a smile pinned on my face as I stared at the camera.

"More hope and less wide, scary eyes, Lanni," Leigh said. "Close your eyes and open them again, but keep the lids relaxed."

"Director Holbeck?" I followed Leigh's instructions, even though I felt like an idiot.

"Pairings for copulation are assigned based on the probability of the most desirable genetic outcome," Holbeck said. "If a lucky couple just so happens to have the DNA we need, then huzzah for them."

Gideon's hand flinched in mine.

"Are you okay?" I looked to him.

"Eyes front, please," Leigh said.

"Are you even supposed to be standing for this long?" I asked.

"He's fine," Holbeck said.

"But he hasn't even been allowed to come back to school," I said.

"I'm okay," Gideon said. "Just overwhelmed by the cameras. I've spent my whole life in the Arc Domes, and I had no idea there were camera crews just up the mountain in Incorporation Headquarters."

"Spoken like a young man raised to be an Outer Guard," Director Holbeck said. "From so close to the action, it's easy to believe that guns and violence are the only way to secure the future. But a well-timed publicity campaign can change the fate of the world. The domes never would have been built if the Incorporation hadn't convinced the right people that our work was necessary. Drop the hands and look at each other."

I squeezed Gideon's hand before pulling free and turning to face him.

"No, body front, face toward your boyfriend," Holbeck said.

"Sorry." I pivoted to have my robed front facing toward the camera.

"Smiles," Leigh said. "Look into each other's eyes, and let us see the love."

I met Gideon's gaze.

Desperation filled his eyes even though he had a smile on his face. I couldn't tell if he wanted to run, or punch Leigh, or leap across the bed and strangle me for having almost gotten him killed in the bombing.

"Without compelling messaging, we wouldn't have gotten the right people to commit to living in the domes, either," Holbeck said. "It was before my time, of course, but I've gone through all the video reels and pamphlets my predecessors created. They were brilliant. They sent those materials out to the best and the brightest, and look at the future those photo shoots helped to create. Now, you're helping to shape the future with the campaign we'll be sending out to the other domes."

"You mean the propaganda." The words shot out of my mouth.

Everyone in the room froze.

Panic filled Gideon's eyes.

Holbeck stood, taking the time to set her tablet back on her seat before stepping toward me.

"Propaganda?" Holbeck didn't sound angry. "Is that what you think this is?"

"I..."

Gideon gave the tiniest shake of his head.

"No, ma'am." I looked to Holbeck, wrinkling my eyebrows in confusion. "Or maybe I do. I'm not sure. I learned about propaganda in school. About sending out information to convince people to believe in something, but maybe I didn't understand the word."

Holbeck reached for me. A chill swept up my arms as I placed my hands in hers.

"Do you often have trouble understanding things in school?" Holbeck wrinkled her brow in a maternal way.

"No, ma'am."

"Are you under too much pressure?" Holbeck let go of my hands, but then she touched my chin, tipping my face so she could look into my eyes, which was so much worse.

"No, ma'am."

"If you're having problems understanding things like the difference between propaganda and the important work we're doing here, maybe we need to lighten your load. Your little sister, Mari, she could stay with your guardian full time."

Bang. The sound echoed through my mind. But a new, high-pitched screaming joined in.

Mari, screaming in terror. Mari, taken away from me so I couldn't help her when the wolves came to kill us all.

"It has nothing to do with Mari." My voice shook. "I can take care of her."

"But is that in Mari's best interest?" Holbeck frowned. "A little girl needs someone who has the capacity to understand the demands that must be met to ensure her safety and happiness. If you're having trouble understanding a simple term like *propaganda*, I think you need to reconsider your priorities."

"I'm sorry, Director Holbeck." The sound of the screaming got louder. The walls seemed to vibrate with the noise. "I promise, I will keep my priorities in order. I won't let myself get confused again." The shaking of the room brought bile to my throat.

"Good." Holbeck squeezed my shoulders. "Someone put more blush on this girl, she looks like a corpse."

A corpse. That's what Mari and I would both be if we'd stayed outside the glass. They'd killed fifty-seven percent of the people in our city. It was better here. We were alive in the glass. Alive had to count for something.

I kept trying to convince myself as they posed Gideon and me just inside the door to the room, giving shy smiles like we were excited to be locked in. Then they made us stand face to face at the foot of the bed. They made Gideon put a hand on my hip, like he was going to lay me down on the white sheet.

I waited for them to pose us on the bed. For them to tell him to climb on top of me and kiss me. I didn't even know if the paired couples were supposed to kiss.

Were they supposed to leave their robes on and just let the most necessary parts touch? If one of the pair wanted more contact than the other, would the doctors intervene? Were there any rules at all?

"One last shot, and then we're done." Leigh tapped on her tablet. "Lanni, hop up on the bed."

"No." Gideon wrapped his arm around my waist, tucking me close to his side. "If people don't know what sex is supposed to look like, they're not getting pictures of Lanni to figure it out."

"Watch your tone." Holbeck didn't look up from her tablet. "Fortune favors the obedient, Gideon."

"Yes, ma'am." Gideon held me tighter. "I'm sorry, ma'am. But if—"

"On the bed, Lanni." Leigh shifted to stand between Gideon and Holbeck. "Sit right up at the top. Gideon, stand behind her."

"I'm okay," I whispered to Gideon as I eased away from him.

I wished there were a way for me to explain it to him. I came from a different world, where desperation made the boundaries of what you wouldn't do so blurry it was easy to consider any option that might keep you and the people you loved safe through another night. If I had to lie on a bed with him to convince Holbeck to let me keep Mari, fine.

I'd been ready to creep into the shadows and sell my body so I could get Vamp for my mom. It would have been my job. Feeding and fucking vampires in alleys. Sex for credits. Blood for medicine. Sex to have more income than I could have earned in the factory even with the extra I made from selling stolen syringes. I hadn't been happy about it, but I was willing to follow in my mother's footsteps for Mari.

But even as I wished I could tell Gideon that sliver of truth about who I'd been, the reality of being in that sterile room sank into my soul.

There was a camera pointed at me. And people ordering me around. And I had no choice but to obey.

The bright lights and clean room were worse than being in an alley with a vampire.

"Gideon, stand right behind her." Leigh looked to the Incorporation Guard at the door. "Bring in the infant."

"Infant?" I froze halfway up onto the bed.

"Hopefully, she's still asleep," Leigh said. "So get into position. We're going to get this shot as quickly as possible."

The guard stepped back into the room, carrying a swaddled baby.

"Whose is that?" I asked.

"Shh. Get into position." Leigh waved a hand at me. "Lanni, hold the baby and look adoringly into her face. Gideon, we want shots of you looking at Lanni and then at the baby."

I climbed onto the bed, and Gideon stood behind me. He put one hand on my hip and the other on my shoulder, steadying me as I shied away from the infant the guard held out to me.

She was tiny. Couldn't have been more than a few days old. "Whose is she?"

"For this picture, she's yours," Holbeck said. "The final product of Project Progeny. A beautiful and healthy child."

I froze as the guard set the baby in my arms. She fussed, scrunching her little nose.

"Less fear, more love, Lanni," Holbeck said.

I tried to make myself smile, but I couldn't.

"This is the goal, Lanni," Holbeck said. "Soon enough, you'll have a little one of these growing inside you."

My hands started shaking.

"You'll bring a life into the world, creating a new citizen for the Incorporation." She kept talking, so I knew the screaming in my head wasn't real.

But the utter sickness in my stomach. The...I don't even have a word for it. Revulsion and loathing and terror and hatred, and wanting to burn the whole world while needing to curl up and cry because you're too weak to move, all at the same time.

"We'll be okay." Gideon wrapped his arm around the baby and me, pulling us closer to him. "Do you remember holding Mari when she was little?"

"I wouldn't go near her for the first week." I let out a long breath, trying to picture tiny Mari in my arms. "Mom had made a big deal about how I had to be careful with her. I was so terrified I would hurt her, I'd scream if Mom brought her within ten feet of me."

Gideon's laugh rumbled from his chest into my back, dulling the edges of my panic just enough for me to force a smile onto my face.

"Once Mom convinced me to hold her, I never wanted to put her down," I said. "I would have carried her all the time if I could've. Mom had to pry her away from me to feed her."

"Look at the baby, Gideon," Leigh said.

He reached down, cradling the back of the baby's head. "What did your dad think about you and Mari?"

I focused on the baby's eyelashes, making sure my voice would come out even before daring to speak. "He was busy with work. I don't think he noticed us."

"My dad was busy, too," Gideon said. "Both my parents, really. But I never felt ignored. I want to be like that with my kids. Make sure they know I love them."

"Perfect," Leigh said. "We have the shot."

The guard stepped forward and scooped the baby out of my arms.

"And don't worry, you two." Holbeck turned off her tablet and tucked it under her arm. "You'll have a chance to prove what sort of parents you'll be very soon."

CHAPTER THIRTEEN

Director Holbeck strode out of the room, two gray-clad guards right behind her.

"Let's pack it up, people." Leigh turned to the photographers. "The medical staff needs to make sure this room is ready for tomorrow."

I leaned against Gideon, shrinking into his arms.

"Tomorrow?" Gideon asked.

"The first pairs are being called down tomorrow." Leigh said it in a cheerful voice, like she wasn't announcing a horror even a kep should know to hate.

"So soon?" Gideon's voice wavered.

"One of the girls from our class will be brought down here. Tomorrow." My voice trembled as badly as Gideon's.

"And we have to make sure all the introductory materials are ready for when your classmate arrives," Leigh said. "So, no time to waste. Let's get you dressed and give the space back to the medical team."

I started to climb off the bed, so desperate to get out of the room I would have bolted in just the white robe if I'd thought I could outrun the guards.

"No." Gideon grabbed my hand. "Five minutes with Lanni. You promised we could have five minutes."

The smile faded from Leigh's eyes. "I suppose I did." She tapped on the tablet in her hand. "The clock starts now." She stared at us, like she expected us to say something.

"Everyone has to leave," Gideon said.

"They're busy," Leigh said.

"You told me I could speak to her alone." Gideon held Leigh's glare.

"All right, everyone out." Leigh shooed the photographers, who'd already been waiting by the door, into the hall like Gideon was choosing to risk the Arc Domes' safety by asking them to leave us alone.

Gideon didn't turn back to me until the door to the hall had swung shut.

"Are you okay?" He took my face in his hands, staring into my eyes like he thought he'd be able to read a report of how damaged I was.

"I'm surviving." I glanced toward the door, not trusting that guards weren't going to come storming in to separate us. "What about you? Have the doctors not been able to fix you? It's all my fault. I'm—"

"I'm healing just fine." Gideon kissed my forehead. "It took a while for my balance to come back, but the doctors say I've avoided any permanent brain damage. My back still hurts where they fused part of my spine, and my leg is weak from the new muscle graft."

"Shit." I backed away from him. "I'm so sorry. It really is my fault."

"Lanni—"

"It doesn't matter what you say. I know it's true."

"We're both alive." Gideon took my hand. "I'm recovering really well."

"Then why haven't you come back to school?"

It was Gideon's turn to glance toward the door. "They won't let me. No one's said it, but I think it's Director Holbeck's doing. She wants me here where it's easy to keep me penned in by guards."

"But if she's keeping you locked up, why hasn't she come for me?"

"Because she's punishing me for speaking out. To make sure my dad has proper motivation to keep the Outer Guard under control."

"What?"

"Didn't you look at the group lists?"

"Of course I did."

Harper. She'll be called soon. They'll lock her in a white room.

The walls started to sway. I reached back, wanting to steady myself against the bed. But then I realized what the bed would be used for in a matter of hours. I moved forward instead, leaning against Gideon's chest.

"Maybe you didn't notice because you're so new to the Arc Domes." Gideon held me close. "They didn't put any married Dome Guard on the list."

"What?"

"I don't know what kind of game Director Holbeck is playing. Married Outer Guard were named but not married Dome Guard. I haven't seen my dad since the list went out. Maybe they're keeping me in here to make sure he doesn't cause trouble because the two sets of guards are being treated so differently."

"It's not just your dad." I wrapped my arms around Gideon's waist, fighting the urge to run from the room and do something deadly stupid. "They've been keeping all the Outer Guard in the barracks. I thought it was because of the attack in the city, but maybe Holbeck is just smart enough to keep the skilled killers she's dicked over contained."

"My brothers were all on the list. Paul is in the first group. He might be called tomorrow. I didn't think it would start so soon."

Gideon eased away from me, like he felt the need to bolt, too. He dragged his hands over his still-regrowing hair. "We helped them do this. They're going to show pictures of us smiling in these awful white robes to my brother. Not even he deserves to be treated this way. I never wanted this to happen."

"I know that. And people are going to blame us. Most of our class blames us. But you were protecting your family. Paul will just have to understand that you only smiled for the Incorporation because you were protecting him."

"I didn't do it for him. I made the deal with Director Holbeck for you."

"What?"

"She came to me after I woke up. I still had tubes attached to my arms while she was explaining Project Progeny to me." Grief filled his eyes. "She said she would assign you to group one if I didn't help. She'd make sure you were the first to be brought down."

I glanced back at the bed where I should've been scheduled to be the next day, where Gideon had saved me from being sent by sacrificing someone else.

"Holbeck told me if I did everything she said, she'd put us both in group three. She said she'd arrange for us to be paired."

"That's not how the pairing works."

"The pairing works however Holbeck wants it to." Gideon took my hands. "That's why I agreed to help. To keep you safe. You won't be locked in this room with someone else. It'll be me. We'll be together."

"And that makes it better?" I yanked my hands away from him.

"Yes!"

We both froze.

I looked to the door, waiting for Leigh to bustle back in and drag me away.

"It won't be someone you've never met waiting for you in here," Gideon whispered. "It'll be me. It'll be your boyfriend."

"Because you decided I should have sex with you?" I bumped into the bed as I backed away from him. "Do you not see how screwed up that is?"

"I know. I know this isn't what either of us would have chosen. We should have been allowed to take our time and decide when we were ready. But you were going to be paired with someone." He reached for me. "At least when they bring you in here, you'll be with someone who cares about you."

I skirted around the bed, trying to put more space between us.

He limped a step toward me. Because he'd nearly died saving my life.

He'd helped me. He'd protected me.

That doesn't make it right.

"Our time's almost up," I said. "I should get changed."

"No, not yet." Gideon limped around me to block my path back to my clothes. "Please, Lanni, we have more time."

I dug my fingers into my hair. The strands felt stiff where the Incorporation lady had slicked it into place.

"My deal was for Mari. I agreed to help Director Holbeck so she'd let me see Mari. You made a deal with Holbeck so you could have sex with me."

"That wasn't it." Gideon hesitated before touching my shoulder. "It wasn't because I wanted to be with you. I mean I do, but not here, not like this. I did it to keep anyone else from touching you."

"That's really not much better." I pushed his hand off of me. "I have to go."

"Lanni, I'm sorry." He followed me to the curtained-off area where I'd changed into the white robe. "I thought I was helping. I thought I was doing the right thing."

"I don't think the right thing exists anymore." I drew the curtain between us, wishing I had a more solid barrier to hide behind.

"I'm..."

I threw my robe into the corner and pulled on my pants.

"Do you want me to talk to Holbeck?" Gideon said.

"And say what? You're sorry for deciding that I'd rather have sex with you than anyone else without even asking me? Tell her you don't want to take any more smiling pictures to convince people to peacefully accept the Incorporation's abuse?"

"I can ask her not to pair us together."

I froze with my shirt in my hands. "I don't want to be moved to group one. I can't. I'm not ready." I hated myself for saying it out loud.

Everyone else on the list were kep, but I still felt selfish for wanting them to be in line for torment before me.

"I could ask her to keep you in group three and just give you a different partner."

I tried to ignore the pain in Gideon's voice as I dragged my shirt over my head. "Do you think she'd even agree?"

"I think we might have enough leverage for that. It was never announced that we'd be paired. It would just be both of us getting tossed into the DNA-matching pool with everyone else."

I closed my eyes, wishing I were at home, hiding in my shower, instead of in a sterile room.

"No." The word fell out of my mouth before I knew I'd decided. "Don't ask her to change anything."

I stomped my feet into my boots.

"Okay," Gideon said. "We'll stay paired."

"Yeah." I walked back out of the curtain, ducking around Gideon and heading to the door.

"Lanni, please don't go. I'm sorry. Tell me what I can do to make this right."

"There's nothing you can do. I guess I'll see you again when they drag me down here."

"Lanni—"

I left without letting him finish.

"You still had another forty-seven seconds." Leigh held up her tablet, showing me the timer she'd set.

"We ran out of things to talk about." I started down the hall.

"Good work today, Lanni," Leigh called after me. "Those pictures of your smiling face will greet every new pair in Project Progeny for years to come."

I sprinted for the stairs, letting the pain in my leg steady my stomach, refusing to puke in front of the Incorporation demons.

CHAPTER FOURTEEN

I didn't go back to class. I couldn't face the girl who'd be hauled into that room in the morning. I couldn't stand the idea of her seeing pictures of me smiling as she faced the worst moment of her privileged kep life.

I sat at the table at home, trying to focus on my schoolwork, so I could at least lie to myself and pretend I'd skipped the rest of class to catch up on what I'd missed.

And getting ahead on my work would mean more time to spend with Mari after I picked her up from school.

Besides, the teachers were going to have to get used to students missing class if the Incorporation fucks were going to drag them away to use them like breeding stock in some sick barnyard nightmare.

"Shit." I set my tablet on the far side of the table, denying myself the pleasure of throwing it against the wall and watching the kep tech crack.

Group one. Group three.

It would take them a while to get to me. Gideon and me.

At least he was nice. At least I wouldn't be stuck raising a baby whose father didn't care that they existed.

I'd never known Amery. Never met him. Didn't even know I had a father until he tore me out of my life and shipped me far away from home.

He was trying to save you. Jaime sat in Mari's chair at the table. *And he was right. What the Plains Domes did to the city...they—*

"Don't." My leg started bouncing, like my body knew I needed the pain from my healing injury to keep from drowning. "Just because the outside world is screwed doesn't mean sending Mari and me to this Hell was right."

Then what should he have done? Jaime leaned across the table, reaching for my hand. *Let you stay in the city and hope you survived the population purge?*

"No. We had to get Mari out of there. Even if we survived, watching that kind of violence would have been too much for her. It would have broken her."

Okay, so what's the other option? Jaime wiggled his fingers, teasing me into taking his hand.

"Being in this Hell *is* the other option." I reached across the table, letting my fingers twine through his.

What's the good option?

"There is no *good* option. It's be in here or be dead."

That's really all you can come up with? Jaime furrowed his brow.

"The world is ending. Mari and I made it into the lifeboat. Whatever they want to do to me, I'll deal with. It's the only way I can protect Mari."

Until they come for her. Jaime tightened his hold on my hand.

"They won't."

Those pictures of you will be shown to pairs for years to come.

"Project Progeny will be over before she even hits puberty."

Evil people don't stop doing evil things. They'll find some new way to torment Mari. If it's not shoving her into a sterile room and forcing her to get pregnant—

"Don't."

—it'll be something else.

"I'll keep her safe." I pulled my hand away from him.

Once they get bored with Project Progeny, the next thing they do to their beloved citizens will only be worse. The demons will want a better win. A bigger high. How many times did we watch that happen in the fighting ring?

"This isn't about assholes punching each other for money."

You're right. It's about keeping Mari safe. So what are you going to do about it?

"I'm already doing everything I can!" I knocked my chair back as I stood. "I'm posing for pictures so I can keep Mari with me. I'm keeping Holbeck happy. I'm doing my best. Mom and Amery did this to us, not me. I'm not her parent. I'm not ready to be a mother."

Then do something about it. Jaime walked through the table. He brushed the tears from my cheeks. *You are Lanni Sampson. You are a fighter. Decide how you're going to fight your way out of this.*

"There is no way out of this."

There is. Trust me. He gave me a crooked smile.

"The last person I should trust is the voice in my head."

Jaime's smile faded just before he disappeared.

"I'm sorry, Jaime," I whispered to the empty room. "I'm sorry."

I wished I could scream the words loud enough they'd be able to hear me in the city back home. So Jaime could hear me if he was still alive. I wished my voice would wash over the domes and the kep would hear that I didn't want to help the monsters who were tormenting them. Not even kep deserve that kind of pain.

"I'm sorry."

My words would never be loud enough for everyone to hear, but I couldn't just do nothing. I wasn't born to survive complacency.

I went to my bed and pulled out the knife I'd hidden under the mattress. I stared at the blade. Made for slicing carrots. Not even as useful as the one I'd carried in the city. This was the best weapon I had.

"One small step, Lanni. Even someone as hopeless as you can manage that."

I tucked the knife into the waistband of my pants before going out into the hall. I stood still for a minute, debating what the best approach would be before heading to the door that led out of the building. I peeked out the door, making sure there were no Dome Guard in sight before slipping outside and cutting through the flowerbed that surrounded our housing unit.

I stopped at Harper's window, looking around one more time before pulling out my knife. I slipped the blade into the side of the window. I'd broken into the room Mari and I shared often enough it only took me a few seconds to flip the lock and slide the window up.

"What the fuck?" Harper's voice came from inside the dark room.

"I was hoping you'd be home." Keeping the knife in my hand, I climbed through the window. The stench of homemade liquor slammed into my nose.

"You can't just climb through my window." Harper was sitting on the floor, leaning against the side of her bed, a plastic jug right beside her. "Haven't you ever heard of a door?"

"I've tried knocking. You never answered." I closed and locked the window behind me.

"And that didn't give you any hints?"

"It's fine that you don't want to talk to me." I put the knife back into my waistband before stepping closer to her. "I hate me, too. But I've been trying to talk to you to make sure you're okay."

"I'm peachy." Harper lifted her jug with both hands and took a long drink. "I'm even better now."

"You just proved I was right to break in." I sat on the floor opposite her, careful to stay out of arm's reach.

"Because I'm sitting in the dark drinking homemade booze? You clearly missed all the fun stories about my adolescence."

She took another drink, then slid the jug toward me.

"Are you sure you want to share with me?" I didn't reach for the nasty wine.

"The royally fucked should stick together." She pushed the jug closer with her foot. "But if you try and pour it out or any other intervention-style shit, I will beat you to death with a chair."

I took a drink of the wine. The sweetness clung to my teeth and dried the back of my tongue. "This is better than the last batch." I coughed as I pushed the jug back to her.

"I've been really focusing on my brewing lately."

We sat in silence for a few minutes. Harper fiddled with the top of the jug as she stared at the wall behind me.

Don't be a coward.

"I'm really sorry, Harper." I pressed my palms to the floor. "Helping the Incorporation lie about Project Progeny is unforgiveable, but—"

"How did they convince you to do it?" She kept her gaze over my shoulder. "What did they do to make you smile while you stood in front of everyone saying that locking people in a room and not letting them out until they've fucked is a great idea?"

"They were going to keep Mari away from me."

"Figured it was something like that." Harper took another drink. "Someone like you doesn't just decide to help the devil for shits and giggles."

"If I could think of a way to make the whole thing stop without putting Mari in danger, I swear I'd do whatever it took."

"I know." She finally looked at me. "The fucks of the Incorporation made sure it would be every man for themselves."

"I know it sounds stupid, but is there anything I can do to help you?"

"Slip me some fruit from your food box." She pushed the jug back toward me. "I have to keep up with my brewing."

"Are you sure more brewing is the best plan?"

I took a drink from the jug, hating the taste, but needing something to do besides sit there.

"Did they tell you they do a full medical exam when your group comes up?" She beckoned me over to sit beside her, waiting until I was right next to her to whisper, "Physical, blood work, the whole thing. Turns out my liver function is shit." She held up the jug and cheersed the air. "I've been bumped to the back of my group while they get me all fixed up and in breeding order. I've already had two injections of some healing shit."

"Then should you be drinking?" I glanced to the jug, wondering how fast I could snatch it out of Harper's reach.

"Don't even think about it." She lifted the jug to her other side. "And, the doctors never said anything about me not being allowed alcohol. Mostly because they don't know that's probably how I screwed my liver to begin with, what with booze technically not existing inside the domes. I bet before society crumbled, a doctor would have figured it out in a minute. Cheers to the apocalypse." She took a drink and passed the jug to me. "Don't be an ass. Take a drink and hand it back."

I took a gulp, letting the sweetness burn through the sour in my throat. "When do they think you'll be ready to be paired?"

"They said two to four weeks before my liver's ready. I'm planning on a solid never."

"They're going to figure out you have alcohol eventually."

"I'm sure they'll find it in my autopsy."

"Harper." A zing of panic shot through my chest.

"Organ failure is probably how I'll go."

"Harper, no—"

"I mean, sure, I could find a quicker way out, but why not indulge in my favorite hobby? What better way to go?"

"That's it." I pulled the jug from her hand. Wine sloshed onto her shirt.

"Don't you fucking dare." Harper elbowed me in the chest,

knocking me back against the bed. She ripped the jug away from me. "Get out."

"I'm not going to just leave while you try and drink yourself to death!" I shouted it too loud.

Both of us froze, listening for any hint of kep coming after us.

"Harper," I whispered, "I care about you. Mari cares about you. This would break her heart."

"And that sucks. And if there were any other way to get out of being tortured by the Incorporation, I'd take it." She bit her lips together like she was trying to stop herself from crying, or maybe screaming. "They tightened security on runs into the city after the attack. As soon as you stood at that podium announcing *Project Proving the Incorporation are Monsters*, I started trying to figure out how to disappear into the city. I'm a driver for the Outer Guard. It should've been easy. Just run away and take my chances in the outside world. It might be a short life, but at least I'd be free.

"But they were so careful to keep my truck guarded, I couldn't get away. And then I got added to group one, so they pulled me from driving at all. I'm on vehicle maintenance now. The way they search the trucks before they head out, there's no chance of me escaping without anyone noticing. I have no way out. Except this." She took another drink.

"Look, I know what the Incorporation is doing to us is evil."

"Beyond evil."

"But you're strong enough to survive. I know you are. After everything we went through to get here—"

"It wasn't about getting here. I never gave a shit about the Arc Domes. I was trying to escape the Plains Domes. It was a ticking clock there. The Plains Domes Council would've decided I had to get married and pop out babies eventually. So Amery helped me get away."

"And it's even worse here."

"I would have drunk my way out there, too. I never..." She

shut her eyes as a shudder shook her shoulders. "I've never even once wanted a man crawling on top of me. Or touching me. Or putting himself inside me. I don't want that. I can't make myself want that. I've tried. I swear, I have tried." She looked at me. Tears clung to her eyelashes. "And the idea of being pregnant, of having a thing growing inside of me. And taking over my body. And forcing its way out of me. I can't. I can't let them do that to me. I'd rather be dead."

Her next breath caught in her throat. Tears slipped down her cheeks.

"You're okay." I knelt beside her, holding her to my chest like I would have with Mari after she'd had a nightmare.

But Harper's nightmare was real. I couldn't scare away the monsters and make everything okay.

"We're going to figure something out." I pressed my cheek to the top of her head.

"We can't. There's no way to stop the project and no way to escape."

"Maybe we can't stop Project Progeny, but if we could just get you off the list, you'd be okay."

"But what about you?" Harper looked up at me. "What about the rest of their victims? What if the project is still running when Mari turns seventeen?"

Nauseating fear tightened my gut. "I won't let them touch Mari."

"They're never going to give any of us a choice." She pulled away from me and reached for the jug.

"I'll find a way to make them." I grabbed her hand, blocking her from the booze.

"You're delusional. None of us are strong enough to fight the Incorporation. If you try, they'll destroy you."

"I need you to trust me." I squeezed her hand before letting go and standing up.

"With what?" She took another drink.

"Get yourself showered, drink some water, and eat some food."

"Why?"

"Because you have to stay alive long enough for me to save you."

CHAPTER FIFTEEN

The feel of the air changed as I climbed the stairs to the Marsh Dome. The scent of salt and tinge of moisture even more present than in the Salt Dome.

The ache in my leg sharpened to genuine pain as I crossed the bridges reaching over the canals that divided the land into islands. School had finally let out for the day, so the guards prowling around didn't stop me as I walked to the single-room housing unit that was almost identical to mine.

Tall grass surrounded the brown building instead of the flowerbeds of Bloom Dome. Grass had been planted on the roof as well, almost like the kep were trying to hide the building. But the structure beneath all the kep camouflage was the same as mine.

I hesitated outside the door while fear and revulsion battled in my mind.

A tool to undo the damage. That's all you need.

I opened the door and stepped inside. Six doors lined the hall. I made myself walk calmly to Walsh's door, trying not to let my panic control my body.

You're asking a question. You have nothing to lose.

I knocked before I could talk myself out of it.

Five seconds passed before he opened his door.

Walsh tipped his head as he studied my face. "Did you get all dressed up to come pound on my door?"

"What?" I backed a step away.

"I didn't think medical would put makeup on you as a cure for vomiting." He pointed at my face. "I was also under the impression you'd never willingly speak to me again."

"I'm not." I tucked my hands into my back pockets to stop myself from reaching for the knife I'd left at home that wouldn't have done me a damn bit of good anyway. "Can I come in?"

"Sure." Walsh stepped aside, bowing me into his room. "Did you bring any of whatever it is you were drinking?"

"I don't know what you're talking about." I didn't let myself flinch as he turned the bolt, locking us into his room.

"You reek of cheap booze."

"Well, I didn't bring any for you."

"I guess that's fine. Smells like it was awful anyway." He pulled out a chair for me.

I leaned against the kitchen counter, mostly in defiance, but I also didn't want to go any farther into his room than I had to.

"So, if you're not speaking to me, why are you here?"

Walsh leaned against the wall opposite me. The space was too small, leaving less than a foot between us.

I glanced toward the chair he'd pulled out for me.

He smiled.

I planted my feet, not letting him chase me from the spot I'd chosen. "Is it safe to talk in here?"

"I suppose that depends on what you're afraid of."

I nodded toward the screen set into the wall.

"Why would anyone listen in on what I say in my room?" Walsh shrugged. "I'm a teenage nobody."

"Lucky you."

"It takes more than luck to stay in the background."

"Well, while you're running around in the shadows, I need your help. I need you to stop Project Progeny."

"Sure, let me get right on that." He nodded, no trace of humor on his face. "It might take me a few hours, but I'll make sure it happens."

"Yes, you will."

"You can't actually be serious?"

"Dead serious." I nodded back at him. "You owe me. So now you're going to stop Project Progeny."

"Lanni"—he shut his eyes and dragged in a deep breath—"it's not possible."

"Make it possible."

"I can't. And trust me, I want to. My name is on that list, too, you know."

"But you'll just slip out before you're called."

He started to pace, his arm brushing against me with each pass. There was an edge to his stride, like the animal the drugs had forced into his body wanted to break free. "Maybe. I don't know if I'll be ready to leave before my group comes up."

"Then it's in your best interest to help me." I put my foot on the wall opposite me, blocking his pacing path. "Not only would you be atoning for the time you almost got Mar and me killed. You'd also be protecting yourself."

"Even if there were a way to stop the project—"

"You'll find one."

"—I can't help you."

"Why the hell not?" I rounded on him. "I helped you when you killed Strand."

"And I'm grateful."

"Just not grateful enough to help me."

He dragged his hands down his face like he wanted to tear his own skin off.

"Kill a few doctors," I said, "blow up the medical corridor. I don't care how it happens as long as Mari stays safe and Project Progeny gets shut the fuck down."

"You're not hearing me, Lanni. I literally can't help you." His shoulders tensed. "It would go against my alpha's orders."

"What do you mean?" I stepped away from him.

A flash of something I think was sadness flitted through his eyes before he backed up and leaned against the door. "I was sent here with a very specific set of instructions. What I have to accomplish before I can leave and what I'm not allowed to do. My alpha ordered me not to endanger my mission."

"Who cares?"

"I have to. It's wired into my brain." He tapped his temple like he could feel where the alpha had driven the orders through his skull. "For my own sake, I want to help you, but I can hear the alpha's voice in my head. It feels like thunder pounding against my brain. If I try to disobey him, it's...it's like my whole body freezes up."

"It makes you a werewolf statue?"

"Closer to overwhelming panic from a fight or flight instinct you can't act on than actual stone."

"But you've helped me take care of Mari."

"It was in the best interest of the mission."

I let out a long breath, trying to convince myself the pang in my chest was anger instead of hurt. "Don't let Mari hear you say that. She really cares about you."

"I care about her, too. I wanted to keep her safe because she's a great kid. I was able to help you watch her because anything happening to Mari could lead to someone looking too deeply into my transfer files."

"A self-serving hero." I buried my face in my hands, trying to think beyond the absurdity of me asking a werewolf for help. "If your alpha's orders weren't interfering, could you stop Project Progeny?"

"I don't know how." He slipped past me to pace between his

bed and the table. "I kill the doctors, the Incorporation brings in doctors from other domes. I destroy the computer files of the pairings, they'll re-run the list."

"There's got to be something."

"It doesn't matter if there is. I can't do it, and you'd be putting Mari in too much danger to try it yourself."

"You were chosen by your werewolf pack to come here on a mission. They blew up the whole depot to get you in here. Sabotage is what you were trained to do. You've got to be able to think of some way to help us."

"I'm sorry. I don't want this to happen to you. I don't want to father a child I'm going to leave behind in the domes." His shoulders sagged. "We're trapped in the Hell the Incorporation built, and there's nothing to do but try and survive."

"Harper won't survive. She's drinking herself to death." I felt the smile curling my lips before all the pieces had actually clicked into place. "Did your alpha give you permission to do whatever was necessary to keep the kep from finding out you're a werewolf?"

"Yes." Walsh froze.

"They're running blood tests on each of the groups. Can't hide from a blood test, can you, wolf boy?"

"Shit." He started pacing again.

"Then you'd better do whatever you have to to stop the project. It's what your alpha ordered. And don't forget, if you put Mari in danger, I'll tell the kep exactly what you are." I turned to leave.

"Well done, Lanni. But don't forget this the next time I need a favor."

"I don't owe you anything." I turned the lock and opened the door. "You're welcome for warning you about the blood test."

I stepped out into the hall, pulling the door closed behind me before letting myself feel a tiny hint of hope.

He was Walsh. He could survive poison and plot assassinations. He'd be able to stop the project. He had to.

CHAPTER SIXTEEN

*L*ast night, I dreamt of rain.

We were lying side by side on the roof, letting ourselves get soaked through. You held my hand and laughed as thunder shook the sky.

The rain was cold as it touched my skin. The chill of it made me feel thoroughly alive, as though I'd been waiting my whole life for the sky to cleanse me of the wounds I'd been born to bear. Feeling the drops fall painlessly onto my body, without the sting of chemicals burning me, I knew I was dreaming. You and I never existed in a place where the rain wouldn't singe our skin.

Knowing I was dreaming didn't peel away the beauty of that moment. Now I have a memory of us lying in the rain. Happy, peaceful. I will hold onto that wonder forever.

I turned to look at you, wanting to memorize the smile that brightened your face.

The first red drop that fell splashed across your forehead. The second fell onto your chest.

A storm of warm blood poured from the sky, coating us both in the truth I've tried so hard to ignore. I wanted to pick you up and carry you to safety, but you were still joyfully watching the rain, unafraid of the horrible way the storm had changed.

I woke up drenched in sweat, wondering if you would accept the blood that has swallowed everything I was as easily as you embraced the change in the rain.

I'll never get the chance to ask you. I have no conscience to rely on but my own. I will have to decide how much of a monster I am willing to become.

See you in the embers,

~C

CHAPTER SEVENTEEN

The morning after I convinced Walsh to help me, the Arc Domes seemed like the same normal Hell. I went to guard training and met the rest of the group in the bay. After hand-to-hand drills, we worked with the guns again.

Walsh was there, but he didn't speak to me or even really look at me. I didn't want to chance interfering with whatever plan he had to save us, so when Beck dismissed the group, I just let Walsh leave without trying to chase after him.

When I got home, I woke Mari up and asked her to make breakfast for three before breaking in through Harper's window again.

Her room smelled worse than it had the night before. I forced her into the shower, found clean clothes in the back of her closet, put her mound of dirty clothes into a bag to be sent to the laundry, and made her brush her teeth.

I promised her I had a plan. I couldn't tell her who was helping me, but the project was going to be called off. She just had to keep her head down and take better care of her liver. She wept on my shoulder until Mari came to get us for breakfast.

It felt good to not be the one who was falling apart for once.

Maybe Walsh would be the one to actually stop Project Progeny, but I'd told him about the blood test, which had convinced him to help. That had to count for something. It had to mark the beginning of my atonement.

I hugged Mari for an extra long time when I dropped her off at school. But Walsh had promised she would be safe. So, I gave her a kiss on the head and went to class.

As Mrs. Hale began our lessons, Elliot's seat was still draped in black and Gideon's seat was still empty. The girl who'd been crying in the Tropics Dome gripped the edge of her desk as tears slid down her cheeks.

I wanted to tell her not to worry, everything would be all right.

I half-listened to Mrs. Hale's lecture on the evolution of the metal recycling process as I kept glancing toward Walsh, trying to guess what his plan might be. But he just sat there taking notes.

Our morning lesson ended, and Mrs. Hale walked us toward the Tropics Dome.

The class moved in its usual blob-like way. Clusters of friends gathered together, taking the few minutes of travel time to talk, the outliers walking along the periphery, enjoying not having to listen to anyone. It was all so beautifully normal. A routine I had learned to survive. Until two gray-clad guards emerged from a stairwell to block our path.

One of them stepped close to Mrs. Hale and said something too quiet for me to hear.

Mrs. Hale shuddered.

Walsh drifted back in the group, coming to stand right beside me.

"Josie Minter." The Incorporation Guard stepped closer to our class.

The girl who had been crying for two days backed away from them. The boy who had comforted her in the Tropics Dome planted himself in front of her.

"Josie Minter, you are late for your scheduled appointment in the medical corridor," the guard said.

"She's not going," the boy spoke over the girl's panicked sobs.

"Failure to comply with the Incorporation's instructions will not be tolerated," the guard said.

The front of the class scattered to the walls as the two guards made their way to Josie and the boy.

"Miss Minter," the second guard said, "I strongly recommend you come with us immediately."

"No!" Josie clung to the boy's back, hiding behind him.

"I'm not going to let you take her, you Incorporation piece of sh—"

The first guard shot a little metal dart into the boy's neck.

The class's screams covered the sound of the girl's sobs as the guards grabbed her arms.

"Get off of her!" I launched myself toward them, but Walsh seized my wrist, painfully holding me back. "Let go of her!" I kicked Walsh in the knee.

He picked me up, pinning me against his side as I uselessly fought to break free.

"Put me down!" I twisted, trying to bite him.

"We can't help her." Walsh held me tighter, squeezing the air out of my lungs as the guards led Josie away. "There's nothing we can do for Josie. I'm sorry."

Josie and the guards disappeared around the arc of the corridor. As her sobs faded, the class fell completely silent.

Mrs. Hale tapped her tablet. "I need immediate medical assistance in the corridor by the Tropics Dome."

"Don't go after her," Walsh whispered in my ear before setting me down.

I didn't realize his grip had been keeping me from breathing until I gasped in air. I coughed, staring down the corridor after Josie like maybe she'd magically break free and run back to class.

"Is he alive?" One of the girls crept closer to the boy the guard had shot.

"You were supposed to stop this," I whispered to Walsh. Tears burned in my eyes. I hated myself for crying over a kep.

"He is breathing." Mrs. Hale knelt beside the boy. "They just tranqued him."

"I still haven't figured out how." Walsh took my hand, drawing me closer to him even as I tried to break free. His lips brushed my cheek as he whispered, "I'm a changed human, not a god. The only solutions I can come up with are a plague, a famine, or a miracle. The first two would put Mari in danger, the third is more than I can manage."

"You said you would stop this." I forced the words past the pain in my throat.

"I'm trying, but I need more time."

"Josie doesn't have time."

"How much time did the guards give the people in your city to flee before they slaughtered more than half the population?"

I tensed.

"At least I'm trying." Walsh let go of my hand. "If you come up with anything brilliant, let me know."

A doctor and two men carrying a gurney ran down the hall toward our class.

"Up into the Tropics Dome, everyone." Mrs. Hale swiped the tears from her face. "Let's give the doctor room to work."

"Meet me in the trees in the atrium at six," I whispered to Walsh as we cut around the doctor tending to the boy. "We'll come up with something."

CHAPTER EIGHTEEN

I went to collect Mari after school. When I hugged her, she clung to me like she hadn't seen me in days. She didn't bounce on her toes or chatter as we walked home.

I should've paid more attention to her mood. But I couldn't get my mind to stop racing through a hundred unworkable plans.

I wasn't a soldier or a spy or anyone who had any business resisting the Incorporation. Every idea I could come up with became either impossible or deadly within the first two steps of the plan.

Walsh is right. There is no way to stop the project.

I shoved the thought aside and tried to come up with another plan.

Destroying the medical corridor would put Mari in danger if she ever needed medical care. So would killing all the doctors.

Burning the food supply so the Arc Domes wouldn't be able to support so many new children might mean Mari not having enough food to eat.

Even if I could spread some kind of illness that would keep kep from mixing with people outside their own households, that would put Mari in danger, too.

"Do you want dinner now?" Mari asked as I locked us into our room.

I hadn't even realized we'd made it all the way home.

"Not yet." I ruffled her hair. "You start on homework while I shower. Then I'll cook for us."

"I'll go get Harper, and then I'll cook for all three of us." Mari tossed her tablet onto her bed. "She needs to eat more actual food. She looks almost like Mom."

"Mar—"

"Don't worry. The doctors here can help Harper." Mari looked back at me. There was something in her eyes that made her seem older, like her time locked in the glass had aged her more than her years in the city had ever managed. "Are you going to tell me?"

"Tell you what?" I set my tablet down and took her hand.

"Whatever it is you're hiding from me." Mari held my gaze.

My mind raced through all the things I hadn't told her. The Plains Domes slaughtering most of our city. Sneaking out with Alec. Holbeck threatening to keep Mari away from me. Promising Harper I could keep her safe. Walsh promising to help me. Walsh being a werewolf.

"I talked to Gideon yesterday when they made me take pictures." I knelt in front of Mari. "He made a deal with Holbeck. He thought he was protecting me. He was wrong, and I'm mad at him for it."

Mari stared at me for a long moment before pulling her hand away from me. "Fine then, don't tell me."

"It's the truth, Mar."

"Not the one you don't want me to know. You cry in your sleep, Lanni. Maybe you'll start talking in your sleep, too. Then you'll tell me what you're hiding, whether you want to or not." She went into the hall and slammed the door behind her.

"Dammit." I buried my face in my hands. "Shit, fucking, dammit."

I was trapped. Penned in from every angle, including by my own little sister.

I took off my boots and headed to the bathroom.

I had no way to give Mari whatever truth it was she was looking for without risking telling her things that would only cause her pain and put her in danger.

No way to stop the project without putting Mari in danger.

No way to save Harper without putting Mari in danger.

No way to fucking breathe without putting Mari in danger.

I stripped and turned the water to hot.

I wondered if they'd let Josie go home yet.

My legs started shaking. I sank down to sit on the floor of the shower.

I forced myself to take deep breaths even as panic made my lungs tremble.

"I'm stuck in the box, Jaime. What the hell am I supposed to do?" I tipped my face up into the water. "The easiest thing would be to give them what they want. Do whatever it takes to survive."

I waited for Jaime to say something.

"What if Mom knew this was a possibility and still thought this was the best place for Mar and me?"

He stayed silent.

"You're supposed to be here to help me fight the monsters. We had a deal. You and me together. Always. We would've figured this out already."

Are you strong enough to take down the Incorporation?

"No." I opened my eyes. Jaime sat in front of me, his clothes soaking wet, his hair stuck to his forehead.

Are you strong enough to kill one person?

"You know I am."

Good. Then you just have to figure out which piece of the puzzle you want to tear out.

"Holbeck." I pushed my hair away from my face. "She's the one behind this."

Jaime gave me a crooked smile. *If you already knew that, why am I in here getting wet?*

"Because I needed you." I took his hand. "I always need you."

You've got to find someone else, Lanni. You can't always—

"Lanni, are you okay?" Mari knocked on the bathroom door. "Is somebody in there with you?"

"Should I take Mari for a walk? Give you some time to finish up in there?" There was genuine laughter in Harper's voice. It was a good thing. I'd missed that sound.

"Nope." I watched Jaime fade away. "Just talking to myself. I'll be right out."

As I scrubbed myself clean, I thought through a dozen different ways to kill Holbeck. I couldn't come up with a plan where I was likely to survive, not when she was always surrounded by so many Incorporation Guard. But the horrible plans I came up with were already sounding better than trying to destroy the medical corridor and crossing my fingers they wouldn't create a sterile room for copulation in some other part of the Arc Domes.

Killing one person seemed possible. Assassinating one person was something Walsh had been sent into the domes to do in the first place.

By the time I was dry and sitting down to eat with Harper and Mari, I couldn't feel the walls closing in around me anymore.

Thank you, Jaime.

The memory of his crooked smile flitted through my mind.

Harper looked a little nauseous as she ate, but she finished all the food Mari put on her plate. When I told them I had to go out for a bit, Mari took Harper's hand and said it was fine, Harper would sit with her. She gave Harper a darling smile, like the older Mari who'd asked about my secrets had been an illusion.

But I knew the awful truth. The beaming Mari, who bounced on her bed when Harper said she'd stay, was the act. She was doing what she'd already done for me, forcing me to stay some kind of human even when I'd forgotten how to breathe.

As I walked out the door, Mari was convincing Harper to build a fort with her so she could do her schoolwork hidden under the blankets.

I wish she could stay a happy little girl.

She's already a better person than I'll ever be.

I practiced keeping my gait even on my way to the atrium, forcing myself to roll heel to toe as I walked, even though it pinched the muscles in the back of my calf. I'd been wounded for too long. Time to stop limping. Time to stop cowering and hiding and crying and guilt puking.

I am not the victim in my own story.

Some will see me as the monster, but their lives are not the ones I set out to save.

CHAPTER NINETEEN

There were no photographers lurking as I walked through the atrium. There wasn't any crowd clustered around the door that led up to Incorporation Headquarters, either. Still, I wandered in that direction. Past the pond where we'd gathered to talk about the vague possibility of the Incorporation inflicting the unforgiveable abuse Holbeck had decided to begin.

Four guards in gray uniforms had been stationed outside the Incorporation's metal door. There had never been guards there before.

Holbeck is right to be scared of us.

Us.

I actually thought the word as I gave the guards a nod and looped back toward the center of the atrium.

I wasn't completely sure I knew which *us* I meant. But whether it was Walsh and me or me and the angry horde of kep Holbeck was determined to make her victims, both pairings were unbelievable. The Lanni who'd lived in a shitty apartment in a doomed city would never have considered allying herself with either.

Josie deserves justice. I sat on a bench near the trees, watching a mother try and entertain her two children while feeding the baby who squirmed against her breast.

Careful, Lanni, Jaime whispered, *don't forget who the demons are.*

"Lanni." Walsh leaned against the back of the bench, smiling at the kids and giving a nod to the couple that hurried past. "Fancy meeting you here."

"I needed a walk after dinner." I stood and headed down the path toward one of the streams that cut through the trees. "Mari made a huge meal. Harper came by and everything."

"How is Harper?" Walsh kept his hands in his pockets as he walked beside me. "She's group one, right? Does she know who her partner will be?"

"Her slot's been delayed." I gave a nod to a passing Dome Guard. "Problems with her medical tests."

I stopped to look at a cluster of bright pink and orange flowers growing through the moss that blanketed the ground of the man-made forest.

"That's too bad." Walsh laid his hand on my arm.

"She'll be fine."

He gripped my arm, pulling me into the cover of the trees as soon as a man carrying a tablet hurried out of sight. Walsh pressed a finger to his lips, as though I wasn't smart enough to know we needed to stay silent as we followed the stream that cut through the woods.

We didn't stop until we'd reached the place where we'd spoken before—well out of view of the path, the bubbling rush of the water beside us the only sound I could hear.

Still, Walsh closed his eyes and tipped his head to the side, listening for a moment before letting go of my arm. He opened his eyes and scanned the trees around us before speaking.

"I have nothing," Walsh said. "I'm sorry, Lanni. I swear to you I've been trying, but every solution I come up with is either very temporary, too dangerous for Mari, or something that would go against my alpha's orders. I'll keep—"

"We're going to assassinate Holbeck." There was no waver to my whisper. No pang of regret or fear in my chest.

"What?" He leaned closer to me.

"She's the head of the snake. We kill her, we stop the program."

"We don't know that. Holbeck is an evil monster, but she's not the only villain the Incorporation has to offer. They've produced far worse demons. Believe me. I've seen their work."

"Even if Holbeck's replacement were to want to continue Project Progeny, it would take them time to step into their new role. Time we could use to convince the Incorporation that what they're doing is wrong."

"And if the new Director is worse?" Walsh dragged his hands over his face.

"We kill them, too." I shrugged. "We murder one evil bastard at a time."

"When I finish my work, I have to leave the Arc Domes. I won't be here long enough to slowly slaughter everyone who lives at the top of the mountain."

"Then teach me how."

"No." He stepped away from me. "Absolutely not."

"Why?"

"Because you becoming the vigilante inside the glass would definitely put Mari in danger."

"Then *you* kill Holbeck."

Walsh shook his head and began to pace.

"Why not? You assassinated Strand. Just put some poison on your palm, shake Holbeck's hand, and be done with it."

"No." His shoulders tensed. He tucked his hands into his pockets as his pacing picked up speed.

"You said you would help me."

"I can't."

I stepped into his path. "You have to. You owe me."

"I literally can't, Lanni." He looked up to the canopy of trees that blocked the stone and glass above us from view. "It would go against my alpha's orders."

"How?" I took his chin, tipping his face down and making him look at me.

He shut his eyes. His breath shuddered in and out of his chest, like he was a regular human who'd run for miles.

"Be vague if you have to," I said.

He worked his lips together for a moment before speaking. "Taking out a high-ranking target like Director Holbeck would make my work harder. I can't do anything that might endanger my mission."

"Fuck." I dug my fingers into my hair, pulling at the roots. "Can you help me do it myself?"

He shook his head.

"Can you..." I looked up into the leaves like Walsh had. "Can you help me once your mission is done? Before you leave?"

"I wish I could." He laid his hands on my shoulders.

I looked into his eyes and found genuine regret. He wanted to help me.

"As soon as I get what I came here for, I have to begin the last—" He shook his head again. "It all rolls together from there. I won't have time."

"Dammit." I leaned forward, pressing my forehead against his shoulder as the idea of standing on my own became too exhausting to consider.

"It's okay." He wrapped his arms around me.

Walsh was solid muscle, like someone had carved him into the perfect instrument of war. But, even though his chest and arms were practically stone, there was something soft in the way he held me.

"There is a way to fix this, Lanni. We just haven't found it yet."

"We're locked in paradise, and I can't stand being caged. My brain freezes when I'm trapped." My voice came out as a strained whisper. "Holbeck is the only plan I can think of. I can't let them do this to Harper."

"How much are you willing to risk?" He loosened his hold on me enough that I could look up into his eyes.

"Everything but Mari."

"Then we make a pact." He stepped away from me and held out his hand. "There's something you're in a position to accomplish that will make my mission faster and easier. You could cut months or maybe even years off my time here. You help me, and my timeframe changes. I could take out Holbeck as payment for your work."

"What do you need me to do?"

"I can't tell you. Not until after you agree."

"Why not?" I looked at his outstretched hand. He'd killed Strand with a simple handshake. A paranoid part of me wondered if he'd coated his palm in poison to get rid of the one person inside the domes who knew what he was.

"Once you agree to join my mission, you're an accomplice in my work. I'd be allowed to tell you how you're going to help me. Right now, you're only someone I'm protecting to maintain the integrity of my cover story." He kept his hand outstretched. "I should warn you—with my kind, the penalty for breaking a pact is death. By order of the alpha."

There's another way, Jaime whispered.

I shoved his voice aside and let out a long breath. "Mari stays safe?"

"You have my word."

"Fine." I took his hand. "I help you. You help me."

We shook hands. It felt like something more should have happened. Like the siren beginning to blare. Or maybe a tingle should've run up my arm. Anything to signify that I'd made a bargain that could very well end with my death.

"So, what do I have to do?" I began to pull my hand free as I took a step back.

Walsh tightened his grip on me, yanking me toward him. He wrapped his arm around my waist, and somehow, he was kissing me.

I tried to pull away from him, but he let go of my hand and laced his fingers through my hair. His lips were firm against mine as he claimed my mouth in such a possessive way my *"The fuck, Walsh?"* didn't even come out as words.

He lifted me off the ground, crushing me to his chest like I was the one thing he needed most in the world. I was his air. I was his heartbeat.

He planted my back against a tree, pinning me between the trunk and the impossibly hard ridges of his muscles.

I snaked my arms free and pushed against his shoulders.

He slid his hands down my hips, gripping my thighs, lifting my legs to wrap around him.

"Hey!" a voice barked. "Both of you step back."

Walsh pulled his lips just far enough away from mine to whisper, "Sorry."

He let go of me.

I stumbled, lurching sideways as my feet hit the ground.

He turned around, holding both hands in front of him as though wanting to prove he didn't have a weapon.

I mimicked his stance, cutting around him to face the two Dome Guard who stood on the opposite side of the stream.

The first guard looked stern enough to make me worried about what the consequences of being found straddling Walsh with my back against a tree might be. The second had a look of mixed humor and shock that sank a stone in my stomach.

"What are you two doing back here?" The first guard kept his hand on his holstered gun.

"Homework, sir," Walsh said.

"Homework?" the first guard said.

"Yes, sir," Walsh said. "Didn't you know? It's been made clear that our primary purpose is mating. We were practicing our technique in preparation for Project Progeny."

The second guard's eyes got wide as she pinched her lips into a straight line.

"That is not entertaining, son," the first guard said.

"Not in the least, sir." Walsh gave a nod that bordered on a bow. "I'm glad you've come to understand our plight. Now, are you going to let Ms. Roberts and me resume our studying, or should I assume you're going to send us home? Last I heard, there was no rule about two students meeting before curfew. So, I believe there's nothing you can report us for."

"An oversight in the current rules," the first guard said.

"Perfect." Walsh wrapped his arm around my waist.

The guards didn't move.

"Should we find a new patch of trees?" Walsh said. "Or will you be leaving now?"

"We'll be on our way." The second guard pulled out her tablet and snapped a picture of us.

Walsh shifted, twisting his shoulders around me like he was shielding me from an attack.

"Rest assured, this will be reported." She gave me a tight-lipped smile, then turned and walked away.

"Our duty to the Incorporation must come first in all things." The first guard glared at us for another moment before following the second guard through the trees.

I managed to stay frozen until they were out of sight, then my legs wobbled beneath me. Walsh gripped my waist, not letting me sink to the ground.

He held up a finger to keep me silent as I opened my mouth to speak. He stayed that way for another thirty seconds before finally looking down at me. "Those guards are prowling everywhere these days."

"So you kiss me?" I whisper-shouted through gritted teeth.

"We're lucky it only had to go that far." Walsh let go of me and smoothed the front of his shirt. "If they had stood there watching us much longer, actual penetration might have been the only option."

"Option for what?" I stood up straighter as anger replaced shock, steadying my limbs.

"Not getting caught plotting the assassination of a top Incorporation official." Walsh furrowed his brow. "Did you not read through the new rules? They didn't create the curfew and gathering limits to keep people from sneaking into the woods to feel each other up. They were worried about the victims of Project Progeny gathering to organize against the Incorporation. Getting caught plotting to murder Holbeck could get us and Mari killed. Getting caught with your legs wrapped around me might get us a slap on the wrist. No big deal."

"It *is* a big deal." I knelt beside the stream to wash my lips.

"I didn't poison you." Walsh sat beside me.

"I'm supposed to be dating Gideon." I scrubbed my face, letting the cool water drip onto my neck.

"And?"

"Do you think word of me making out with you isn't going to fly through the Dome Guard and head right to the Outer Guard?" I dried my face with the front of my shirt.

"Captain Pace being pissed at you is better than being accused of attempted murder. And do you really care if someone tells Gideon? I didn't think you were actually attached to the dome trash."

"If the Outer Guard start whispering about this, Alec will find out." I pushed myself to my feet. Pain didn't zing through my calf. I missed it. I needed the ache to center me away from my panic.

"So Alec hears about us kissing in the atrium." Walsh stood and stepped around me, blocking my path back out of the trees. "I'm sure you can come up with some decent lie to tell him as soon as they let the guards back out of the barracks."

"I don't want to lie to Alec."

Walsh laughed. "Think through what you just said. Think about what we're planning to do, about who you are, and tell me that lying about kissing me to that dome butcher really matters."

"Of course it matters. I care about Alec. He's a good guy." I dodged around Walsh.

"He's an Incorporation soldier trained to kill people like us." He caught my arm. "Monster. Murderer. Butcher. Tell me he doesn't deserve any one of those titles."

"You don't know him." I yanked my arm free, hating knowing that Walsh had been willing to let go. I wouldn't have been able to break free otherwise. "I care about Alec. He cares about me. And I don't want him to get hurt because you planted my back against a tree."

"What's more important to you—stopping Project Progeny or keeping Alec happy?" Walsh tucked his fucking hands into his pockets again. "Figure your shit out, Lanni."

I turned to walk away.

"We'll have another rendezvous tomorrow," Walsh said. "I have another romantic place picked out."

I held up my favored finger over my head.

"And don't forget to break up with Gideon," he called after me. "Can't fish with too many lines in the pond."

CHAPTER TWENTY

I waited at the top of the stairs that led up from the barracks, listening to the sounds of the rest of the trainees running on the level below. I stretched out my calf, pressing through the tight spot where my injury was still working on healing.

Guard Beck was the first up the stairs. I stepped into his path just enough to make sure he saw me before shifting back out of the way.

"This isn't the vehicle bay, Roberts." Beck didn't even sound out of breath.

"I know, sir." I started running just behind him. "But if I don't start trying to run, I'll never be back in shape. Let me finish with everyone else."

He shook his head, but didn't say anything, so I kept running, letting myself slow down enough to be near the back of the group where the pace was more of a jog than an actual run.

Walsh slowed to run beside me. "The doctors let you rejoin the pack?"

"Nope."

"Good for you. Same time tonight. Aviary Dome, head toward the back."

"Great." I pushed myself to run faster. Partially to avoid suspicion, but mostly because I had this strange sense that the wolf within Walsh might somehow scent my thoughts. I didn't want his opinion on any of it. Not the way I felt about Alec, and certainly not what I should do about Gideon.

I'd never dated in the city. There had never been time for it. I had to keep Mari fed and safe.

Worrying about my relationship with one boy who liked me was strange enough. Having to consider the emotions of two boys was more than I could manage.

I kept practicing what I wanted to say over and over in my head as I went through the physical drills. In hand-to-hand, I pictured Gideon as my partner as I flipped one of the boys and pinned him to the ground with his arm twisted behind his back.

Each dart I shot for target practice was a curse I wanted to hurl at Gideon.

By the time our session ended, I was sweaty, sore, and felt stronger than I had in a long time.

When Beck dismissed us, I kept to the center of the group, hiding from his line of sight as we filed out of the vehicle bay. While the rest of the students took the stairs up to the housing domes, I cut away from the pack and toward the stairs that led down to the Outer Guard barracks.

"Lanni." Walsh grabbed my arm a full ten steps before I thought he would.

"Go home and shower," I said. "You smell like a dirty dog."

"Low blow." He didn't let go. "Your room is the other way. Do you need me to escort you?"

"Nope." I gave him a grin. "Just have to make a quick stop on the way home. So step back before I decide to test how fast you heal."

He shook his head and let go of my arm. "Don't do anything stupid."

"I'm fixing the damage you did. You can thank me later." I

kept my smile pinned in place as I waved to him and hurried down the stairs.

There wasn't much on the barracks level. Smaller rooms that were probably storage and offices lined the hall, but I'd never been in any of them. There were a few maintenance corridors that cut through in funny places, too.

I didn't pass many people as I walked toward the barracks. Still, I kept my face pleasant and my shoulders back, nodding to everyone in a *good morning* sort of way.

I'd started to feel confident in my plan until I saw the ten gray-uniformed guards stationed outside the barracks entrance. I didn't bother trying to give any of them a friendly nod as they glowered at me.

I hadn't been down to that level since the bombing in the atrium. I didn't know how long the Incorporation had been so blatantly watching the Outer Guard.

Bang. I flinched at the remembered sound.

I'm done falling apart.

"I'm here to see Captain Pace." I spoke to the line of Incorporation Guard.

None of them responded.

"May I please be allowed to see Captain Pace?" I tried again, stepping up to the centermost guard and staring him right in the eye.

"Do you have an appointment?" the guard said.

"Yes." I smiled. "Lanni Roberts here for my 7:45 meeting with Captain Pace."

"Has this meeting been approved?" the guard asked.

"I assume so." I wrinkled my brow. "It must have been approved if Captain Pace allowed it to be scheduled. He is in charge of the barracks, right? Can you call and ask him?"

The guard ground his teeth together before lifting his wrist to his mouth. "Captain Pace, I have Lanni Roberts here for a meeting. She said the meeting has been approved."

I held my breath, drowning in the quiet of the hall as the guard's wrist stayed silent.

"She's two minutes late," Captain Pace's voice answered. "Send her in."

The guard stepped out of my way.

"Thanks." I passed through the line of guards and into the barracks.

Wide, swinging doors on either side of the hall had been propped open. I peeked through them as I passed. Beds lined the rooms. Some were filled with guards either sleeping, reading, or talking to their fellow kep. From the length of the rooms, they held enough beds the Incorporation could keep the guards trapped down there for as long as they damn well pleased.

I walked by a room with punching bags and weights, then passed a dining hall that smelled like overcooked vegetables, before Captain Pace stepped out of a door toward the end of the hall.

"Miss Roberts." Pace held a hand to the side, inviting me into his office.

My shoulders tensed, like my body knew damn well I was walking into an enemy's lair even though I kept my smile fixed on my face.

"Good morning, Captain Pace." I gave him a nod before stepping into his office.

I hated that nod. That stupid kep nod everyone in the Arc Domes gave so often, it had become a common gesture to me. The kep way of saying, *Greetings, fellow privileged asshole. The murderer in me sees and honors the murderer in you.*

"Take a seat." Pace closed the door behind us.

Two plain chairs faced his bare desk, with a more comfortable looking seat ready for the Captain. The only decoration in the entire room was a painting on the wall behind his desk—an image of a man and woman standing on either side of a tree.

It was the same image they'd made Gideon and me stand in front of when we'd announced Project Progeny.

I took a seat, swallowing the bile that crept into my throat.

"To what do I owe this unexpected pleasure?" Pace sat in his chair. He stared at me questioningly, but not with any anger or malice.

He hasn't heard about Walsh.

I let out a long breath.

"First of all, I wanted to apologize." I tucked my hands behind my back to keep from balling them into fists. "Your son was injured while protecting me. I didn't ask him to do it, and I'm sorry he was so badly wounded. I hate that he's suffered for his bravery."

Pace locked his hands together on top of his desk. He looked down at them for a moment before speaking. "My son has always been gifted with courage. I'm not surprised he didn't hesitate to protect you. In fact"—he met my gaze—"it makes me proud."

"Have you seen him? Since the announcement?"

"I've been unfortunately busy." Pace's jaw tightened. "But I receive daily updates on his progress. I'm told he'll make a full recovery given the proper care."

"That's what he told me when I saw him two days ago."

"Does he look well? Has he said anything about going home?" Pace leaned forward. "Has his mother seen him?"

"He's..." I looked at Pace, making myself see the kep instead of the frightened father. "He's recovering well for someone who's being forced to create propaganda by Holbeck."

"Miss Roberts—"

"Don't worry. I know not to say that where Incorporation lackeys might hear."

Pace widened his eyes before glancing up to the corner of his office.

I turned, following his gaze.

A little black disk stood out from the gray of the wall.

I bit my lips together, choking down my desire to scream everything I thought of Holbeck at the top of my lungs.

"I came here to tell you that Gideon and I are no longer together. We broke up." I turned back to Pace. "He made a deal with Director Holbeck to make sure he and I would be paired."

Pace leaned back in his chair, lifting his clenched hands to cover his mouth.

"We're still going to be paired, that hasn't changed. But he bargained his way into having sex with me, and that's not something I can forgive." An unexpected heat burned in my eyes. "I wanted you to know what your son did and who the mother of your grandchild will be."

I stood to leave.

"Miss Roberts—Lanni, wait." Pace got slowly to his feet, like he'd aged twenty years in the span of a few seconds. "I'm so sorry."

"For your son's mistakes or for the Incorporation offering me to him as a reward for good behavior?" I took a step closer to his desk. "Either way, a simple *I'm so sorry* isn't enough to fix anything."

"An apology on my son's behalf is all I can offer. Working for the good of the Incorporation—"

"Justifies every horrible action?" A low laugh slipped out of my throat. "I didn't come here for apologies or explanations. I came here to tell you that if you want to do what's best for your future grandchild, convince Director Holbeck to see Gideon and me as people and not just props. Make her leave us alone. We're the two most hated people in the Arc Domes right now. What do you think that's going to do to our kid?"

Pace froze for a moment before nodding. "I'll see what I can do."

"Thanks, Grandpa." I stepped out into the hall and closed his office door behind me.

A wave of exhaustion washed over me, sweeping away all the adrenaline the training session had pumped into my veins.

One lie gone.

I wanted to slide down the wall and sit until my legs stopped feeling like jelly, but guards were already peering out of the rooms lining the hall, staring at me like I was a mix between a dangerous intruder and an exotic bird.

They really have been keeping them locked down here.

I pushed my sweaty hair away from my face and started walking slowly down the corridor.

"Good morning," I spoke as loudly as I dared to the group lurking in the dining hall doorway. "Sorry to be intruding in the barracks. And for all of you being stuck down here for so long."

"For the good of the Incorporation." One of the female guards glared at me and walked away.

"You would know more about that than me," I spoke even louder, digging my nails into my palms to keep my hands from shaking. "I'm just a student. They put a script in front of me and told me to read. Understanding, agreement—they weren't required. Only obedience."

Two more of the guards walked away.

"I'd think the Outer Guard of all people would understand that." I started walking again, searching through the people watching me as I headed toward the corridor beyond the barracks.

My heart tightened with each group I passed until Alec stepped out of one of the wide bunkroom doors near the end of the hall.

His hair was out of place, and red lines of sleep marked his left cheek. I wanted to run into his arms and see if he still held the warmth of his bed. Just bury myself in the comfort he offered and forget anything else in the world existed.

I gave him a kep nod, barely resisting the urge to reach for him.

"Miss Roberts." He stepped farther out into the hall. "I hope you're well. It's unusual to see students in the barracks."

"I had an unusual reason for visiting." I moved closer to Alec, dropping my voice to something just above a whisper I hoped wouldn't seem too intimate to the horde of kep watching us. "I don't suppose it's too often someone pays a visit to Captain Pace to inform him they broke up with his son."

Alec's neck tensed.

"But with everything that's going on in the domes," I said, "I didn't want the captain hearing any rumors. The captain has enough on his plate without worrying about his son's dating status."

"You're probably right," Alec said. "I hope all parties involved move on amicably."

"We—" I dipped my chin, looking at the ground like maybe the way to explain everything to him without the whole hall knowing what Gideon had done would be written on the perfectly polished floor. "As peacefully as Project Progeny will allow."

I tried to force a smile onto my face, but the tears burning in my eyes wouldn't let me.

"Lanni." Alec raised his arms, reaching toward me.

I stepped away from him. "Any news from your family back home?"

"I..." Alec tucked his hands behind his back, like he was having trouble resisting the urge to seek comfort in touching me, too. "I haven't gotten any messages since I've been down here."

"Right."

Mom, Jaime, Amery.

Gone. Silent. Too far away to ever find out what had happened to them.

"I'm sorry," Alec whispered.

"I have to go make sure Mari's up. Get her ready for school."

"Of course. Tell Mari I say hi."

"Any idea when you'll be able to tell her yourself?"

He shook his head. "The situation is still in flux."

"Sure. Well, be careful." I gave him one more stupid nod and walked away.

I wanted to scream and tear down the ceiling and melt all the glass in the domes.

I just needed him to hold me and tell me everything would be all right. Such a simple thing.

But the Incorporation had made that tiny comfort impossible.

Not just for me. For all the Outer Guard they'd ordered to stay hidden in the barracks.

The Incorporation forgot that animals get more vicious when they're cornered.

CHAPTER TWENTY-ONE

Josie didn't come to class that day. No one raised their hand to ask where she was. I don't know if everyone else knew but me, or if all of us were drowning in the dark, trying not to look at her empty chair, too afraid to find out some new horrible part of the fate that awaited us all.

Not if I can help it. I have a plan. We can stop the Incorporation.

I wanted to scream the words, but I just kept repeating them over and over in my head instead.

We can stop the Incorporation.

I knew it wasn't entirely true. Stopping the Incorporation would take the work of an army that didn't exist. But stopping Project Progeny would save my peers, and that had to be enough.

They took us to the Haven Dome for afternoon lessons. Half the group worked on tying up vines while the other half planted new seeds.

Walsh stationed himself near me. He didn't have to try very hard to manage it since everyone else in the group was doing everything possible to stay away from me.

"Did you make it home in time to feed Mari breakfast?" Walsh propped up a vine and passed me a piece of twine.

"She and Harper were already eating when I got home," I said. "But I still had plenty of time for breakfast. My meeting with Captain Pace only took a few minutes."

"You saw Captain Pace?" One of the girls on the other side of the trellis peeked between the vines. "Have they let the guards out of the barracks?"

"No," I said.

The girl's shoulders rounded.

"I went to Captain Pace's office," I said. "But I did walk through the barracks and saw a lot of the guards."

"Are they okay?" the girl asked.

"As long as you count bored as hell and stir-crazy as okay." I leaned closer to her. "Everyone I saw was up and moving around with no sign of injury from fighting in the city. I'm sorry, I wish I could tell you more."

She opened her mouth like she was going to say something but disappeared back through the trellis as Mrs. Burton came down the row.

I quickly tied a vine in place.

Mrs. Burton stopped beside me, pursing her lips as she examined my work. "You're going to break the plant if you tie the twine that tight. Give it a lighter touch, Lanni."

"Yes, ma'am." I untied the twine, carefully retying it as Mrs. Burton wandered down the row smiling at the more competent students' work.

The girl stayed on her side of the trellis until Mrs. Burton had moved on to examining the planting trays the other half of the class were working on.

The girl watched me for a moment, the wrinkles on her brow growing. "At least you know where your boyfriend is. At least you get to see him."

"I don't have a boyfriend." I lifted my hands away from the vines, knowing I wouldn't be able to manage a gentle touch. "That's why I went to see Captain Pace. To make it very clear that just because the Incorporation has decided to stick their hand up my ass and make me their puppet so I can smile for the cameras with Gideon doesn't mean I'm dating him. The Incorporation may have decided that I'm supposed to lie back and let Gideon use my body to lose his virginity, but that doesn't mean I'm going to let him touch me outside of that sterile fucking room. It's all—"

"Lanni." Walsh gripped my arm hard enough to hurt.

I looked toward him. Half a dozen other people had popped their heads through the trellis to stare at me. Everyone on our side of the row had stopped working to watch my tirade.

"Sorry." I pressed a smile onto my face. "I had a long morning. I guess I should be careful to get more sleep. I have to stay in top shape for the good of the Incorporation."

"Exactly." Walsh let go of my arm.

I shook my hands out and went back to work, carefully tying the vine Walsh held in place.

"Did you really need to bother Captain Pace with his son's relationship status?" Walsh whispered. "Don't you think he has more important things to worry about?"

"He's not the only one I needed to make sure knew."

"Lanni." The girl peeked through the trellis. "I'm sorry the Incorporation has their hand up your butt, and about Gideon."

"Thanks. I'm sorry you can't see your guard."

She swiped a tear from her cheek. "We're both group four. So that's something. I wish I knew how—"

A siren cut over the girl's words. Red lights flashed from the peak of the glass high above, transforming the Haven Dome into a place of panic in the span of a heartbeat.

"Everyone to the bunker below seed storage," Mrs. Burton shouted as she ran for the stairs that led out of the Haven Dome.

The class scrambled to follow her.

"Where does the Aquaponics Dome evacuate to?" I called over the siren.

No one answered me.

I broke free from the scrum of students trying to get down the stairs and bolted to Mrs. Burton. "Where does the Aquaponics Dome evacuate to?"

"Get to the bunker." Mrs. Burton pushed me toward the steps.

"My sister was scheduled to be in the Aquaponics Dome." I rounded on Mrs. Burton. "Where will they send her?"

"To the bunker below seed storage." Mrs. Burton waved me toward the stairs. "This whole level goes to Bunker B. Now move."

"Thank you!" I shouted back to her as I let the crowd funnel me down the steps.

A hand took mine.

I knew it was Walsh without having to look. There was something in the firmness of his grasp and the unnatural heat of his skin against mine.

At the bottom of the steps, people started to run, all heading the same way down the red-lit corridor.

Walsh didn't let go of my hand.

"Tell me Mari's not in danger." I looked to him.

Something glinted in his eyes. Maybe danger or hunger or pure frustration at knowing he could outpace us all in the race to safety but having to keep to a normal human speed.

"Walsh?"

"Not from us."

A ding cut through the siren.

"All guard program trainees report to the Root Dome." The siren went silent as the voice spoke. "All guard program trainees report to the Root Dome."

"I have to get to Mari." I kept running forward.

Walsh looped his free arm around my waist, lifting me out of the stream of fleeing kep and heading the other way.

"Put me down." I elbowed him in the ribs.

"If whatever is happening is bad enough to need trainees,

don't you think you'll do Mari more good by following orders? She'll be with her class." He carried me all the way to the stairs before letting my feet touch the floor.

I tried to pull away from him, but he gripped my hand harder.

"You can't afford to defy an order right now," Walsh said. "Whatever they're calling us to do, we get it done. That's how we keep Mari safe."

I looked down the corridor. Every instinct told me I should run back into the horde of people packing into the bunker and find Mari.

Shit.

Shit.

We can stop the Incorporation.

"Okay." I shook my shoulders out and forced my lungs to accept air. "Let's get this done and get to Mari."

He loosened his grip but didn't let go of my hand as we ran down the stairs to the housing level. I could have pulled free if I'd wanted to, but there was something comforting in knowing I ran hand in hand with a man-made beast.

If his pack had come to attack us, then I wanted to be standing with him so he could tell them I wasn't a kep. Mari and I didn't belong in the Arc Domes and we should be spared from the werewolves' wrath.

If it was some other demon come to seek vengeance for the evils of the Incorporation, I still wanted to be fighting by Walsh's side. Even knowing all the things he'd done, I'd feel safer with him watching my back.

The Root Dome was beyond the housing domes, tucked into a curve of the mountainside where the rocks blocked more of the sun than in any of the other domes. Whether the placement had been chosen because the roots didn't need as much light or if the stacked trays of edible roots weren't impressive enough for the Incorporation to give them a prominent place, I didn't know.

A line of Outer Guard ran up the steps into the Root Dome

ahead of us. All of them were dressed in jackets and helmets like they were going outside.

"What the hell is happening?" I said as we bolted up the stairs behind the pack of guards, knowing I wouldn't get an answer but unable to hold the question in.

Things didn't get any clearer once we'd gotten into the Root Dome.

Shouted orders came from the right where the Outer Guard gathered.

Guard Beck stood to the left of the stairs with five other Outer Guard. All of them were in full gear, too.

"Trainees to me." Beck waved us over. "Suit 'em up," he ordered the guards behind him.

Those guards came toward Walsh, me, and the few other trainees who'd already arrived.

They gave me a vest and put a gun in my hand.

"What is this?" I asked the guard as he roughly fastened the vest in place.

"A gun." He moved on to the next trainee.

"Move out, move out!" The call came from the Outer Guard pack on the right side of the dome.

"We don't have time to wait." Beck's lips pinched into a thin line. He looked to one of the guards. "Get the rest suited up as they come. Trainees, if you have a gun in your hand, follow me."

He led the seven of us who'd been handed weapons toward the right side of the Root Dome.

"We've had a breach in the glass," he shouted over the siren. "The Outer Guard are stretched thin. You're going to aid in guarding the gap. If I say shoot, do it. If anyone not in an Outer Guard uniform attempts to enter the glass, shoot them. If anyone not in an Outer Guard uniform attempts to leave the glass, shoot them."

"What sort of darts do we have, sir?" I asked.

"That doesn't affect your orders," Beck said. "Do you understand?"

A band tightened around my chest.

"I said do you understand, Roberts?" He rounded on me.

"Yes, sir." I forced the words out.

We cut around the last set of tiered planting trays, and a new level of panic squeezed my lungs.

Part of the dome was just...gone.

The glass had been shattered, leaving a hole big enough for a truck to drive through in the barrier that protected the kep from the outside world. Shards of glass littered the singed ground, sparkling in the sun.

The Outer Guard had all gone through the gap, charging down the mountain's slope. I squinted after them, trying to see what they might be racing toward.

"Did any of the attackers make it inside?" The other girl from the training program took her place beside me. She held her gun the way they'd taught us, ready to shoot to kill.

"No one was trying to come in." Walsh pointed to the blackened ground bordering the line where the glass should have been. "The blast came from the inside. Someone was trying to get out."

I looked down the slope again, searching for a single dot of a person running away instead of a horde the Outer Guard were preparing to face in battle.

I found it just above the tree line. Not one dot, but two, running close together as they raced toward the shelter of the forest.

"What will happen to them if they're caught?" I stepped closer to the break in the glass.

"Turn around, Roberts," Beck ordered. "Watch for people coming from the stairs."

"You mean more people trying to escape, sir?" Walsh turned around with me, almost like he didn't want to watch what was happening outside.

"It's not escape," Beck said. "It's desertion."

"So, they'll be kicked out of the Arc Domes?" a boy with short, black hair said. "Then is it really worth chasing them?"

"Their punishment will be decided by the Domes Council," Beck said.

Run faster.

I didn't even feel guilty for wanting the kep to escape.

"Back, get back!" The shout came from by the stairs that led up into the Root Dome.

I tried to listen for the pop of a gun but couldn't hear well enough over the still-wailing siren.

Two men ran into view, holding hands as they tore around the corner toward the break in the glass.

One of them fell, tumbling to the ground with a glint of silver sticking out of his neck.

"No!" The other man looked back to his fallen partner even as he kept running toward us.

"Defend the gap," Beck ordered.

I let out a breath as I raised my gun.

"Don't." Walsh hit my arm with his elbow, knocking my gun aside.

One of the other trainees took the shot before I could even look to Walsh to ask him why it mattered whose dart sealed that poor man's fate.

CHAPTER TWENTY-TWO

I don't remember the first person I watched die. It might have been my parents. I'll never know for sure.

By the time my real, solid memories start, living in the boys' home had dulled Death into a less shocking thing.

For the ones who got sick, there was a simple pattern to their end. Illness, pain, the release of death. Some were trapped within the horrible death rattle for hours. Others were lucky and went more quickly. But the pattern remained.

Death brought on by the violent world outside the boys' home came in many forms. A blow to the head that would instantly end a life. A slash to the gut that would take hours to kill. An infected wound that would make the injured scream for Death's embrace before their time finally came.

I thought I knew Death in all his forms. He had become an old friend to me. Always waiting nearby, watching the world as I did, telling me in a whisper that it wasn't my time yet.

I was wrong.

Death is not a friend to me. He is not one consuming force that treats us all the same.

Death is a predator. He hunts us all with his many weapons.

I learned that the first time I became the blade in Death's hand.

I stabbed that woman in the chest. I watched the pain and fear in her eyes as her blood touched my skin. I pushed her weight away from me as I ripped my knife free. I stood over her as Death claimed his prize.

He took the woman's life and seized the part of my soul it had cost me to kill her. But a soul doesn't get lighter as parts of it are ripped away. It gets heavier. Weighing you down. Sinking you into the ground as Death draws you into his clutches one sliced throat at a time.

My soul is heavy from being one of Death's favored weapons.

I wish I were naïve enough to believe there was some sort of redemption that might wipe away the tally of the lives I've taken.

Even if it were possible, it would be foolish of me to ask for forgiveness now. I will shed many more pieces of my soul before my work is done.

See you in the embers,

-C

They caught them. The couple who'd tried to escape. They were married. Maybe five years older than me. The Outer Guard carried them back in through the same break in the glass.

They looked dead, but I knew they weren't. Just like the two men who'd tried to escape weren't. The Incorporation needed their DNA. Simple as that. They were worth too much alive.

An awful sick feeling rolled through my stomach as they loaded the woman onto a gurney and strapped her down.

The black-haired boy lunged toward her. "Addy. Addy!"

Walsh wrapped his arm around my waist as I swayed.

"Let her up!" The boy tore at the straps. "Addy!"

"Step back," Beck ordered.

"Let her go!" the boy shouted.

Beck shot a dart into the boy's neck.

Walsh held me closer, putting one hand on the side of my head, tucking my face close to his neck. "Don't react. We cannot afford to react."

I gave the tinniest nod and nestled closer to Walsh, letting his strength form a shield to block out all thoughts of what Addy's fate might be.

The voices of the doctors with the gurneys had faded before Beck spoke again. "Trainees, turn in your weapons and vests and get down to medical. They'll treat and release you."

"None of us are hurt." I eased away from Walsh. "I need to get down to the bunker. My sister—"

"Can wait," Beck said. "Get to medical."

"But—"

"Yes, sir." Walsh took my hand as he cut across me.

"Yes, sir." I couldn't manage the same level of conviction as Walsh.

He kept his hand locked with mine as we walked over to the guards waiting for our guns and vests.

A head of bright blond hair caught my eye.

Alec stood behind them, hurt in his eyes and wrinkles on his brow as he watched me clinging to Walsh's hand.

"I feel steadier now." I pulled my hand away from Walsh. "Thanks for the help."

"Anytime." He thumped me on the back.

Alec shook his head and stared down at his own hands. By the time I'd turned in my vest and gun, he'd disappeared.

I looked between the tiers of planters as I headed back to the stairs but couldn't find any sign of him.

"Quick question." I stopped beside one of the two guards flanking the top of the steps. "While an Outer Guard is stationed down in the barracks, will they get any messages I send through PAM?"

"No," the guard said. "It's considered a security risk."

"Thanks." I tucked my hands into my pockets to hide their shaking as I walked down the stairs.

"You okay?" Walsh kept pace beside me.

I missed the siren filling the hall. It had made me feel less alone in my panic.

"I just watched some people get hauled back into the domes,

and I'm pretty sure Alec is pissed at me. Why wouldn't I be okay?"

Walsh tipped his head back, studying the ceiling as we walked. "You need to forget about Alec being mad at you."

"Why is that?"

He wrapped his arm around my waist.

"Don't." I tried to elbow him away, but he only gripped harder.

"Distractions are deadly in the work we're doing." His breath warmed my neck as he whispered in my ear. "You're already worried about Mari. Add anything else to your plate and you'll get sloppy. You can care about people once our mission is done."

"Is that what you do?" I whispered back to him, digging my elbow into his stomach as hard as I could. He didn't flinch. "Do you just not care about anybody?"

He turned his face toward mine, our lips close enough that anyone who didn't know I was trying to mash his stomach into his kidney would have thought we were about to kiss.

"I care about people, Lanni. I care enough to put my sanity on the line to help them. But I'm also a hell of a lot better at this than you. Don't pretend you're a big wolf, pup. That's when you slip up and die."

He held my gaze even as he steered me around the corner to the stairs.

"You're a real shit sometimes," I said.

"I'm trying to help you. If you fail in something like this, there is no second chance."

"Fine." I relaxed my now aching arm, hoping Walsh had noticed at least a bit of pain from my elbow driving into his gut. "I can't do anything about Alec right now anyway."

"That's the way." He let go of me but stayed right by my side as we went down the stairs to the medical corridor.

I tried not to feel like he was staying close in case he needed to restrain me again.

As we passed Captain Tate's office, angry voices carried

through her door. But I couldn't slow down to listen, not with the rest of the tainted trainees surrounding me.

"This way." A doctor at the end of the hall beckoned us toward him. He kept motioning to our group, waving as if we should hurry past the Dome Guard stationed along the walls.

We all picked up our pace, jogging toward him, though the doctor didn't bother to call out and tell us why we should race to be purged of whatever toxins had seeped into our systems in the short time we'd stood by the gap in the glass.

"If you'll all just file in here." The doctor held the door to the last room in the corridor open. "Take a seat and someone will be around to help you."

Walsh shifted to walk in front of me as we entered the room.

Two kep in maintenance uniforms set out little rolling trays next to each of the chairs stationed around the room.

Three doctors bustled around large carts in the center of the space, and another worked on a tablet, glancing down at the carts every few seconds like he was checking off a list.

I followed Walsh to the seats nearest the door. I didn't know if he'd picked them because he thought he'd be treated first and be done with the kep nonsense of thinking breathing the unfiltered air of the outside world for an hour could kill you, or if he wanted to be ready in case of attack. Either way, I trusted his judgment.

A tentacle of self-loathing wound around my throat. The werewolf who'd almost gotten my sister killed was my teacher and ally. Walsh was my protector.

Was the world always this complicated, Jaime? I sat in my chair, waiting for Jaime to speak.

He stayed silent, just like the trainees seated around the room. Even the doctors working on their carts of supplies whispered to each other.

The doctor from the hall stood in front of the door, flanked by two Dome Guard, blocking us in.

Trapped. Caged in. Locked up.

My heart started to beat faster.

I wiped the sweat from my palms onto my pants before raising my hand.

The doctor in the doorway sighed and walked toward me.

"How long will the treatment take?" I asked before the doctor could reach me.

"Shh." He stopped right in front of my rolling tray and bent down to speak in a hushed tone. "If all goes well, we should have the lot of you out of here in about two hours."

"Will everyone be let out of the bunkers before then?" I asked, raising my voice to just above a normal volume.

"I don't know." He leaned closer to me and spoke in a whisper.

"My little sister is in the bunker below seed storage." I kept my volume the same. "If she gets home and I'm not there, she'll panic. Can someone tell her where I am?"

"Please lower your voice." The doctor's eyebrows shot up his forehead.

"Why?" I asked in the loudest whisper I could manage. "Is it supposed to be a secret that we're down here?"

"Some activities are more productive when uninterrupted." The doctor spoke through clenched teeth.

"What do you..." I looked at the two guards stationed by the door. Just like the guards who had been stationed along the hall. "You sick fuck."

"There is no need for—"

"You don't want your sterile rooms contaminated with our noise?" I leaned toward the doctor. "Can't let the people you've locked in know that we might hear them fucking?"

"That is completely uncalled for." The doctor straightened up and backed away from me.

"They're down here now?" One of boys stood from his seat, staring at the wall we shared with one of the sterile rooms. The look of disgust and hatred on his face was everything I wished I were brave enough to show on mine. "You didn't send them down to the bunkers when the siren went off?"

"This corridor is well-protected." The doctor stepped back to stand between the two Dome Guard that flanked the door. "I assure you everyone was safe."

"Why did you bother keeping them down here?" a different boy asked, speaking even louder than I'd dared to. "I can promise you none of your subjects were *productive* with the siren blaring."

"Enough," one of the door guards barked. "You will sit and receive the prescribed treatment. Any further disturbances will be reported directly to Captain Tate."

I leaned back in my chair, gripping the tops of my legs hard enough for my fingernails to hurt my thighs.

"Yes, sir!" the boy who'd stood shouted. He gave a salute and sat back down in his chair.

I was proud of him for that small defiance. Though it probably wasn't worth whatever punishment Captain Tate would give him.

The doctors started at the far end of the room, handing each person a cup of green goop and making them gulp it down before strapping a breathing mask onto their face.

Walsh leaned toward me as the doctors worked on the boy beside me. "You go home to Mari tonight. We can meet tomorrow."

"We're meeting tonight. We're not waiting."

I chugged the nasty green goop then let them strap a mask to my face and pump the metallic tasting medicine into my lungs.

We can stop the Incorporation.

I had to keep believing it. It was the only way I could survive.

CHAPTER TWENTY-FOUR

I met with Walsh in the Aviary Dome that evening. We crept deep into the trees and hid in a patch of berry-filled bushes. We sat silently for a while, Walsh cocking his head as he listened for any hint of someone coming to spy on us.

When he finally decided we were alone, he pulled a box smaller than my thumb from his pocket. He shuddered as he held it out to me, like he could hear the voice of his alpha screaming in his head.

It only took him fifteen minutes to explain exactly what he needed me to do. What his pack had killed hundreds of people and sacrificed so many of their own to get him inside the Arc Domes to do.

A computer file. That's what it all came down to. A bit of information that could change the fate of the world.

Plant a tiny touch-tech chip where it needed to be. Let the virus in the chip invade the system so hackers could dive into the Incorporation's database, steal the file, and save thousands of lives.

The weight of a chance for survival pressed down on me,

threatening to bury me alive before I could even begin my part in helping Walsh to succeed.

He checked four times, making sure I understood everything he had told me before pressing the tiny box into my hand and disappearing into the trees. I couldn't get myself to follow him.

My legs had gone numb. My whole body had decided it didn't want to work anymore. I couldn't even hear the calls of the birds that surrounded me. I'd slipped into a void where not even Jaime's voice could reach me.

I probably would have sat there forever, just melted into the bushes and let myself decay, but instinct kicked in. I had to get back to Mari before curfew. I had to make sure the monsters that had slicked the world in innocent blood didn't hurt my little sister.

For her sake, I could make myself keep breathing.

I hid the box in the ankle of my boot, crawled out of the bushes, and went home.

Harper was there with Mari, helping her with her homework.

Harper didn't know the murderous secret hidden deep within the Incorporation's computers. There was no way. Someone as good as Harper couldn't laugh with Mari while knowing that the information stored in the computers up the mountain could have saved my mom, and Jaime, and all the people the Plains Domes had slaughtered. She couldn't possibly know the terrible truth.

But what if she did?

What if Alec knew? Or Amery?

After I tucked Mari in, I sat on my bed, leaning against the wall, staring at my tablet.

It was past midnight before I managed to convince myself to write the message. When I'd finally finished an hour later, I read through the words a dozen times, waiting to wake up and find out that all of it had been an awful nightmare.

Maybe I'd fallen asleep and missed my meeting with Walsh in

the Aviary Dome. Or maybe I was sick and I'd wake up at home in the city, sweat-drenched and lying in the bed I shared with Mari. Jaime would bring me canned peaches to make me feel better, and I'd tell him all about the nightmare that had nearly stolen my mind.

I read through the message one final time.

Dear Director Holbeck,

I'm writing to offer my sincerest apologies for my previous behavior. The shock of learning what my role within Project Progeny would be overwhelmed my reason.

But after being present at the break in the glass in the Root Dome, I now fully understand the importance of the work you've asked me to do. There is a monumental difference between the message you're creating to help ensure peace within the domes and propaganda meant to misinform Incorporation citizens.

Through my recent interactions with my peers, I believe I have gained valuable insight as to where some of their fears lie and how providing them with further information and experience-oriented messaging might aid in the smooth rollout of Project Progeny.

I would be honored if I could be granted a meeting with you where I could offer my apologies in person and share my ideas.

My only aim is to do my part to aid the Incorporation as they protect the lives of those who will come long after us.

Thank you for your time,

Lanni Roberts

I scrunched my eyes closed, giving myself one final chance to wake up from the nightmare.

I waited until spots danced in front of my eyes before finally opening them.

Mari slept in the bed opposite me. The scent of the vegetables she'd cooked for dinner still lingered in the air.

I clicked send and turned off my tablet. I lay down on my bed and watched Mari sleeping.

I was still watching her when PAM told me it was time to wake up for guard training the next morning.

CHAPTER TWENTY-FIVE

The first day I didn't hear from Holbeck, I told myself she was busy. Being the Director of the people who decided to fuck over the world couldn't be an easy job.

The second day, Josie was back in class. She looked like a shell. She flinched when anyone tried to speak to her. She threw her tablet at the wall when the guards came to collect her. But when they reached for their guns, she stood and followed them out of the room without fighting back.

None of us picked Josie's cracked tablet up from where it had landed. I think we all needed to be able to see it. As a memorial for the bit of Josie the Incorporation had stolen.

The absolute rage that burned through my body made me pretty sure taking out everyone in the Incorporation was a better plan than doing as Walsh had instructed. But getting myself killed while fighting against an enemy I was too small to defeat wouldn't help Josie.

It wouldn't stop the demons from coming for whichever classmate was next on their list.

The third day, I made dinner for Mari, then ignored my homework to write another message.

Dear Miss Leigh,

I sent Director Holbeck a message a few days ago, but she's so busy she probably won't have had time to read it. I've included that message below.

I'm sure you're busy as well, but if you have a moment, maybe you could meet with me and then take my ideas to Holbeck. I also thought that maybe it would be a good idea to get some pictures of Gideon and me staged somewhere other than the medical corridor. I'd be happy to explain why if you'd like, but in listening to my peers, I think more causal photos would really help the message you're trying to send the younger participants in Project Progeny.

Thank you,

Lanni

I hated myself. Even knowing what I was working toward and how worthwhile my goal was, I hated myself.

Because I was right. I could help Leigh and Holbeck take the edge off the evil that was Project Progeny.

I set my tablet on the table, leaned back in my chair, and dug my knuckles into my eyes.

"What's wrong?" Mari asked.

"Nothing, Mar." I pressed harder until spots danced through my vision.

"Sticking with lying?"

"I'm not lying." I opened my eyes to find Mari standing next to me, arms crossed and lips pursed. She looked like our mom had back when she'd had the energy to be truly angry at me. The mom I'd had before she got sick.

"Fine. I'll go see if Harper wants to talk to me." She started toward the door.

"Mar"—I caught her arm—"I am stressed, but it's nothing you need to worry about."

"Because I'm too little." She twisted her arm away from me.

"That's not it."

"Then what is it?" Mari stared at me, just waiting for me to tell her why I was a mess and what I was plotting.

She's just a little girl, even if she doesn't want to be.

"I broke up with Gideon," I said.

"You never really liked him." Mari cocked her head to the side. "You like Alec."

"Mar—"

"Don't lie to me." She stepped closer to me. Since I was still sitting, she managed to glare right into my eyes.

"Gideon and I are going to be partnered. He bargained for it, and it disgusts me."

She studied my face. "That's still not what you're hiding. I don't like who you are in here. Things aren't better in here. It was better at home."

"I know. Some things were better at home. But you have all the food and water you need here. You're safe here."

"Until I'm old enough for Project Progeny."

"No, Mar." I took her shoulders. "I would never, ever let them do that to you. Do you hear me? I will find a way to protect you. I promise."

"But it's okay if they hurt you?" She wriggled away from me. "I have to protect you, too. You're my sister."

"I'll be okay. I have—" I looked to the computer set into the wall. Would the Incorporation bother listening to someone as unimportant as me?

"Have what?"

"I have a plan. I know how to make sure you and I are both happy and safe."

"I have a plan, too. We're going to break through the glass and run, like those other people did. But we're faster than them."

"Mar—"

"We'll be smarter and run away at night so it won't be so easy for the kep to find us."

"It wouldn't matter."

"We can take the road and go all the way home. When we get back to the—"

"Mari Roberts, enough!" I shouted, drowning out her words.

She flinched like I'd hit her.

"I understand you're upset. I know that moving here from so far away was hard. But this is where we live now." I picked up Mari's boots and handed them to her.

She dropped them on the floor. "No we don't. We're leaving."

"You're right." I stomped my feet into my own boots. "We're going for a walk to calm you down. Right now. Put on your shoes or you're walking barefoot."

She glared at me for a few seconds before shoving her feet into her shoes. "You were nicer before."

"Yeah well, parenting a seven-year-old is hard." I took her hand, dragging her toward the door.

"So is parenting a teenager."

I got her into the hall and closed the door behind us, then scanned the walls and ceiling for any hint of a black disk that could be listening to us. Nothing.

I bent over to whisper to Mari. "I'm not sure if they can hear us in our room. So come with me and stay quiet until I say we can talk."

Fear filled Mari's eyes. She switched her grip to cling to my arm as I led her out of our building.

I didn't have time to take her to the atrium, not with curfew starting so soon. Even if I'd had time, I didn't want to force her to walk that far once I'd broken her heart. Mari deserved more from me than making her parade her pain through kep-filled halls.

I froze in front of our building, needing a moment to make sure I wouldn't crumble, before cutting up toward the fountain at the center of Bloom Dome then turning to follow the path Gideon had taken me down during our first and only date.

By the time I helped Mari step over the flowerbeds so we could weave between the trees, she was shaking.

I'm supposed to protect her. I'm failing.

You're not, Jaime whispered. *Protected and unaware aren't always the same thing.*

I stopped beside the weeping willow tree as the sudden fear I'd push the branches aside and find Gideon waiting for me twisted my gut.

"What's wrong?" Mari whispered.

"Nothing." I held the branches aside with my free arm. "This is a safe place to talk."

Mari stared up in wonder at the canopy of branches draping over us. From inside the protection of the tree's limbs, the glass around us disappeared, almost like we were free.

"Sit with me." I moved to lift her up onto the sturdiest branch of the willow. But she'd need more secure, steady ground when I tore her heart apart.

I sank down to sit in the soft dirt.

"Are they really listening in our room?" Mari kept her grip on my arm.

"I'm not sure. But we have to be careful, and there are some things we can't risk saying where the Incorporation might hear us."

"And they won't hear us here?"

"Nope." I picked her up and settled her in my lap.

"We have to go home. We can't stay where they're going to hurt you."

"I'll be fine." I kissed the side of her head. "I have a plan. The Incorporation isn't going to hurt me or Harper or Alec or Walsh and especially not you. We're all going to be okay."

"What's your plan?"

Walsh's secrets aren't mine to tell. Not yet.

"It starts with me having a meeting with Miss Leigh," I said.

"That's not going to change anything."

"You don't know that."

"Yes, I do." Mari pushed away from me. "And even if Miss

Leigh wanted to help, which she won't because she's awful, the Incorporation would still make you an Outer Guard so you'd have to shoot people. Or they might take me away from you and make me live with Miranda. Or do a ton of other awful things. We can't stay here. We're going home."

"No, Mar. That's impossible. We live here now, and we just have to make the best of it."

"We're going home." She stood and glared down at me.

"Please take a breath. There's something we need to talk about."

"Either you help me figure out how to get us out of here or I'll tell them we aren't kep and they can kick us out!"

A shock of fear zinged through my whole body.

"We're leaving. We're going home." Mari turned away like she was going to storm through the trees and start shouting that we were city scum to anyone who would listen.

"We don't have a home anymore. The Plains Domes cleared the city out. They killed a lot of people, anyone who wasn't following their rules."

I took Mari's elbow as she swayed.

"But Mom"—Mari's breath hitched in her throat—"Mom's still in the city."

"I know. I've tried to find out about her, but Alec hasn't been able to get word from Amery. I'm so sorry, Mar."

"But the man who drove me into the plains said he'd protect her. The man who came to get me with Alec and Harper. He promised me." She swiped the tears from her face. "He promised he would get Mom medicine and make sure she had food. He said he'd make her better. He looked me in the eye and promised."

"Who are you talking about, Mar?" I caught Mari as she fumbled back into my lap.

"The man who came to get me at our apartment. Him and Alec and Harper, but you weren't there so Alec and Harper went to get you and the man drove me into the plains to the bunker. He promised she'd be okay." She choked on her tears.

I held Mari tight. "Maybe Mom is safe. Maybe Amery is busy protecting her and that's why we haven't heard from him. We just don't know. But we can't go back to the city. If they purged the population once, they'll do it again."

"But Jaime can take care of us." She clung to my neck. "We'll hide with Jaime and we'll be safe."

Tears burned in my eyes.

I'm sorry, Lanni, he whispered.

"Jaime's gone, Mar. With all the trading he did at the hall..." My voice got stuck in my throat. "We have to stay here. I am going to fight to make this place as safe and wonderful for you as I can, but we've got to stay. We don't have anywhere else to go."

She wept in my arms, sobbing and shaking.

I didn't blame her. Kep had murdered the people we loved, and pretending to be kep was the only way we could stay alive.

By the time her crying had calmed enough for her to breathe properly, the top of her head was soaked with my tears.

"We've got to get back." I kissed her forehead and scooted her off my lap.

"We already missed curfew." She wiped her nose on her sleeve. "We should just stay here."

"And risk Miranda finding out I let you sleep in the dirt?" I stood and picked Mari up, settling her on my hip and letting her wrap her legs around my waist and cling to me like one of the monkeys from the Tropics Dome. "You can't say anything about this, okay? I know what I told you is sad and scary, but you have to pretend everything is normal. You can only talk about this to me, Harper, and Alec. You can't let your friends or even Miranda see you upset."

"I know." Mari rested her head on my shoulder. "I don't want us to starve outside. I just wish there were someplace else we could go."

"Me, too. I love you, Mar."

I could feel her ribs shaking as I carried her through the trees and over the flowerbeds. Her crying had turned back into hiccupping coughs by the time we reached the fountain at the center of the dome.

We'd turned onto the path to go home when a bright light shone in my eyes.

"You, stop," a voice ordered. The beam of light kept me from seeing who'd spoken.

"Hop down." I eased Mari off my hip and set her behind me.

"Name?" the voice said.

"Lanni and Mari Roberts." I raised my hand to shield my eyes from the light.

Two Dome Guard stood on the path between us and our housing unit, both with their flashlights aimed at my face.

"Students," the smaller guard said.

"Yes, sir," I said, not that he'd been asking.

"Are you aware of the curfew that has been instated by the Domes Council?" The taller guard stepped closer to me.

"It's my fault." Mari peeked out from behind me, gripping the back of my shirt as she stepped on my heel. "I got upset and ran away to cry. Lanni followed me, cause she's my sister and she loves me and it's her job to take care of me and..." She dissolved into gasping tears.

"You're okay, Mar." I rubbed her back while still keeping her behind me. "I will always take care of you." I looked to the guards. "Sorry. We lost both our parents before we transferred here. Neither of us is really great at being an orphan." I wiped my tears away with my free hand. "I was just trying to get her calmed down and home."

"But it won't be just our home anymore!" Mari wailed. "There'll be a baby soon, and you'll love the baby more than you love me. And then I won't have parents or a sister." She crumpled to the ground, sobbing on the path.

A pain twisted in my gut.

"Let's get you two home." The taller guard put away his flashlight and stepped forward to pick Mari up.

"I can do it," I said.

He ignored me and scooped her off the ground.

"The baby will cry and take all your attention, and you won't care about me," Mari coughed through her tears.

It's not going to happen. I'm going to stop Project Progeny. I'm going to help kill Holbeck.

But that wasn't a truth Mari was ready for. Not yet.

When we got back to our room, I thanked the guards for their understanding and locked the door behind them. My tablet was still sitting on the table where I'd left it. A little icon flashed in the corner.

Message from the Incorporation.

I waited to tap *open* until I'd convinced Mari to take a hot shower.

I am excited to hear your ideas.
    Will discuss tomorrow,
    Miss Leigh

CHAPTER TWENTY-SIX

Fire the dart, picture Holbeck's face.

Fire the dart, picture Amery lying about protecting our mother.

Fire the dart, picture the kep guards who slaughtered our city.

The pop, pop, pop of the guards' guns filled the bay. I liked the sound. It was calm. Controlled. So much easier to manage than the scream still burning to tear from my throat and the bang that still wouldn't leave my head.

Pop. Sink a dart right into Holbeck's neck.

Beck dismissed us at the end of the session. He looked my way when he said he was happy to see how quickly we were improving.

"Walsh." I said his name quietly, knowing that, even though he was leaving the bay at the other end of our group, he'd be able to hear me.

He lingered outside the bay door, rolling his ankle back and forth as though anything we'd done in training might have actually hurt him.

"Nice work today." He fell into step beside me.

"Thanks." I gave him a little smile. "I'm starting to feel like I'm actually getting the hang of training."

"You are." Walsh stopped to lean against the wall and roll his ankle around again.

"Do you need to go to medical?" I asked as the last of the students passed us.

"Just tweaked it." He started walking again, keeping to a pace that dropped us well behind everyone else. "Careful not to get too good in training, or they'll force you to become an actual Outer Guard."

"That's what Alec said."

"And you decided to ignore precious Alec's advice?" Walsh raised an eyebrow at me.

We headed up the stairs together.

"No." I pushed my sweaty hair away from my face. "But running and punching people makes me feel a lot less like I might explode."

"Pity we didn't meet sooner. You would have done well with my pack." He kept walking even as I froze halfway up the steps. He beckoned me over his shoulder then tapped his ear. "Don't worry. We're good."

I ran up the stairs to reach him. "You do know they have microphones listening in on people now."

"I know." Walsh bowed me around the corner to the housing domes corridor. "Which is why you wanting to talk to me is strange."

He gave a kep nod to a passing pair of maintenance workers.

"I have a meeting with Miss Leigh today." I kept my tone bright and excited. "We're going to talk about some of my ideas for how the Incorporation can approach Project Progeny with our peers."

The muscles in Walsh's jaw tensed.

"I'm hoping if Miss Leigh likes them enough, she'll let me talk to Director Holbeck," I said.

"That would be a huge honor."

"It really would. But I—" I stopped speaking as a Dome Guard came around the curve of the hall.

Subtle, Lanni.

I tried to blush but it came out as a wince. I made myself match Walsh's steady pace instead of giving in to the want to bolt down the corridor and hide from all kep.

"You what?" Walsh asked when the guard was right beside us.

"I need you to help me keep an eye out for Mari." I matched Walsh's volume. "She had a rough night. She misses home, and she wants to go back."

Walsh reached out, his fingers brushing my palm in a movement so quick I barely even felt it.

"Mari can't talk about home." My throat got tight.

"It's not healthy to cling to the past."

I stopped and turned to Walsh, ignoring the people passing by as I stared into his eyes, begging him to understand what I was trying to say.

"If I get too busy meeting with Miss Leigh or Director Holbeck," I said, "just make sure Mari doesn't talk about our life before the Arc Domes enough to make people worry about her. This is where we live now."

"Even if Mari would rather go home?" Walsh stepped closer to me, holding his arms toward me, giving me the option to seek comfort.

I leaned into him, burying myself in his strength, waiting until he wrapped his arms around me to whisper, "We don't have anywhere to go back to. It's stay in here or starve out there. This is the only chance we've got. Keep her quiet."

He held me tighter, pressing his cheek to my hair for a moment before kissing my forehead. His lips brushed against my skin as he whispered in my ear, "Be careful, and I won't have to."

He locked eyes with me as I stepped away from him, and the painful edges of my panic and anger shifted. Not dulling or weakening, more like changing angles. Tipping away from slicing my soul and pointing their danger toward my enemies.

"See you in class." Walsh squeezed my hand before jogging away and disappearing around the arc of the corridor.

CHAPTER TWENTY-SEVEN

"While the war decimated an unfortunate portion of the world's population, the most horrific tragedy came in the environmental consequences." Mrs. Hale paced in front of the full-wall screen. "In spending all their power plotting destruction, the greatest governments in the world ignored the growing danger our planet faced while wasting irreplaceable resources on a cycle of violence that only furthered the problems of poverty and want that created the conflict in the first place."

I gripped the edge of my desk, trying to burn my restless energy out through my hands when what I really wanted to do was sprint circles around the room.

"The long-term ramifications of regional pollution created by the battles of—"

"So sorry to interrupt."

I was halfway out of my seat before I realized I recognized the voice speaking from out of sight.

Miss Leigh walked up the stairs, her tablet in hand. "I need to speak to Lanni."

"Of course." Mrs. Hale's jaw tensed as she gave a pinched smile. "Lanni, you're dismissed. Rejoin us—"

"We're going to need the room," Leigh said. "Your students should be heading to their afternoon lesson soon. Why don't you all enjoy a leisurely stroll through the corridors?"

Mrs. Hale blinked for a few seconds. "I think stretching our legs would be a wonderful idea. Come along, class." She waved the rest of the students toward the door.

I stood up with everyone else, choosing to stand beside my desk rather than let Leigh tower over me.

Walsh didn't look at me as he left with the other students. Not so much as a glance in my direction.

He's better at this than I am.

He was trained for it.

Mrs. Hale hesitated by the top of the stairs once the students had all fled. "Lanni, rejoin the group as soon as you're done."

"Yes, ma'am." I gave her the best smile I could.

Leigh waited until the door had closed behind Mrs. Hale before speaking. "It's been so long since I've been in one of these classrooms. It's cheerier than I remember."

"The classrooms in Incorporation Headquarters don't look the same?" I asked.

"Of course not." Leigh laughed. "Those rooms are smaller and have windows overlooking the valley. But I wasn't born up the mountain. I am one of those rare gems that floated all the way to the top. I am what every child in the domes should aspire to be."

"Being so perfect must be hard." I forced myself to relax my fists.

"Constantly." Leigh patted my desk. "Sit, Lanni. I'm excited to hear your ideas, but my schedule does not allow for wasted time."

"Of course. My primary concern is how you're addressing the teens. I think you've forgotten—"

"I asked you to sit." Leigh patted my desk again.

"I'd rather not ma'am." I looked down at my leg. "I'm still recovering from the bombing and standing helps with the pain."

"Pity medical couldn't do a better job healing you." Leigh typed something on her tablet.

My fingers itched with the want to snatch the tablet from her hands.

Not yet. Stealing the tablet wouldn't help you. Eye on the mark, Lanni.

"You were saying?" Leigh looked up from her tablet.

"Right." I shook my head, trying to bang my thoughts back into order. "I think you and Director Holbeck have forgotten what it was like to be teenagers."

"Is that so?"

"Yes, ma'am. Take my classmate, Josie Minter." I pointed to Josie's desk. It had been empty again that morning. "Pulling her out of class is humiliating."

And traumatizing. And evil. And I'll fucking kill you for it.

"Doing her part to ensure a bountiful future for the domes is humiliating?" Leigh's perfect smile frosted over.

"Having her peers know she's not in class because she's copulating in a sterile room is. And then there's the problem with the doctors and guards lurking outside the sterile rooms in the medical corridor."

"The program has been carefully planned—"

"For people who aren't terrified and fascinated and humiliated by and obsessed with sex!"

"Miss Roberts, there is no need to speak in such incendiary terms."

"I'm just telling you the truth. Sending a virgin who blushes at the thought of penetration into a room to have sex while guards stand outside the door and all their classmates know exactly where they've gone? Even if you let them pick their partner, the teens would still hate you for it."

"So we should put the genetic future of the Arcadia Domes at risk to appease our teenage population."

Smile now. Vengeance later.

"You should change tactics." I forced placidity onto my face. "A veil of choice and privacy will go a long way toward creating acceptance for Project Progeny."

CHAPTER TWENTY-EIGHT

Leigh's smile had shifted from pinned-in-place to genuine joy before I'd finished feeding her my ideas. She'd paced and made notes on her tablet, nodding while I played naïve and desperate to prove my worth.

It was all so easy.

I rejoined the class, feeling like I might actually be capable of helping Walsh complete his mission so he could kill Holbeck for me. I slid into place beside him in the Tropics Dome, squeezing his hand and giving him a little nod.

My plan was working. I had become a worthy assistant in his mission that could save thousands of lives, and I would earn his help in stopping Project Progeny.

It was all going to be wonderful.

I made dinner for Mari, and laughed with Harper, and didn't hear Jaime's voice in the shower.

The message came just before curfew. Incorporation Guard were going to be coming to collect me for the new photo shoot. We would be working after curfew to ensure privacy.

I set my tablet on the table and let out a long breath.

"What?" Mari looked up at me, a wrinkle pinching between

her eyebrows. Red ringed her eyes from where she'd cried while I was in the shower.

I let her think I didn't notice. She deserved the opportunity to grieve without me fretting over every tear she shed.

"Lanni?" She set her tablet down.

"Can you get ready for bed on your own tonight?" I reached across the table and took her hand.

"Why would I have to?"

"I have a meeting with Miss Leigh."

"After curfew?" Mari clung to my hand. "Why? Why can't they see you in the morning instead? How long will you be gone?"

I stood and shifted to her bed, pulling her with me. I bundled her onto my lap and whispered in her ear, "This is a good thing, Mar. Just go with it."

She squeezed my hand extra hard before nodding. "Promise you'll be back before morning?"

"Sure." I kissed the top of her head. "And you promise to finish your homework and not stay up too late?"

"Yeah."

"Then get to work." I hugged her one more time before setting her back on her feet.

I dried my hair as well as I could and brushed my teeth, then changed into a shirt that fit more snuggly, showing off the small amount of cleavage I had to offer.

Mari kept looking up from her tablet and wrinkling her brow at me. I'd wink and nod for her to go back to her work.

Fifteen minutes after curfew began, two Incorporation Guard knocked on the door.

"Miss Roberts," the female guard said, "follow us."

"Just a second." I crossed back to Mari.

"Now, Miss Roberts," the male guard said.

I kissed Mari on top of the head. "Call Harper if you need anything."

"Don't stay out too late, Lanni," Mari called as I went to the door.

"Go to bed, Mari," I called back.

The male guard closed the door before I'd finished speaking.

"This way," the female said.

"Where are we going?" I asked.

Neither of them responded.

This is a good thing. This is what you wanted.

I shook my shoulders out, forcing myself to stay calm.

When we left my building, we didn't head toward the stairs leading out of Bloom Dome. Instead, the guards cut along the path to the fountain. It wasn't until they turned down the next tree-lined path that my stomach started to tense.

A swatch of the flowers separating the houses from the trees had been dug up and moved into a temporary planter nearby. Lights shone from the woods, back where I'd led Mari to tell her what the kep had done to our city.

Don't react, Jaime whispered. *Don't hand them any power.*

I followed the guards straight toward the weeping willow. The space had been invaded. Curtains had been strung between the trees. A makeup station sat off to the side, complete with a big mirror that glowed with its own special lights.

"Lanni." Leigh bustled toward me, reaching for my hand like she was genuinely glad to see me.

The prize is worth the pain.

"Miss Leigh. What is all this?" I tried to sound amazed as she led me into the curtained-off area.

"After our talk today, I wanted to dive straight into your ideas for the new, youth-oriented messaging." Leigh snapped her fingers, and a man hurried forward, carrying hangers full of clothes.

"That's great," I said.

Leigh held a black shirt up to me, crinkled her nose and pulled a pale yellow shirt out instead. "More youthful?" She looked to the man with the hangers.

"Definitely," he said.

"Get changed." Leigh passed the shirt and a pair of black pants to me. She pulled a curtain, hiding me in the little fabric changing room. "You can keep the clothes. It'll be a nice treat for coming up with such a fun idea."

"Did Director Holbeck like it?" I switched shirts. The new yellow one clung to my body and had a lower neckline than I'd ever seen a kep wear.

"I haven't spoken to Director Holbeck yet," Leigh said.

"Oh." I froze with my hands on the button of my pants.

Don't panic.

"Do you think she'll be mad I talked to you?" I asked.

"Not at all," Leigh said. "But Director Holbeck is an extremely busy woman. If we want to convince her to use your ideas, we need to present her with a full concept. We're going to do the photo shoot tonight. Then, depending on how my team can use the materials, I'll come up with a presentation to take to the Director."

"That's great." I dragged on the new pants. They were more flexible than I was used to and hugged my ass like I was planning on heading to the Misery Drain to make some money from the blood drinkers.

The Misery Drain is gone.

I pressed my hands to my stomach, forcing away the sick feeling that rolled through my gut, before pulling the curtain open.

Leigh studied me from the ground up. "Perfect. Now let's deal with your face."

"Thanks?" It just slipped out. "Sorry. I didn't mean—"

"You're a very pretty girl, Lanni." Leigh brushed a finger along my cheek. She did it gently, like she thought she was being kind and couldn't at all sense my burning desire to bite her finger off. "But no one looks good barefaced in front of a camera."

"I guess I'm still not used to makeup being an option."

"Well, it's not down here." She waved me over to the makeup station, sitting me in one of the three chairs.

Gideon sat opposite me. Creases formed in the corners of his eyes like watching them drape a cloth over my new clothes caused him physical pain.

I held his gaze. Not flinching. Not looking away or offering him any hint of pity.

"Makeup, fancy clothes—they'd be a waste down here." Leigh kept talking as the woman brushed powder all over my face. "In the Arcadia Domes and all its sister sites, status symbols would be entirely destructive. The only way to achieve a high status must be through outstanding service to the domes and the Incorporation."

"It's not like that at Headquarters?" I asked.

"Eyes closed," the makeup lady said.

"Of course it is," Leigh said. "But a little bit of glamor and a few exclusive incentives keep the common Incorporation citizen striving to rise and give those who have devoted every fiber of their being to our cause a little treat for their boundless labor. Getting to wear a bit of perfume as a reward for finding a way to consolidate assets and reduce a location's reliance on outside labor ten years ahead of schedule is a tiny use of resources. But it makes those at Headquarters feel truly appreciated for their work."

"It sounds amazing up there," I said.

"Eyes open and straight ahead," the makeup lady said.

I fixed my gaze on the carved wooden pendant around her neck. The image was a series of swirls that seemed to make a maze with no way out.

"I'd love to see it someday," I said. "Headquarters, I mean."

"Who knows?" Leigh patted my hand. "An ambitious girl like you might just be the kind of diamond who rises to the top."

My heart fluttered in my chest.

"What about her hair?" the makeup lady asked.

"Pull it back," Leigh said. "We want a full view of her face."

The makeup lady stepped behind me, clearing my view of Gideon. The chair next to his had been filled. Walsh sat beside Gideon, wearing brand new clothes. His hair had been carefully combed.

I choked on my next breath.

"Good, everyone's almost ready." Leigh beamed at the three of us.

"But why is Walsh—"

"Your idea was a little too small, Lanni. You and Gideon have already been seen together. Everyone views you two as the most dedicated young couple participating in Project Progeny. If we want to really catch the attention of your peers, we need a new pairing. I wanted you to be comfortable enough for the pictures to come out well, so I dug around in your file." Leigh raised her eyebrows as she looked from Walsh to me. "Based on the report from the guards who found you two in the atrium, we should have no problem getting a few convincing pictures."

"What?" The hurt in Gideon's eyes made me want to scream.

"Don't pretend you get to care," I said at the same moment Walsh asked, "What exactly did they put in the file?"

"Let's play nice, children. We don't want to be here all night." Leigh beckoned over the photographers.

"Yes, ma'am," Walsh said.

The photographers eyed Walsh, Gideon, and me.

"I think we should start with Lanni and Gideon." Leigh pointed between the two of us. "Then we'll move on to the second pairing."

"Pairing?" I gripped the seat of my chair.

"It's only pictures, Lanni." Leigh flashed me a smile before tapping away on her tablet. "Let's set up the shot."

"Over here." The red-haired photographer waved me toward the willow tree while the black-haired one fiddled with Gideon's collar.

"You really are lucky, you know." Leigh didn't look up from her tablet. "We are the only publicity and marketing team the Incorporation has bothered to maintain. When the River Domes attempted their preliminary version of Project Progeny, there was nothing but a memo sent by the Domes Council."

"And how did that go?" I held still as the redhead tugged at the front of my shirt, making sure I showed as much cleavage as possible.

"We'll never know," Leigh said. "The attack on the River Domes stole a pivotal Incorporation asset and deprived us of any insight we might have gained through the breeding program instated at that location."

"You're wrong." Gideon took his place beside me. "We know exactly how much of a failure that project was. Lanni and I were almost killed by the bomb that was set off because of that *breeding program*."

"Hmm." Leigh blinked at him. "I suppose that makes the messaging we're working on now all the more important."

"No amount of—"

I gripped Gideon's arm, cutting him off. "Let's just take the pictures."

"First shot is the two of you holding hands." Leigh stepped back, pursing her lips as she studied the tree. "More light through the branches. I want a fairy tale feel."

I took Gideon's hand.

"Are you sure you want to touch me?" Gideon asked.

"You've made sure I'm not going to have any choice in that," I said.

"Smiles from both of you," Leigh said.

"She wants us to hold hands for the picture. The sooner we give her what she wants, the sooner we get to be done." I looked at the camera, digging deep into my soul, trying to find a bit of joy to light up my eyes.

Holbeck will be dead soon. She'll be nothing more than ash, and this whole project will crumble.

"Beautiful, Lanni," Leigh said. "Gideon, give me something to work with."

"When were you and Walsh in the atrium?" Gideon asked.

"None of your damn business." I spoke through my smile.

"Turn to face each other," Leigh said.

"Hold one hand or both?" I asked.

Leigh stepped farther back and tipped her head. "Both. It'll help with the progression."

We turned to face each other.

"I thought we were a couple." Even as Gideon smiled, a pinch of pain furrowed his brow. "I thought you cared about me."

"I thought you respected me enough to let me make my own decisions," I said.

"I'm so sorry, Lanni." Gideon let go of my hand and reached out to touch my face.

"I like it. Keep going," Leigh said.

I fought my need to cringe as Gideon caressed my cheek.

"I only wanted to help," he whispered. "But if you were sneaking around with Walsh, then we were never really together."

"And you shouldn't have risked your life to save me." A tiny tinge of regret twisted my resolve to hate him. I hadn't been sneaking around with Walsh, but I had been meeting Alec in the Salt Dome.

"I would have tried to protect you from the blast anyway." Gideon let go of me. "But I wouldn't have let them force me into doing all of this. I would have protested. I would have let them lock me in the cells before I helped them."

"We need happy faces for these pictures," Leigh said. "Smile, or the cells can still be arranged."

"Then lock me up." Gideon turned to her. "I'm already a prisoner in the medical corridor. I'd rather be in the cells. Do you know what it's like to wonder who's in the room next to me? To not know if they're happy to be doing their duty for the good of the Incorporation or if they've been dragged in there and drugged?"

"You need to take a breath so we can finish these pictures." Leigh smiled at Gideon. There was something in her eyes that made her seem more dangerous than if her tablet had been another bomb.

"No." Gideon stepped toward her. "I'm done playing your game. I don't care—"

"It was after you told me." I grabbed Gideon's hand, making him look back at me. "I didn't kiss Walsh until after you told me the deal you'd made."

Gideon stared down at our joined hands.

"I am furious with you. I feel completely betrayed." I tipped his chin up, making him meet my gaze. "But you getting yourself locked in a cell isn't going to make things any better. You made a deal with Holbeck. If you break your word, what do you think she'll do to you? What could she do to me?"

Gideon closed his eyes. Tears ran down his cheeks.

"We're too deep into this." I wiped his tears away. "The only way out is through."

He shook his head.

"Don't abandon me now, Gideon. I'm scared. I don't want any of this. But if I'm going to have to drop my pants for someone, I don't want it to be someone I've never met. I don't want a stranger to be the father of my child." Pain sliced from my throat to my chest.

I tried to take a breath, but it felt like my lungs had swollen shut. I couldn't drag in any air.

"Lanni." Walsh reached my side in four long strides. "Breathe, Lanni." He stepped between Gideon and me.

"We're not ready for your pictures yet, Walsh," Leigh said.

"Look at me." Walsh stared right into my eyes. "You're okay, Lanni. I promise you're going to be okay."

"I know." Forcing the words out somehow let me draw in a

little air.

"We really don't have time for this," Leigh said.

Walsh leaned in to kiss my cheek. "I won't let them hurt you." His breath warmed my skin as he whispered the words. "They don't know that we're the monsters."

The pain in my chest ebbed.

"I'm okay." I forced my shoulders to relax.

"Then let's keep moving." Leigh waved Walsh back toward his seat. "I would like to sleep at some point tonight."

Walsh gave me a nod before going back to stand by his chair.

"The next shot we need is Gideon and Lanni kissing." Leigh tapped on her tablet.

"No." Gideon stepped away from me. "I'm not going to kiss her for the cameras."

"Yes, you are." I took his hands, drawing him toward me. "Just relax. It'll be okay."

"I'm not going to kiss you with your new boyfriend watching."

"I'll close my eyes," Walsh said.

"He's not my boyfriend." I shot Walsh a glare.

"Why do we have to do this?" Gideon looked to Leigh.

"Because you need to look in love in order for the narrative to make sense," Leigh said. "Now, kiss the future mother of your child and let's move on."

Another wave of panic tightened my chest. I glanced to Walsh.

He winked at me.

We're the monsters.

I placed Gideon's hands on my hips. "Just close your eyes."

"Lanni—"

I stepped closer to him as I wrapped my arms around his neck and kissed him. Gently brushing my lips against his. Giving a little sigh, like I'd finally found the place I was supposed to be. I melted against him as I kissed him again. And finally, he started kissing me back.

"Lanni," he sighed my name.

"And we've got the shot." Leigh clapped her hands.

I eased away from Gideon, letting his hands linger on my hips. He stared into my eyes with something like hope.

"Walsh, you're up." Leigh waved him over. "We need you standing just inside the branches of the tree."

"Yes, ma'am." Walsh ducked into the safety of the willow and disappeared from view.

"Gideon and Lanni hold hands as Gideon pulls aside the branches of the tree, presenting Lanni to Walsh," Leigh read from her tablet.

"What?" Gideon planted himself between the cameras and me.

"Why do you think I asked you if there was a special place where you would want to create a romantic setting with Lanni?" Leigh said. "The two of you are already comfortable with each other. The idea we're working on is creating a conducive and romantic environment for people to feel confident enough to enjoy intercourse outside their relationship."

"It would mean fewer people being brought to the medical corridor." I stepped around Gideon to face him. "It would mean not getting pulled out of class. When our group is called, I would much rather meet you here than in an awful, sterile room. We wouldn't have someone monitoring us." I took his face in my hands. "We can work with medical to figure out the best days for my body, then schedule where to meet on our own. If we have to do this, I want to meet you in the trees for lots of sweaty sex, not in the medical corridor for copulation. That's the idea I want to present to Holbeck."

Gideon looked past my shoulder.

"Please, Gideon," I whispered. "You never finished showing me your favorite hiding places. We can work our way through them. And no one will drag me out of class and lock me in a sterile room. Please, do this for me."

Gideon took my hand. "It shouldn't be like this."

"No. But it's the best option we have." I squeezed his hand.

He turned around, stepping toward the tree.

"Smiles from both of you," Leigh said. "The first shot we need is Lanni and Gideon looking at each other. Then Gideon's eyes stay on Lanni as she looks to Walsh."

I kept my gaze fixed on Gideon, willing him to keep his smile on his face while he gripped my hand hard enough to hurt my fingers as he pulled the boughs of the willow tree aside.

We're the monsters.

We're the monsters. This is all a part of our plan.

The photographers came closer.

"Eyes toward Gideon," Leigh said as soon as my gaze wavered toward the cameras.

The black-haired photographer ducked into the shelter of the trees.

"And we've got the shot," Leigh said. "Lanni, look toward Walsh."

I looked into the haven created by the branches of the willow. They'd hung tiny lights, making it look like fairies had somehow snuck into the domes seeking refuge inside the glass.

I hadn't been dumb enough to believe in magic for a long time, but for a breath, it seemed like maybe I could be whisked away to a world where salvation didn't require murder.

Walsh stepped out of the shadows, reaching for my hand. The fairy lights glistened off his hair. Hunger filled his eyes, like the wolf hidden beneath his skin wanted to devour me. Or maybe the boy who lived tangled up in secrets just wanted a moment to hold someone and forget.

"Lanni, let go of Gideon and take Walsh's hand," Leigh said.

I stepped forward, pulling away from Gideon's grip and locking fingers with Walsh.

"And we've got the shot."

CHAPTER TWENTY-NINE

"We're done?" Walsh didn't let go of my hand.

"Gideon's done." Leigh stepped into the shelter of the willow tree. "We're just getting started with you two."

"What pictures do you need?" I asked.

"Something lusty," Leigh said. "A little moment right where you are, and then maybe pin her against the tree. According to the security report, that's where you two are comfortable."

Gideon stepped forward. "How do you—"

"Someone keep him quiet." Leigh clapped her hands.

"Why don't you just send me back to my cage?" Gideon asked.

"And split up my guards?" Leigh didn't even look toward Gideon. "Sit quietly, little boy, before word leaks to Director Holbeck that you don't want to help the Incorporation anymore."

"So kiss her out here for a shot, and then we'll take a picture by the tree?" Walsh said before Gideon could speak again.

Leigh pursed her lips and cocked her head, studying us.

Walsh let go of my hand and wrapped his arm around my waist, holding me close to his side like he was shielding me from Leigh's glare.

"We need steamier than a kiss," Leigh said. "More visceral.

Just forget we're here and go at each other like two teenagers in heat. I'll let you know when we've gotten all we need."

"This is ridiculous," Gideon said.

"He's distracting me from the process." Leigh said. "Can someone please restrain him?"

Walsh turned to me, blocking my view of whoever it was that grabbed Gideon.

"I'm sorry about this," Walsh said.

"It's not like you haven't kissed me before," I said.

He leaned close, whispering so I could barely hear. "But that was life or death."

I took his chin, moving his face so his lips were a breath away from mine. "So is this."

I kissed him carefully, as unlike the first time as I could possibly imagine.

He moved his hands to my waist, keeping space between us as he started to kiss me back.

I wrapped my arms around him. My fingers found the skin on the back of his neck. Delicious warmth radiated from him. The heat of safety, and fire, and rage that could burn the whole world. I teased his lips with my tongue, tasting him.

He held me closer, pressing me to the ridges of his body.

Perfect stone. Steady. Solid.

He stole his mouth from mine, kissing the side of my neck, moving down to my collarbone as his hand trailed up my side.

I tipped my head, offering him more of my skin, gasping as his thumb teased my breast.

I pulled his head back up. Wanting to kiss him. Needing to claim him as my own.

His hand shifted under my shirt, trailing across the small of my back.

I dug my fingers into his hair, arching against him.

His hands left my breast and my back. I missed their touch. He slid his grip down to my thighs and lifted me.

I wrapped my legs around him, wanting to hold him closer. Certain that filling my body with his would make everything else in the world disappear.

He wanted me, too. I could feel it. The pulsing. The heat.

He placed my back against the tree with a tender hand, like I was a precious thing that needed to be protected.

He kissed down my chest as far as the low front of my shirt would allow.

I gripped the back of his shirt, pulling it up, wanting to feel his skin burn my palms.

I gasped as he pressed his hips to mine, steadying me against the tree as he pulled off his shirt and tossed it aside.

"Lanni," he whispered my name as he kissed me again, trailing his hands up my sides, lifting the bottom of my shirt.

I snaked my hands between us, unfastening the button on the front of his pants.

"Enough!" The shout cut through the haze of lust that had filled my mind.

I tightened my legs around Walsh, desperate to hold on to the bliss of forgetting.

Walsh's hands found my bare breasts.

I moaned as wanting pulsed through me.

"And we have the shot." Leigh clapped her hands.

Walsh pulled his lips away from mine, resting his head on my shoulder as he panted. He lowered the bottom of my shirt, covering the skin he had exposed.

"Excellent work, you two," Leigh said.

Walsh lifted me off him, setting my feet back on the ground.

"I have high confidence that the messaging we're going to be able to create from this shoot can be turned into something Director Holbeck will love." Leigh stepped out of the shadows, a beaming smile on her face. "Passion like that elicits strong responses. I'm very impressed with your work."

"We all must do our part for the Incorporation." I forced a

smile onto my face and grabbed Walsh's shirt from where it had gotten caught in the tree branches.

"It was a very convincing display." Leigh winked. "I didn't think it would go quite so well with the cameras watching."

"We're teenagers with a strict curfew." Walsh pulled on his shirt, covering the muscles on his back I'd been enjoying just a moment before. "I'll take just about any chance I can get to touch Lanni."

"Then maybe I should let you two walk each other home as a little reward for your help," Leigh said.

"No." Gideon spoke from just beyond the parted tree branches where he sat flanked by two guards. "This is grotesque. Taking pictures of them groping each other like that is just wrong."

"I don't think you'd be so mad if you'd been the one doing the groping, Gideon. Take him back to medical," Leigh said.

The two guards grabbed Gideon's arms.

"Lanni, I'm sorry for everything," Gideon called as they hauled him away. "Please don't do this."

"Pity that one is already a part of the branding for Project Progeny," Leigh said. "You two are a much easier couple to work with."

"We're happy to help the Incorporation in any way we can." Walsh laid his hand on the back of my waist.

"And that is the attitude I love," Leigh said. "Now run along. I'll have the Dome Guard give the area around Lanni's house a wide berth until morning." She gave a wink that made my gut twist and my fingers tingle all at the same time. "Have fun."

"Actually," I said, "if you did want to give me any kind of treat for coming up with the idea or for being in the photos tonight, I'd really love to be there when you present the idea to Director Holbeck."

Leigh frowned.

"I understand if it's not possible," I said, "but the more I hear about life at Headquarters, the more I find it's something I want to strive for. Helping with this messaging could be a huge rung on my climb to the top."

Walsh's hand tensed on my back.

"I'll see what I can do." Leigh began tapping away on her tablet. "Now run along, you two. I have a massive amount of editing to do."

Walsh switched his grip to my hand and led me out from beneath the willow tree. The makeup lady handed him a pile of our clothes and no one stopped us as we walked into the dark.

I didn't start to believe Leigh actually meant she'd keep the guards away from us until we passed the fountain at the center of the dome.

There was no hint of angry kep coming to yell at me for being out of my room. Leigh really wanted to give Walsh and me time to sneak into the trees and fool around.

A flustered heat I hadn't felt when we'd been kissing for the cameras rose into my cheeks.

"I should get back to Mari," I said. "Make sure she isn't worrying about where I am."

"Not the best idea." Walsh raised our locked hands and kissed the inside of my wrist.

"Why not?" I looked up the path behind us, trusting Walsh to guide me as I searched for guards waiting to pounce out and grab us.

"Two teenagers were just given permission to dive into the trees together. If we're seen doing anything but that, Leigh might start to doubt we're an item. The less she considers the possibility of you being dishonest, the better."

"So we should just slip into the woods and have sex?" My throat got a little tight as I whispered the words.

"No." Walsh stopped and turned to face me. He brushed his lips against mine, then pulled off the elastic holding my ponytail back. He ran his fingers through my hair like he was trying to memorize its texture. "But we should slip into the trees and stay there for a bit."

"Lead the way." I tucked my hair behind my ears, even though it would have felt safer to tip my face away from him and hide behind the black curtain it provided.

He cut off the path, leading me between two single housing units, heading farther east than I'd explored, away from the little hidden patch of solitude where I'd taken Alec. It seemed like forever since Alec and I had been able to steal that time together.

"We should be more careful," I said.

"What do you mean?"

"About kissing in the trees. I had to rip your shirt off this time. Don't want the third time to be the charm for actually having sex."

"We are developing a nasty habit." Walsh gave a low laugh. "We got pretty damn close...again."

Boiling heat flared from my heart to my cheeks. "Next time we'll pretend to be fighting instead."

He ducked beneath the thick limbs of a twisted tree. I followed him into the darkness.

"Right over here." He put his hand on top of my head, guiding me beneath the branches to a little patch of bare earth.

"It feels like we're little kids playing fort." I sank to the ground.

The dirt was cool, like the heavy leaves of the tree blocked out the sunlight during the day.

"I never really played games." Walsh sat beside me, his leg pressing against mine.

I was glad our tiny fort didn't leave space for him to be farther away.

"You didn't play any games?" I asked. "No jump squares? No finger knots?"

"I've never even heard of those."

"Maybe they had different names in your city."

"Maybe. But I spent my childhood avoiding other kids. And whenever I had any time, I'd read. I went through every book I could find."

"You had a tablet?" I sat up straighter.

"Old paperbacks from before the world fell apart. The science books were outdated, but they taught me enough. It's one of the reasons I was groomed for this mission. Most of the pack members my age hadn't read a book since they were dismissed from school at ten."

"Mar and I had a tablet. Mom made us do lessons every night." It was such a small confession. Still, I held Walsh's gaze. Even in the dim light I could see the question in his eyes. *How did city scum get a tablet?*

I waited for him to ask, but he didn't.

"Mari is lucky to have you, you know?" he said.

"Sometimes, she takes better care of me than I do of her."

"But I've seen what you're willing to do to make sure she stays safe." Walsh looked down at our locked hands. "I'm sorry if tonight made you uncomfortable. I promise I didn't want any of that."

"I hope kissing me wasn't too awful for you." I tried to pull my hand away as I failed to keep the hurt out of my voice.

"That's not what I meant." He held on tighter, holding my hand in both of his. "I didn't want to put your back against a tree for the Incorporation's cameras. Frankly, you're an excellent kisser and if things were different, I wouldn't mind finishing what we started. But putting you in an intimate position that you might find embarrassing—"

"My mom was a sex worker." I cut across him, saving him from himself. "At least that's what she let me believe, I don't actually know the truth about anything anymore. But I grew up thinking Mom went into alleys with men and came home with more credits and rations."

"She found a way to provide for her kids."

"She did." I looked away from Walsh and leaned against the tree's knobbled trunk. "I almost followed in her footsteps. She needed Vamp and offering up my body was the only way I could get her a dose. I was going to work at the blood suckers' club. Be a meal and a lay all in one. But then Al—" I shut my eyes, making my brain slow down. "I lost my chance. I would have done it, though. Fucking strangers would've gotten the Vamp for my mom and credits to take care of Mari."

"I'm sorry things were that bad." Walsh pulled his hands away from mine.

I tensed, ready for him to call me filthy or a whore or—

He wrapped his arm around my shoulders. "Everyone outside has to make tough choices to survive. If selling sex was going to give you a better life than working in a factory, you would have been making the right choice."

"It felt like the only choice." I leaned closer to him.

He kissed the side of my head.

"I didn't tell you that to make you feel sorry for me." I reached across him, taking his other hand. "I just wanted you to know that I'm fine. Nothing back there bothered me. It was just two bodies enjoying the things we were designed to find pleasure in."

Walsh's laugh rumbled through my back. "So you liked it."

"Don't be an ass." I dug my elbow into his gut. "But yeah. It was nice. If things were different, it might have been really nice. But I'm with Alec."

"The Outer Guard of your dreams. A true knight in murdering outsiders armor."

"You don't know him."

"Does he know you?" Walsh shifted, leaning away enough to look me in the eye. "You say you're together, but everything he knows about you is a lie. He thinks you're from the Ice Domes."

I flinched. My heart rocketed into my throat as the lines between the secrets I had to keep blurred. "Where I was born doesn't—"

"You told him." Walsh pulled away, backing as far from me as our tiny hiding place allowed. "Are you insane? You date a guy for, what, a few weeks *while* you're actually dating someone else and you decide to risk your life for him?"

"That's not fair."

"Did you tell him about me? Does he know what I am?"

"Of course not. Why would you think I'd do that?"

"You put Mari in danger by telling him you're outsiders, why should you protect me?" Anger flared in Walsh's eyes. "I trusted you. I told you why I was sent here. You know how many lives are at stake."

"I didn't tell Alec anything!" I shifted to my knees as my body screamed that I should be ready to run. I'd locked myself in a cage with a predator I had no hope of fighting. "Alec helped Mari and me sneak in. Our father is a kep guard. Mari and I never knew him, but he smuggled us in here. Alec knows my father. My father convinced Alec to help us. I never told Alec shit. He knew before I'd ever met him."

"The hacking happened inside the domes." The anger in Walsh's eyes vanished. "When I found out you and Mari were outsiders, I thought you'd found a way in yourselves. But the hole in the computer files really did come from the inside."

"I guess. I don't know how it was done. I didn't even know Mari and I were supposed to be leaving home until Alec kidnapped me."

"Alec and Harper." Walsh sank back. "The way she is with Mari and you. She's in on it."

"You can't tell anyone. They'd be thrown out into the open at best. Be mad at me if you want for not telling you sooner, but don't punish them for helping Mar and me."

"I'm not going to tell anyone." Walsh kissed the back of my hand. "I have to think."

"About what?"

"Paths to victory." He got to his feet and ducked beneath the branches, leaving me alone.

"But tonight went well." I grabbed our pile of clothes and scrambled after him. "I think I have a real shot."

"We absolutely have a shot." He turned around, took my face in his hands and kissed me. Just one kiss. Just enough to leave a pull in my chest whispering that I wanted more of him as he stepped away. "You're brilliant, Lanni."

He disappeared into the darkness, leaving me alone with the taste of his lips.

CHAPTER THIRTY

PAM woke me up late the next day. I leapt out of bed as panic surged through me, but the computer spoke calmly.

"Lanni Roberts, your alarm was manually reset by Liaison of Incorporation Outreach Kinley Leigh."

I sank down onto my bed, trying to convince my heart not to explode out of my chest.

"A schedule adjustment has been added for Lanni Roberts," PAM kept talking. "There are two messages waiting for Lanni Roberts."

"PAM, you're annoying in the morning." Mari threw her pillow at the computer screen.

"At least it's not my fault I slept through training." I stood back up and went to the computer on the wall.

Schedule Adjustment for Lanni Roberts.

Meeting today:

11:00 a.m. Domes Council chamber.

"What did they add to your schedule?" Mari took my hand.

"A meeting with the Domes Council. They probably want to talk about the new pictures. I'm sure it's fine."

I tapped over to the first message.

Lanni,

Director Holbeck caught wind of my crew being in the Arcadia Domes at night. She's already seen the photos from the shoot. She loves the concept and wants to begin the new campaign ASAP!

Congratulations on winning the Director's approval,

Leigh

My heart sank. My ticket up to Incorporation Headquarters had just vanished.

I'd have to come up with another plan.

I could find a way to get past the guards. I could see if there was a vent I could sneak through.

If either of those things were possible, Walsh would already be gone.

I closed my eyes, refusing to let panic send me spiraling.

"What do the messages say?" Mari jiggled my hand.

"Holbeck liked my idea." I clicked over to the second message.

It was from Harper.

My liver function improved faster than the doctors had planned. I've been paired. I'll be called to the medical corridor in three days.

My legs buckled. I sank to the ground.

"Lanni!" Mari was beside me in a second. "Are you okay? Should I get a doctor? What's wrong?"

I bundled Mari into my arms, holding her close as tears threatened to leak from my eyes.

"Lanni." Mari squirmed free so she could see my face. "What happened?"

"Nothing."

"Why are you lying?"

"I'm not." I kissed her forehead. "Everything is going to be okay. I just have to work a little faster, that's all."

"You're sure?" Mari frowned at me.

"Positive. Can you make breakfast? I need to reply to the messages."

"Fine. But if I find out you're lying, I'm going to spit in your food every time I cook for you for the rest of forever."

"Deal." I lifted Mari onto her feet. I didn't get up right away. I just sat there, staring at the wall, trying to think.

I'm the monster now. I have to think like one.

By the time I figured out what to say, I barely had time to type out the two messages before I had to take Mari to school.

Harper,

> *Getting paired sooner will be great!*
> *Trust me. Things are going to work out perfectly for both of us.*
> *Lanni*

Miss Leigh,

> *I'm so glad Director Holbeck liked the pictures! I have a few more ideas I'd love to share with her if she has time.*
> *Thank you for having faith in me,*
> *Lanni*

Mari squeezed me extra hard when I dropped her off at school. As soon as she was in her classroom, I hurried down the hall.

I didn't mind the people glaring at me, or the averted gazes. I didn't have time.

Three days to save Harper.

It was possible. Harper had risked everything when she'd helped Mari and me. I couldn't let her down.

"Lanni." Walsh said my name the moment before he took my hand. "Did your alarm get pushed back, too?"

"Yep."

"That was nice of Miss Leigh."

A group of our classmates came from the other direction.

Walsh let go of my hand to slide his arm around my waist.

"What are you doing?" I whispered.

"We're a couple. Can't let it look like there's trouble in paradise."

"We're not a couple." I began to ease away from him, but he tightened his grip.

"Are you going to tell that to Miss Leigh?" He smiled for a passing pair of Dome Guard.

"We're fuck buddies at best." I leaned into him like I wanted to feel more of his body against mine. "And we have to make sure we're careful about who sees us until I can tell Alec why we're doing this."

Walsh veered us to the wall just far enough away from our classroom that anyone lurking in the stairwell wouldn't be able to hear us. "Is he really your biggest concern right now?"

"No, Harper is, but Alec still matters."

"Harper is one person." Walsh waved to a passing maintenance worker.

"Harper got moved back up the list. We've got three days to get this done."

"You've already planted the seed. If Holbeck—"

"It won't work. Leigh already told Holbeck about the pictures."

He gave a nod to a pack of younger students.

Standing with him was an exhausting exercise in greeting every kep who passed.

"I have an idea that's either brilliant or catastrophic." I leaned close enough to whisper in his ear. "I have to go to the Council room this morning. If something decent doesn't come of that, I'll need your help, but I think I can get up to Headquarters soon."

"Count me in." Walsh kissed my cheek and led me to our classroom.

I sat quietly in class, tapping on my tablet to check the time whenever Mrs. Hale wasn't looking.

When 10:50 finally came around, guards hadn't shown up to haul me away, so I raised my hand.

"Yes, Lanni?" Mrs. Hale said.

"I have a meeting at eleven," I said. "May I be dismissed?"

"Wonder what you'll become the poster girl for this time."

I couldn't tell who'd spoken.

I kept my gaze fixed on Mrs. Hale. She didn't say anything about the comment, though there was no way she hadn't heard.

"It's in the Council chamber," I said. "I don't know what the meeting is for, but PAM told me—"

"You're dismissed," Mrs. Hale said. "Come back to class when you're done."

"Yes, ma'am." I took my tablet and left, trying not to care that every classmate who glared at me would hate me even more before my work was done.

I kept my eyes front as I walked to the Council chamber, clutching my tablet to my chest, ignoring the people I passed.

I missed Walsh walking beside me. Even if I hadn't known he was changed and could probably slaughter a dozen kep without breaking a sweat, he had a solidness to him that made it easier not to slip into the dark and horrible place that clawed at the edges of my mind.

I'm the monster. I'm the monster. I repeated the thought over and over.

Walsh was a werewolf roaming through the kep halls, biding his time until he could complete his mission.

I was a regular human, but I'd seen pure humans do horrible things to each other. I could be just as much a monster as Walsh. I didn't need to shove drugs into my veins for my mission to succeed.

You don't have to be a monster, either, Jaime whispered. *The hero can look evil from the villain's side of the battle. You're a hero, Lanni. It doesn't matter if no one else sees it yet.*

I stopped in front of the Council chamber door, checking the time on my tablet again.

10:58

I leaned against the wall, closing my eyes. But it wasn't pure black that waited in my mind.

Walls of solid concrete surrounded me. A metal ladder led to the trapdoor up above. A man stood beside the ladder, grinning as he raised the knife in his hand.

"Miss Roberts."

The voice yanked me back into the present.

Captain Tate stood in the entrance to the Council chamber, holding the door open. "We're ready for you."

"Thanks." I pinched a smile onto my face as I followed her.

Everything inside the chamber was the same as it had been during my other visit.

The Council members sat at a long table, all facing front.

I went to the single seat in the center of the room, while Captain Tate took her place behind the table.

The chair beside her, Captain Pace's chair, was empty.

Fuck.

I scooted my seat forward an inch. Just enough to make myself feel less like I was about to be strapped down.

"Miss Roberts," Captain Tate said, "do you have any idea why you're here today?"

Fuckity fucks.

"I suppose it could be a few different things." I furrowed my brow. "It could be something to do with Project Progeny, though it would be strange not to have Director Holbeck or Miss Leigh talk to me instead of the Council. Since Captain Pace isn't here"—I pointed to his empty seat—"it's probably not about guard training."

"We're very concerned for you," a woman in a doctor's uniform said.

"Concerned?" I ran through everything in my mind, trying to

find where concern might come in. "Is this because I broke up with Gideon? Did Captain Pace ask you to call me here because I don't want to date his son?"

"No." Captain Tate glanced to the doctor. The two of them shared a look like I'd just confirmed something for them.

"You and your sister are both students," the doctor said.

"My sister?" I gripped my tablet until my fingers hurt. "Mari and I are good students. We're both doing really well in school. You can ask my teachers—"

"How have you been feeling since the bombing in the atrium?" the doctor leaned toward me.

"Fine." I didn't let myself react to the doctor's frown. "I'm working up to being able to run in the guard training program again."

"I have a report of you feeling stressed, anxious even," the doctor said. "It was recommended by one of my team that you receive counseling. That never happened."

"It never showed up on my schedule," I said. "I promise I would've gone if PAM had told me to."

"Your work with Project Progeny had to be given priority," Captain Tate said.

"And I've done everything Director Holbeck's asked," I said.

"How has that work affected your sister?" a man toward the end of the table said.

"She doesn't like the idea of the project, but she's little. It's got nothing to do with her."

"And your interactions with her. How have they changed?" the man asked.

"They haven't." I dug the edge of my tablet into my thighs, confining my panic into one small point of pain I could manage. "Mari and I are doing well. I make sure she does her schoolwork. She's always clean. I make sure she sleeps."

"We're concerned about more than basic needs," the doctor said.

"What do you mean?" I asked.

"You were found in a compromising position with Connor Walsh in the atrium," Captain Tate said.

"I broke up with Gideon," I said. "And if you want to be mad at me for making out with Walsh, you should talk to Miss Leigh, because the Incorporation has no problem with me kissing him."

"You and Mari were also found outside your housing unit after curfew," Captain Tate said. "That is unacceptable behavior, which has unfortunately become a clear pattern of defiance."

"No. There was no defiance." My chest started to get cold. "I explained that to the guards. Mari got upset and ran off. I was comforting her. I was taking care of my little sister and we missed curfew."

"Why was Mari upset?" a woman in a lab coat asked.

"Because she's a seven-year-old orphan who's lost everything she's ever known but me! Because she's a little girl, and Project Progeny scares her. And the idea of bringing a baby into our home scares her. And Dome Guard patrolling all night scares her. I know we weren't supposed to be out, but please don't blame Mari. She's just a kid."

The whole Council stared at me.

"The problem, Miss Roberts, is that you're just a kid, too," Captain Tate said. "And the Council thinks raising your sister has become too much of a burden for you."

"Mari is not a burden." The cold raced through my arms and legs, stealing the pain that had saved me from overwhelming fear. "Mari is everything to me. I would do anything for her. She's my sister."

"Then I hope you'll want what's best for her," the doctor said. "And we believe that it is in Mari's best interest to be raised by an adult."

"No, it's in Mari's best interest to stay with me." Somehow, I was standing. "We have to stay together."

"You're seventeen," Captain Tate said. "The responsibility of raising a grieving child is too much for this Council—"

"But you think I can raise a baby?" I shouted.

"We think caring for an infant *and* your sister would be too much for you," the woman in the lab coat said.

"Then pull me out of Project Progeny." I stepped toward the table. "Or let me wait until Mari is older."

"You've already been assigned to a group," Captain Tate said.

"Then *un*assign me!"

"It can't be done." Captain Tate smacked her hand on the table like she was ordering my execution. "Project Progeny must take priority. There is no point in arguing for that solution."

"Then keep me in the project. I can manage Mari and a baby. We'll be fine."

"It is the opinion of this Council that you and your sister would be better off if she were removed from your care and sent to live with your guardian Miranda," the doctor said.

"No." I stepped all the way up to the edge of the table. "Please. I promise we'll be okay, but Mari has to stay with me."

"As orphaned students, choices affecting your wellbeing are to be made by this Council," Captain Tate said. "Our decision is final."

"You can't do this." The cold in my chest darkened into a void. "Please, I'll do anything you want. I don't care what it is, just let Mari stay with me."

"There is no bargain to be made, Miss Roberts," Captain Tate said. "Your guardian has already collected Mari's belongings from your room. She'll be taken to her new home after school."

"I won't let you take her!"

"Outbursts will not aid in your plea," the doctor said.

"Please don't take her." Tears streamed down my cheeks.

"You're dismissed, Miss Roberts." Captain Tate pointed me toward the door. "I suggest you return to class."

CHAPTER THIRTY-ONE

I can't bring myself to regret the path I've chosen. Even after the sacrifices I've made and the lives I've taken have been tallied, I still believe the good I'm doing will be worth the cost.

But if the skies were to open and give me the chance, I wouldn't choose to bring you on this journey with me.

The pain I've endured. The blood that will never wash off my hands. I could never ask you to carry those burdens.

I will gladly wade through blood and become a monster to put an end to the Incorporation's reign of terror, but how horrible a demon would I be if I dragged you along my path? Can a monster who sacrifices the soul of someone they care for to make themselves a little less lonely even hope for redemption?

Even as I miss you, I am glad you're far out of reach and bringing you with me was not a choice I had to face.

We were born into a world of suffering. The last thing I ever wanted was to cause you more pain.

See you in the embers,

-C

CHAPTER THIRTY-TWO

Everything went numb as I walked back to class. I couldn't see the faces of the people I passed. They were all blurry. Inhuman. Demons who had come to join my nightmare. But their chosen torment sliced deeper than simple terror.

The feeling that carved out my lungs wasn't fear. It was bigger than that. Sharper.

Trapped. Cornered. No way to protect her.

The walls of the corridor swayed, but somehow my feet kept moving.

I stopped at the bottom of the steps to the Tropics Dome. Captain Tate had told me to go back to class, but why should it matter if I disobeyed? They'd already taken everything from me.

Broken. Caged. Alone.

I leaned against the wall. I wanted to scream, but I couldn't draw in enough air.

Keep moving, Jaime said. *You still have more to lose.*

"I don't," I whispered.

You do. A smile brightened his eyes. *They haven't stolen your plan. Fight them, Lanni.*

"I can't."

You have to. You're not allowed to give up. Just keep breathing. He brushed his lips against my forehead. *Do it for me.*

"Okay." I swiped the tears from my cheeks. "Okay."

I made myself climb the steps into the Tropics Dome.

The class had lined up behind rows of tables, working on grinding roots and dried leaves with mortars and pestles.

My feet carried me toward Walsh before I knew I'd chosen where I wanted to be. I slipped into place beside him.

"Back already?" He tapped the powder off his pestle. "I thought you'd be recording a new speech."

"It wasn't a meeting with Leigh." I planted my hands on the table, trying to make the trees stop swaying.

"What happened?" Walsh dropped his pestle and gripped my hips, holding me upright.

The girl beside Walsh turned to stare at me.

"Not here." I slid my hands off the table, trusting Walsh to keep me steady. "Promise you'll walk me home?"

"Anything you need." Walsh pulled me closer to him, letting me lay my head against his shoulder. "I've got you."

"Hands should be used for working." Mr. Jackson cut between the tables, heading straight toward us.

"Sorry, Mr. Jackson." I stepped away from Walsh and brushed my tears from my cheeks.

"We don't have time for petty drama." Mr. Jackson pushed an unclaimed mortar and pestle toward me. "Class is going to be cut short today as it is."

All the students within hearing distance froze.

"Why?" the girl nearest me asked in a voice loud enough to attract the attention of the rest of the class.

Mr. Jackson sighed before addressing the now panicking students. "An announcement has been prepared for all Arcadia Domes residents between the ages of seventeen and twenty. The announcement will be made just before the end of the school day. As you are not in a classroom with a big enough screen for you all to receive the update together, it was decided you would all be sent home early to view the announcement individually."

"What are they doing to us now?" a boy asked.

"Are they canceling Project Progeny?" Tricia looked to me. There was genuine hope in her eyes.

I gave the tiniest shake of my head.

Walsh slid his hand across the table, letting his pinky drape over mine. I wanted to cling to him and beg him to find a way to steal Mari back from Miranda and stop the Incorporation from hurting anyone else.

But Walsh couldn't help me. His mission was too important.

"Back to work, everyone," Mr. Jackson said. "I don't want to have to haul these tables out again tomorrow."

Walsh handed me his mostly ground up root.

He couldn't be my savior, but having him beside me as I worked kept the hollow feeling from coming back.

The Domes Council hadn't stolen my plan from me. Help Walsh. Kill Holbeck. Get my sister back.

I'd wasted so much time searching for a simple, discreet solution. A way to calmly be invited up into Incorporation Headquarters. But the Incorporation didn't deserve calm.

The kep had destroyed my city. I'd lost my mom and Jaime.

The Incorporation owed me at least a few corpses.

Mr. Jackson dismissed our class twenty minutes before the end of the day.

Walsh offered me his arm as we headed for the stairs. Half the group hurried down into the corridor. The other half lingered by the tables, like they were trying to postpone their new doom.

"Should we see if we can grab Mari early?" Walsh asked as we neared Mari's classroom.

"I'm not supposed to pick her up anymore." Pain stabbed at the base of my lungs. "Mari lives with our guardian now. The Domes Council decided she couldn't stay with me."

"What?" Walsh turned to me, taking both my arms like he knew saying it out loud had made the walls start swaying again.

"I'm too young to be expected to take care of a seven-year-old and a baby. So they took Mar." The pain punched into my throat. "What if they're right? What if she's—"

Walsh pulled me into a tight hug as he whispered, "Don't say that. Don't you even fucking think Mari would be better off with anyone but you. No one else would protect her like you do. No one else would fight for her or love her like you do. Do not ever doubt that."

I nodded as I curled into the strength of his embrace.

"We'll fix this." His shoulders shuddered.

I pulled away.

He'd scrunched his eyes shut like pain was shooting from the back of his head.

"You can't help us." I touched his cheek. "Your orders won't let you."

"Yes, they will." Walsh cracked his neck. "I'll find a way."

He took my hand, leading me down the corridor to Bloom Dome.

Dread settled into my stomach as we reached the building where Mari and I lived. Had lived. Our room was just mine now.

"They already took all her things away." I gripped Walsh's arm.

"While you were gone?" He looked to me with a mix of rage and horror in his eyes.

I couldn't manage anything more than a nod.

He kissed my cheek. "We're getting her back." He didn't shudder that time.

"Promise?" The word cracked in my throat.

He slid his hand to the back of my neck, steadying me and making me meet his gaze at the same time. "I swore to you I would help you keep Mari safe. Safe means with you." He rested his forehead against mine. "We're not letting them turn her into another Incorporation demon."

He shoved open the door to my building, keeping me tucked close to his side as we walked down the hall.

I didn't have time to hesitate before going into my room. I could already hear PAM dinging through the door.

My heart stuttered as I stepped inside.

They'd taken Mari's bed away. The space looked empty without it.

"Mandatory message from Incorporation Headquarters beginning in ten seconds," PAM said.

The closet door was open. A giant gap had taken the place of Mari's clothes.

"It's temporary." Walsh herded me to the computer screen just as the images began.

"Project Progeny will ensure genetic prosperity for years to come," Leigh spoke in a soothing tone as the picture of me holding a baby while Gideon looked lovingly at me showed on the screen.

I sank into Walsh's side.

"But the process of pairing should be a joyful experience." The image shifted to Gideon and me standing beside the bed in the Medical Corridor.

"While some prefer the well-regulated environment provided by the domes' medical staff, others may find the experience to be embarrassing or frightening." The picture of Gideon and me holding hands in front of the willow tree appeared. "Beginning immediately, the Incorporation will offer the option for discreet copulation." Gideon and I were kissing by the tree.

"Should both members of the pair agree, coupling may take place outside the medical corridor, where a more traditional intercourse experience is possible." Gideon pulled aside the branches of the willow, presenting me to Walsh.

"Rendezvous locations can be chosen by the pair, where they can couple in privacy, creating an intimate setting for a new life to begin." Walsh was kissing me, clutching me close like his survival depended on our bodies joining together.

"Copulation reports will be filled out by both members of the pair and sent directly, and confidentially, to our medical staff after each session of intercourse." He had my back against the tree. "A mandatory, weekly meeting with a doctor will be scheduled outside of school and work hours to update our medical team on the progress of each pairing." My nails dug into Walsh's bare back. I arched my spine, offering him more of me to explore.

"Details of both discreet and supervised coupling options will be given to each pair as they reach their assigned start date, and the domes' medical staff will help each pair choose the experience that's right for them." I was unbuttoning his pants. "The good of the Incorporation must come first in all things. But the wellbeing of our citizens is never forgotten."

Walsh I and walked hand in hand toward the fountain.

"They were still taking pictures of us?" I pulled away from him. "How long did they follow us?"

The screen faded to black.

"They stopped just after we passed the fountain." Walsh sank down onto my bed.

"Why didn't you tell me?" I rounded on him.

He tapped his ear and gave a sweeping gesture around the room.

"Walk with me." I reached for his hand. "I don't want to be here right now."

"Let's go explore some potential coupling hideouts." Walsh winked at me and led me from the room.

CHAPTER THIRTY-THREE

I made him circle the trees three times while I waited in our little fort hidden in the twisted branches. I had to make sure no one would be able to hear my plan.

I thought he'd refuse, tell me I was taking too many desperate risks. But it didn't even take me long to convince him my idea was our best option. Maybe I imagined it, but for a split second, it almost looked like he was excited.

I left our sanctuary first, sneaking the long way through the trees to cut around to Miranda's house. Two Dome Guard waited out front. They had been ordered not to let me see Mari. They called it an adjustment period. A necessary step in Mari and me starting our separate lives. The kep told me I'd be able to see her again in seven days.

I could hear Mari screaming for me from inside the house.

I pictured the Dome Guard with their throats slashed open, soaking the ground with their kep blood. I wanted it to happen. I would have done it myself if I could. But killing them wasn't part of my plan. I'd have to find other ways to make them suffer.

I shouted to Mari that she would be okay and went back to

my room. I sat where her bed should have been while I typed a message to send to Director Holbeck and Miss Leigh.

I think something might be wrong. I need to speak to one of you. I can't talk to anybody down here.

Please, it's important.

Lanni

I set my tablet down and leaned against the wall. They wouldn't answer me right away. They might not answer me at all. What sort of important person would want to waste their time listening to the worries of a teenage girl?

An hour passed before I finally managed to convince myself to get up and eat something. If they thought I wasn't taking care of myself, I'd have an even harder time getting Mari back.

I tried not to picture Mari crying in her new room. I didn't know if she'd be crying or screaming her rage at Miranda.

I couldn't taste the apple I made myself eat.

It was just before midnight when the siren started.

I let myself enjoy a quick smile before running out of my room.

CHAPTER THIRTY-FOUR

Red lights flashed in Bloom Dome, warning all the kep to flee for safety. I cut through the darkness, running to the quickest path from Miranda's house to the stairs leading down into the corridors.

People bolted through the night. Some crying. Some angry at having been woken up.

I stood beside the path, waiting as they ran by.

"No!" Mari's shout cut over the siren. "Let go of me. I am not going with you!"

I sprinted up the path, heading toward her voice.

"I have to get my sister," Mari screamed. "Lanni! Lanni!"

"I'm here, Mar." I dodged through the pack.

"Lanni!" Mari reached for me. One of the Dome Guard was carrying her. She kicked back, catching him in the knee. "Put me down, or I'll bite you."

"We don't have time for this. Just let me carry her," I said.

The second guard blocked me as I grabbed for Mari.

"It's fine," Miranda said. "I'll stay with them."

"Yes, ma'am." The guard put Mari down.

She vaulted into my arms, clinging to me. "I didn't want to go with them. I tried to fight them, I promise."

"I know, Mar." I carried her down the path, trying to ignore the guards and Miranda walking right on my heels. "I heard you screaming for me. I'm sorry I couldn't get to you."

Mari hiccupped a sob, then pressed her tear-soaked cheek to mine. "I won't let them take me away from you again."

"I need you to trust me, Mar," I said just loudly enough for her to hear me over the siren. "You have to do everything they say for now, but I promise I'm going to get you back."

She tucked her head onto my shoulder as I carried her down the stairs. "Do you really promise?"

"Just be good, and don't fight them."

She nodded but didn't loosen her grip on me as I followed the crowd toward the bunker below seed storage.

We had managed to get down to the bay level before the siren stopped so a voice could speak. "Members of the guard training program, report to the atrium immediately. I repeat, members of the guard training program, report to the atrium immediately."

A wave of triumphant relief eased the ache in my chest.

"Hop down, Mar." I tried to lift her off me.

"No." Mari tightened her hold on me, squeezing her little legs around my stomach until I could barely breathe. "You can't go."

"This is a good thing, Mar." I turned my face away from the Dome Guard, hiding behind my hair as I spoke in her ear. "Go with Miranda." I pried her off me.

"But what if they won't let me see you when you're done?" Mari clung to my hand. "How will I know if you're okay?"

I looked to Miranda.

"You can have a quick check in at my house." Miranda's jaw tensed, like she was convincing herself she had a right to steal my sister. "But the adjustment clock will start again after that."

"Thank you." I kissed Mari on top of the head. "Be good, Mari."

"Be safe, Lanni."

I bopped her nose and ran down the hall, away from the safety all the other kep fled toward.

By the time I'd neared the atrium, I'd joined a new pack. Trainees and guards all running together.

Not enough guards. They should all be running this way.

Fear replaced triumph as I ran up into the atrium. The siren had been silenced and the lights turned brighter than I'd ever seen them.

"Guard Trainees over here." Beck waved us toward him.

Only ten from the program had beaten me to the atrium. Walsh wasn't with them.

"Line up the team heading west," someone shouted from the northern side of the atrium, away from the staircase.

"Line the glass," a different voice ordered.

I glanced toward the glass that overlooked the valley on the eastern side of the atrium. A group of Outer Guard in full gear fanned out toward the edge of the dome.

"Eyes front," Beck said. "We're taking the center path. Anyone but a guard tries to cross that path, you stop them."

"Weapons ready, sir." A guard knelt beside Beck to open a big black case.

"Who are we looking for, sir?" I asked. "What happened?"

"Don't let anyone cross the center line." Beck handed me a gun. "That's all you need to know."

"Yes, sir." I checked the clip in my weapon and hurried down the path, following two of the others.

From the way their shoulders tensed and their heads swiveled as they glanced from one side of the path to the other, it looked like they thought a monster was going to charge out of the trees to devour them.

You're halfway right, kep shits.

I copied their stance, trying to look afraid of what might leap out of the trees.

Leaves rustled to my right.

I raised my weapon as a bit of black came into view.

A Dome Guard looped to the very edge of the path, staring up into the branches before cutting back between the trees.

Come on, Walsh. Get out of there before they find you.

"What the hell is going on?" the boy in front of me asked.

"I don't know," I said. "I'm just glad my sister is in the bunker."

We reached the end of the path, right near the entrance to Incorporation Headquarters.

Captain Tate and Captain Pace stood together, watching a team of doctors and guards prowl between four kep corpses.

I swallowed the laugh that bubbled into my throat.

All four Incorporation Guard who'd been watching the entrance had been killed. The one nearest the door had a knife sticking out of his chest. The next had one poking out of his throat. I couldn't tell how the third one had been killed. The fourth lay right beside the tree line. His head was tilted at an odd angle and his limbs were twisted, like whoever had snapped his neck had tossed him back out of the trees for good measure.

We're the monsters now.

I wished I could have been there to watch the kep fall, but seeing Pace and Tate hovering over the corpses, not knowing who'd killed the precious Incorporation elite, held its own sort of satisfaction.

The boy beside me dodged behind a tree to puke.

"Take slow breaths," I said. "It'll help."

I took the boy's place in our line, claiming a spot closer to the kep corpses.

Pace and Tate both tipped their heads, listening to their earpieces.

Pace raised his wrist to his mouth. "Search again. Search every damn inch of glass in this place. If someone got in here, we need to know how."

Keep moving, Walsh. They think the bogeyman broke in.

I bit the corners of my mouth, making sure I didn't accidentally smile.

"Don't move!" The shout came from the northern side of the path, right ahead of me. "I said don't move!"

I turned that way, holding my breath as I raised my weapon.

The other trainees ran up the path, surging toward the voice.

"I'm a guard, same as you, asshole! Point your weapon at someone else," another voice shouted.

"Sorry, Warren," the first voice said. "False alarm. Keep searching."

"Who are they searching for?"

I spun toward Walsh before he'd even finished speaking.

He had a guard-issued weapon in hand, concern on his face, and not a trace of blood on him.

You're amazing.

"Someone killed four Incorporation Guard," I said instead of throwing myself into his arms and squealing with glee at the chaos he'd caused.

"Damn." Walsh stepped around me to get a better look at the kep he'd killed. "Where's Mari?"

"In the bunker with Miranda."

"At least we know she's safe." He squeezed my shoulder.

The trainees fanned back out along the path.

I kept watching the trees, trying to look like I was afraid that a killer might leap out and attack at any moment.

My feet had started to ache from standing for so long before Beck finally called the trainees to the front of the atrium. Everyone looked somewhere between terrified and confused as we gathered around our fearless leader.

I decided to go with confusion. Terrified took too much effort.

"The atrium has been cleared," Beck said. "They're locking down this area. The Council has ordered a floor-by-floor sweep of the domes. The Dome Guard have already started searching the Council chamber level."

"So, we're done?" I didn't have to fake my confusion anymore. "Are you sending us to the bunker?"

"I did not give you permission to speak." Beck glared at me.

"Sorry, sir." I tipped my chin down and backed away a step.

"By Incorporation order, Dome and Outer Guard will be working together to complete the search as quickly as possible," Beck continued. "We're going down to the growing and learning domes. Pairs of trainees will be stationed outside each dome as it's searched to prevent any suspect from changing locations. Are we clear?"

"Yes, sir," the group spoke together.

There were sixteen of us. Three fewer than there should have been. I didn't know if the three had been in training that morning. Leigh had made sure I'd miss it.

I cut through the group to walk right on Beck's heels as he led us toward the stairs.

"Sir," I said, "I need to send a message. I don't have my tablet. If I could just use a—"

"We don't have time for messages, Roberts." Beck didn't even glance over his shoulder at me.

"Sir, I need to send a message to Miss Leigh from Headquarters," I said. "It's important."

"As important as protecting your fellow citizens?" Beck hurried down the steps to the Council chamber level.

"It's about keeping everyone safe." I spoke in a low voice. "Please, sir."

Beck stopped at the bottom of the stairs, finally turning around to look at me. "If you have any information, it is your duty to give it to your commanding officer. That would be me."

"I can't, sir." I raised my chin and kept my hands plastered to my sides. "I don't have authorization to talk about Project Progeny without permission from Miss Leigh."

Beck chewed his cheeks like he was swallowing all the things he wanted to shout at me. "There's a computer just inside the Salt Dome. Send your message, then get down to the bottom of the stairs. You'll be stationed there. If you happen to get murdered while standing at a computer all on your own with a killer lurking in the domes, that's on Miss Leigh's head."

"Yes, sir." I gave him a kep nod.

Outer Guard were already sweeping the corridor by the time we got down the steps to the growing and learning domes.

Beck left two trainees at the first staircase. Like two students would be able to fight against someone who'd managed to kill four Incorporation Guard and not get caught.

"I'll stay with Roberts, sir." Walsh stepped up beside me as we reached the stairs to the Salt Dome. "I can watch the steps on my own until she gets down."

"Stay alert." Beck looked to me. "If anything happens to Walsh, I hope your message is worth his life."

"It is, sir."

I bolted up the stairs, not letting myself look at Walsh.

Just act scared. There's a murderer on the loose.

And I told him who to kill.

They'd turned the lights all the way up in the Salt Dome. The glow glared off the lines of tanks, stealing the calm that usually filled the space. Two Outer Guard stood on the walkway that led over the aquariums, watching in either direction as more guards prowled through all the tiny passages between the tanks.

I tapped on the computer screen, logging into my messages.

I had told Walsh to target the Incorporation Guard. It was my fault they weren't going to go home to their Incorporation families at the top of the mountain. I'd stolen those guards' chance to sit in the safety outsiders had died to give them, laughing about making the ordinary kep fuck each other and pop out babies.

I tried to find a shred of regret for their deaths. I couldn't feel anything but satisfaction.

Director Holbeck and Miss Leigh,

I think I know what happened. I need to talk to you where they can't hear me. Please. I'm afraid. I think they might try to kill more people. I can't put it in a message.

Send Incorporation Guard to get me.

Lanni

I hit send and headed back toward the stairs.

"I need someone smaller. I can't fit through the gap."

"Alec." I turned toward his voice. He was in the corner of the dome, where piping cut behind the glass of the tanks. "I can do it." I ran toward him.

"Lanni." His face brightened for a moment before turning to stone, like he had put up some kind of barrier between us. "What are you doing here?"

"I was sent to help." I held up my gun. "I'm good with small spaces. I can go back and search."

I peeked into the narrow gap. It would be a tight squeeze, and I'd have to crawl. But I could make it.

"You should leave." Alec stepped in front of me, blocking my path to the gap.

"I can help."

"It's not safe."

"I'll be fine." I touched his arm.

He flinched.

"Alec." I slid my hand down to take his. He didn't curl his fingers around mine. "What's wrong? Did you know one of the Incorporation Guard?"

"No." He pulled his hand from mine and took a step back. "I don't even know their names."

"Then what—"

"I saw the pictures, Lanni." He kept his gaze fixed above my head. "Everyone in the barracks saw every picture in that damn video."

"The pictures with Walsh and Gideon? The ones the Incorporation staged?"

"Beach section clear." The shout carried over the tanks.

"I'm sorry I couldn't warn you." I stepped as close to him as I could without cornering him. "I wanted to, I swear."

"Warning wouldn't have made seeing them much better."

"I'm sorry they made you watch that." I held out my hand, waiting for him to take it. "None of it meant anything. It's all part of the Incorporation's bullshit. I promise, it was just something that had to be done."

"It always is with you." He finally looked at me. "Dating Gideon had to be done. Staying with him had to be done. Letting Walsh touch you like that had to be done."

"I didn't even know he was going to be at the photo shoot until I showed up." I gave up on waiting and grabbed his hand. "I have to keep the Incorporation happy. It didn't mean anything."

"You're right. It's just two bodies giving each other pleasure. Just sex, right?" He finally squeezed my hand.

"I didn't have sex with Walsh."

"Close enough."

"That's not fair." I pulled my hand away from him.

"I volunteered to be moved to group one." Alec stepped aside, clearing my path to the dark gap. "Another guard's wife just found out she's pregnant. He doesn't want her to have to deal with his being paired with someone else while she's in her first trimester. If the trade is accepted, I'll start with my partner next week."

I stumbled back a step. My legs had forgotten how to hold me up. "Alec, please don't do this."

"Why should you care? It's only sex."

Pain pummeled the air out of my lungs.

"Careful crawling back there," he said. "There's a murderer on the loose."

"Don't worry. A whore's daughter is used to scary men." I slid into the gap, keeping my gun pointed into the shadows I knew couldn't hurt me.

"Lanni, I'd never call you that."

"Don't." I stepped farther into the darkness. "Tell me if you hear from Amery. Other than that, fuck the hell off."

I crawled under the pipes and into a tiny niche where I could crumple without kep Alec being able to see me.

CHAPTER THIRTY-FIVE

The sun had started to rise before they declared the growing and learning level clear. The Dome Guard went to sweep the housing domes, and the Outer Guard were ordered down to the medical corridor and vehicle bay level.

They broke the trainees into groups again. I let myself be assigned to stand on the staircase to make sure no one tried to switch levels.

Walsh volunteered to guard the vehicle bay. No one else wanted that job. After all, if the killer wanted to escape, the vehicle bay was the only way out of the domes without breaking through the glass.

I waited until everyone had switched floors before digging into the ankle of my boot to pull out the little black box Walsh had given me. I tucked my weapon into my waistband then pried the box open. The black disk inside was barely larger than the tip of my pinky and so flat I was afraid of cracking it as I peeled it out of the box.

The back of the disk was sticky enough to cling to my skin. I stuck it to the inside of my forearm, just high enough I wasn't in danger of my sleeve slipping and letting it show. I shoved the box into my waistband and pulled my gun back out.

And then, I waited.

I could see up and down the stairs from my position, but there was nothing to look at besides concrete.

I hated it.

It's worth it. Be patient. It'll be worth it.

I wanted to hear Jaime's voice. To let him tell me those Incorporation Guard deserved to die. That I hadn't lost my mind and helping Walsh really was worth a few new corpses. Worth a sea of Incorporation blood.

He would've told me I was right. Saving city scum lives was worth any number of kep deaths. But I couldn't afford the distraction of talking to Jaime.

I paced on the stairs, trying to keep myself awake.

I listened to the sounds of people charging through the corridor on the housing level and wondered what they thought they'd found.

The killer was in the vehicle bay, safe and sound as he helped search for himself.

"Lanni Roberts, report to the atrium. Lanni Roberts, report to the atrium."

I closed my eyes and shook out my hands, banishing any trace of the girl who wanted the Incorporation to burn, then ran up the steps, sprinting like someone who was terrified a killer might be on their heels.

By the time I'd made it to the atrium, fear was easier to fake. My breath had started coming in labored pants, and my calf had cramped up. I embraced the urge to limp as I ran toward the six gray-clad Incorporation Guard who waited by the path to the pond.

"I'm Lanni Roberts." I held up my weapon-free hand as I neared them.

"Drop the weapon," one of the guards said.

All six guards aimed their guns at me.

I let my own gun fall into the grass. "I was asked to come here."

"This way." The same guard spoke again.

"Yes, sir," I said.

I followed three of the guards who headed down the center path. One of the others grabbed my gun before filing in to walk behind me.

I slipped the tiny black box out of my waistband, keeping it hidden in my palm as we neared the pond. I waited until the last moment to veer off the path.

"Miss Roberts, get back in line," the guard with my gun ordered.

"It was right here," I said, like I hadn't heard him.

"Miss Roberts—"

"She just disappeared." I knelt beside the new tree they'd added to replace the one the bomber had killed.

Someone had planted flowers around the trunk. I hoped they weren't a memorial. She didn't deserve a pretty remembrance.

"I can still hear the bang sometimes, you know?" I slipped the black box between the flowers, hiding the evidence beneath the colorful blooms. "I don't want to, it just echoes in my head."

"Miss Roberts, we were ordered to escort you to Incorporation Headquarters. Walk willingly, or you will be forced to move."

I looked up at the guard. "The guards who died tonight, there was no bang when they were killed. What's going to stay stuck in the minds of the people who found their bodies?"

"Move," the guard said.

I stood and brushed my hands off on my pants. "I'm in the guard training program, but I don't think I can become a guard. I'm not built to be okay with murder." I stayed quiet and obediently followed them to the entrance of Incorporation Headquarters.

Someone had taken the corpses away. I wondered if they'd be

sent to the incinerator where they burned normal kep bodies, or if they'd be given some special treatment for being Incorporation butchers.

Ten guards stood in front of the door to Headquarters, all dressed in full riot gear.

They parted, letting our group pass. One of my guards pressed his wrist to a scanner on the side of the door then pressed his palm to the same reader.

Fancy.

The door silently opened, allowing my lowly factory rat self into the Headquarters of the Incorporation.

It didn't look like much at first, just a square room that led to another door.

I pressed my hands to my thighs as the door to the atrium closed.

Trapped. Prisoner. Doomed.

The door in front of us opened, letting us enter another square room, this one with shiny metal walls. I followed the guards in, not understanding the space I had entered until the floor shifted.

I'd heard of elevators before but had never actually been in one. I listened to the faint hum of the machine as we were carried higher up in the mountain than normal kep were ever allowed to go.

One of the guards lifted his wrist to his mouth. "Arrival imminent."

"Are you taking me to see Director Holbeck or Miss Leigh?" I asked.

None of them answered.

"Four of your people were murdered." I pressed my palms to my cheeks, like I was trying to wipe away my tears before they could show. "That's what I need to talk to Director Holbeck about. The search of the Arcadia Domes isn't going to find anything. And I don't think the killer is done yet."

All six guards tensed.

"I'm risking my life to try and save your asses," I said. "Please don't treat me like I'm a stupid kid."

The doors slid open, and I finally understood why Leigh had been so desperate to claw her way up to Incorporation Headquarters.

White marble walls took the place of concrete in the long corridor. Fancy glass and metal light fixtures that had been polished until they sparkled hung from the ceiling. Potted plants stood at regular intervals, with massive paintings positioned in between.

At the end of the hall, a carved archway led out into the Incorporation's version of an atrium.

A waterfall took up the back wall. Stairs and slides had been carved into the rock of the mountain, giving the Incorporation butchers a chance for a thrill on their way into the massive swimming pool at the bottom. The glass of the dome arched more than six stories up, and beside the waterfall, balconies looked out over the whole beautiful paradise.

Faint strains of music filled the air as the guards led me toward an elevator made of glass. Fruit trees lined the path. I watched a woman reach up and pluck a peach from a tree. She bit into the fruit and walked away like she hadn't just done something completely miraculous.

A loathing so strong it made me want to vomit twisted in my gut.

We are the monsters now. We are the monsters now.

The guard didn't even have to use his wristband to get us into the glass elevator. He just touched a button, and the doors slid open.

We got inside, and he pressed another button to take us to the sixth floor, right in the center of the eleven levels the elevator could reach.

I'd always thought of Incorporation Headquarters as a lair

where a dozen hateful people and their evil guards lived at the top of the mountain. But it was a whole city inside the mountaintop just as large as the Arcadia Domes below.

Does the Arcadia Domes Council even know how many Incorporation kep are living in paradise right above their heads?

The Incorporation scum deserved a name worse than kep. Worse than murderer. Butcher. Monster. Destroyer. I couldn't think of a word bad enough to describe demons who had sacrificed civilizations so they could eat fresh peaches as the world crumbled.

I watched the ground get farther away as the elevator rose, but distance didn't make the scene below any better. Flowerbeds had been laid out in a maze-like pattern, giving the killers a pretty place to walk. Children raced around on the grass, playing some sort of game. A man jumped from the top of the waterfall, diving into the pool far below.

I looked away. I couldn't stand watching them enjoy the luxury they'd bought by spilling so much outsider blood.

Near the elevator doors, a computer screen had been set into the wall. I judged the distance from me to the screen.

One stumble, like I was too tired to stand, and I could plant the black disk without any of the guards noticing. I'd made a living stealing syringes from a desperate man. Planting a tiny thing under the noses of smug assholes would be easy.

Not yet. You can find a better place. You have one chance, Lanni Sampson.

I liked hearing my real last name, even if it was only in my head.

The doors slid open on the sixth floor. The guards led me onto a walkway that looked out over the massive atrium.

I kept my gaze fixed on the guards in front of me. Better not to let loathing distract me from my mission.

Walsh's mission.

The difference didn't really matter much in that moment.

We reached a door flanked by two gray-clad guards with golden trees stitched onto their uniforms.

"Fancy," I said.

The gold-marked guards turned their stern gazes toward me.

"They just have badges down below." I shrugged.

"We've brought the girl," one of my guards said, like I was trash they'd been told to scrape up as punishment.

One of the gold-marked guards opened the door, letting us into the fanciest fucking office the apocalypse had to offer.

A plush red and gold carpet covered the marble floor. A crystal chandelier hung from the ceiling, and matching sconces dotted the sidewalls, lighting a collection of paintings and sculptures.

Some of the art seemed familiar, like maybe I'd seen the sad-looking sunflowers in a picture on my tablet.

But I didn't take the time to study the rest of the paintings to see what I might recognize. I was too drawn to the far side of the room.

The back wall was filled with massive computer screens, each marked with the name of one of the sets of domes. Arcadia Domes was the top right. The screen showed a view of the outside of the domes. The sun glinted off the glass set into the mountainside in an almost beautiful way.

I scanned the rows.

The screen marked *River Domes* had a black band running through the middle of the live feed, like some sort of digital tribute to all the kep who'd died there.

I found what I needed to see near the middle. *Plains Domes.* Smoke clouded the image, like the kep had chosen to let the fires around the city burn. I wanted whatever camera was watching the domes to turn so I could get a glimpse of home.

Pain crashed into my gut as I remembered that, even if the buildings were there, fifty-seven percent of my home had been exterminated like vermin.

"Is it a hard thing to see?" Director Holbeck said.

I finally looked toward the massive shining wooden desk in the center of the room where Holbeck sat in a fancy leather chair.

"Seeing your former home from so far away must be shocking," she said.

I backed up a step, ready to try and uselessly run for my life before realizing what she meant.

I fixed my gaze on the screen labeled *Ice Domes*. "Honestly, it feels like a place I've never even been. It looks so different from here."

"You poor thing." Holbeck waved a hand and one of my guards took a chair from beneath a painting of a woman holding a baby and set it in front of Holbeck's desk. "Have a seat."

"Yes, ma'am."

The carpet beneath my boots made the ground seem foreign and unfriendly in a weird way, like the comfort of it had been designed to lure me into submission.

I stayed on my feet as long as I could, walking past my seat and all the way up to the edge of Holbeck's desk.

There was no computer on her desk, just the tablet she always carried. There were seams in the wooden top of her desk, but even if some sort of computer hid beneath the shining surface, there would be no way for me to discreetly plant the disk.

I slunk back, trying to look like I had been too enamored of the majesty of it all, and sank into my seat.

"Your message sounded urgent." Holbeck furrowed her brow.

"I..." I looked to the guards. "Am I safe here?"

"Of course." She gave me a comforting smile that made me wish Walsh had come with me so I could watch her die as she sat at her fancy desk.

"Can you..." I made my voice wobble. "Can you make sure they don't hurt my sister?"

"Who on earth would want to hurt a little girl?" Holbeck said.

You, you sick fuck.

"I think I know who killed the Incorporation Guard. I over-heard some things I shouldn't have, and now they have my sister." I dissolved into noisy tears.

CHAPTER THIRTY-SIX

"Take a breath, and tell me what happened." Holbeck crossed around her desk to sit on the edge right in front of me.

"I heard"—I choked on my tears—"I knew people were mad at me for working with Project Progeny. I was just trying to help and prove that I want the Incorporation to succeed. But the Domes Council decided I couldn't keep my sister with me anymore. They said it would be better if she lived with our guardian."

I took a breath, trying to replace the anger in my tone with fear.

"Yesterday, I went to try and see her at our guardian's, just to say goodnight." I swiped the tears from my cheeks. "They wouldn't let me near her. I could hear her screaming for me from inside the house, and the Dome Guard made me leave without seeing her."

"I'm sorry the Council wants your sister to live with someone else, but that has nothing to do with—"

"It does." I sat up straighter. "I couldn't just walk away and leave Mari like that. So I cut around through the trees and went back to our guardian's house. I just wanted to talk to Mari through the window. Make sure she knew I was okay and hadn't forgotten about her. That she knew how much I'd begged the Council to let me keep her. But, when I got close to the house, I heard the Dome Guard talking."

Holbeck leaned toward me like she was finally interested.

"They were talking about Project Progeny." I shifted forward in my seat. "One said something about how it was nice to finally see the Outer Guard be put in their place. And the other said he was happy because married Dome Guard hadn't been put into the groups. Then he said leaving them out of the pairings was a mistake. The Incorporation shouldn't have let them have so much respect, because now the Dome Guard had their chance. Both of the guards started laughing, and I wanted to sneak away, but I was scared they'd hear me. I finally started to move, but then the laughing went quiet, and my body just froze.

"The first guard said the Incorporation had finally set themselves up to fall, and that he was excited for a chance to see if Incorporation Guard bled normal red. The second guard said something about climbing up to paradise. They started laughing again, and I snuck away. I didn't even get to wave to Mari." I gripped the edge of my chair. "I sent the first message to you when I got home. I thought maybe it was just two guards being dumb. But I wanted to tell you or Miss Leigh instead of Captain Tate, because the guards were watching my sister, and I didn't want her to think I was making things up to get Mari back."

"And then my guards were murdered," Holbeck said.

"But the guards I overheard were watching Mari when your guards died. So if it wasn't them, then there must be more Dome Guard in on it. There are Dome Guard watching my sister right now. If they find out I told you what I heard—" I dissolved into wracking sobs.

"I want a full lockdown of the entrance to Headquarters." Holbeck strode behind her desk. "Pull our guards out of the Arcadia atrium. Get Tate and Pace in the Council room, now."

"No, please don't." I leapt to my feet and lunged toward Holbeck's desk.

One of her guards grabbed my arm.

"Please, you called my name over the system." Pain shot into my shoulder as I tried to twist away from the guard. "They know I've been talking to you. They have my sister in the bunker. What if they hurt Mari?"

"Move all guards out of the vehicle bay and override the locks for the outer doors from here." Holbeck kept talking like I wasn't begging for my sister's life. "I want this problem contained, now."

"I came here to help you!" I shouted. "I'll tell you which guards I heard if you protect my sister."

Holbeck folded her hands on her desk and looked up at me. "Do you really think you're in a position to bargain?"

"No, ma'am. But panicking about Mari's safety might affect my ability to remember who I heard talking." I stomped on the guard's toe then looped my leg behind his, forcing his knee to buckle. I yanked my arm from his grip as the guards along the sides of the room aimed their guns at me. "I heard things when I visited the Outer Guard barracks, too, but it's hard to sort through everything when the sound of Mari screaming for my help keeps banging around in my head."

A smile curved Holbeck's lips, almost like she was proud of me.

"Have Mari Roberts delivered to the Arcadia atrium." Holbeck looked to the guard nearest the door. "Our guards can keep her right inside our door."

"And once I tell you everything?" My voice trembled.

"Then I'll send you down to meet her," Holbeck said. "While you're up here, we'll record a new video for Project Progeny. It seems you're a more useful asset than I'd hoped, Lanni Roberts. I have a new mole living in the Arcadia Domes. I'd hate to waste that by letting everyone know you so willingly came racing to me with information."

"Thank you, Director Holbeck." I used the sleeve of my shirt to wipe the tears from my cheeks.

Holbeck pressed a button on her desk and the wooden top shifted, sliding away as three computer screens rose up.

My fingers itched. I just needed to get close to them. Two seconds to plant the disk, and I'd have paid for Walsh's help in ending Holbeck's reign of terror.

Holbeck tapped on the leftmost screen. "Leigh, bring a team to my office. We're going to be making a special recording with Lanni."

"Yes, Director Holbeck." Leigh's voice came out of the computer.

"Now tell me, Lanni," Holbeck said, "what else do you know?"

"The Outer Guard know you've been confining them to the barracks because the married Outer Guard have been included in Project Progeny. They know you left the married Dome Guard out," I said.

"It couldn't have taken them long to figure that out." Holbeck waved a hand like she was shooing the information away. "You're going to have to do better than that if you want my guards to endanger themselves to protect your sister."

Shit.

The bang of the bomb echoed through my head.

I'd been trying to make everything safer for Mari but was so fucking dumb I'd turned her into a pawn.

Don't panic, Jaime whispered. *Holbeck has no idea who she's up against.*

"Captain"—I let out a long breath—"Captain Pace knows you're listening to him."

"He'd have to be an idiot to think we weren't." Holbeck circled around to perch on the front of her desk again.

"But he seemed worried about it. Like he had to be careful of what he said in his office. And the Outer Guard, the way they looked at me when I was down there, it was more than them being angry that I was helping the Incorporation. It was like they wanted to get me out before I saw something they didn't want me to."

Holbeck kept watching me.

"I want to think I'm wrong, that I'm making it all up in my head. But I thought someone was targeting Dr. Kain's work, and I was right. The bomber in the Arc Domes' atrium almost killed me. And think about all the Outer Guard that were lost at the River Domes. They worked with the Outer Guard that are still in the Arc Domes. Those guards lost so many of their friends and colleagues. If they blame the breeding program like the bomber did..." I let my voice trail away.

"Sorry for the wait, Director." Leigh bustled into Holbeck's office with a camera crew behind her. "What can I help you with?"

"Get Lanni ready. She's going to be recording a statement on behalf of the Incorporation." Holbeck waved the makeup lady toward me.

"Is the statement written out?" Leigh tapped frantically on her tablet. "I can have a prompter brought in."

The makeup lady tsked as she started working on the bags under my eyes from not having slept in more than a day.

"There is no written statement. I want to hear straight from Lanni's heart," Holbeck said.

"I'm sorry, what?" I peeked around the makeup lady to look at Holbeck.

"You have to hold still." The makeup lady grabbed my shoulders, pushing me back into place.

"I want you to tell your peers in your own words why you believe in the importance of Project Progeny," Holbeck said.

"Eyes closed." Makeup lady tipped my chin up.

"But I already read that statement in the atrium with Gideon," I said. "I don't think I can say it any better than that."

"Don't be silly," Holbeck said. "I've witnessed firsthand the love you have for your sister. Mari's under the Incorporation's care right now. Being kept out of harm's way. On my orders."

My eyes flew open as fear jolted my gut.

"Keep your eyes closed." Makeup lady flicked my forehead.

I batted her hand away and stood. "Director Holbeck, I am so grateful to you for taking care of Mari." I rubbed my hands on my arms as though the reality of the cruel world had somehow frozen me from the inside. "Mari is an amazing kid. She's an asset to the Incorporation."

"And you are helping to ensure her future." Holbeck squeezed my shoulder. "I'm sure you'll do wonderfully, Lanni."

"Yes, ma'am." I pulled the little black disk from my arm. "Is the video going to go out to all the domes?" I stepped away from Holbeck, drifting toward the side of her desk as though feeling the pull of the computers set into the back wall, displaying all the places the kep had chosen to comfortably wait as they watched the rest of us die.

"That depends on how well you do," Holbeck said.

"It would be so strange to have people on the other side of the world hear what I think." I kept moving slowly toward the screens. "And if I help those people see the importance of the work we're doing here, I might still be making a tiny bit of difference long after I'm gone."

"That is the hope we all carry," Holbeck said.

I reached out, brushing my fingers across the screen labeled *Ice Domes*.

"I don't think I ever really understood." I turned around, my back mere inches from the wall. "Even after having traveled so far to get here, and living in two different sets of domes, it never really clicked how big the Incorporation is."

I pressed my fingers to the middle of the screen labeled *River Domes*, sticking the tiny disk in place.

"We're the only hint of civilization left in this terrible world." Holbeck came to join me. "Every time I face a difficult decision, I stare at these screens and remind myself that this is all the world has left."

I brushed my fingers against the disk, making sure it had stayed in place, before turning around to stand beside Holbeck.

"Out of billions of people, the lives held in the domes you see on these screens are all that will survive," Holbeck said. "We are the last hope for the human race. Whenever it seems that the sacrifices the Incorporation demands of me are too great, I remember how much depends on our success. Can there be a more important calling?"

"No, ma'am." I tightened my throat as I spoke, like she'd actually made me feel anything other than the urge to stab her in the neck. "I think I know what I want to say."

"Perfect." Holbeck smiled. "Get the cameras ready and put some blush and a clean shirt on the girl."

I ran through what I wanted to say over and over in my head, trying to pick better words, even though I knew it wouldn't come out the way I planned.

When they'd finished primping me, Holbeck had me stand in front of the doors to her office, away from the wall of screens and works of art.

"Whenever you're ready, Lanni," Leigh said. "And if you get stuck, just remember we can do more than one take."

"Thanks." I gave her the best smile I could manage. For some reason, staring into the camera made my hands shake worse than they ever had, even when I'd stabbed someone or been blown up.

"Camera's on," Leigh said in a soothing tone. "Take a breath, Lanni."

I took a big breath.

"And go."

"My name is Lanni, and I am a seventeen-year-old girl who has only seen a tiny portion of our world. Our ruined world. My name is Lanni, and I live on a planet that was destroyed by greed and war, but somehow, I've survived. I am here, and I am breathing.

But millions, no, billions of people weren't so lucky. Me and you, we're alive. But most of our world is nothing but a graveyard.

"We have survived, but our survival does not come without a cost. We have a duty to continue to fight for the world that has been left in our care. We have to fight every day to make sure there will be something left for the ones who come after us. Something better than the mess we've inherited. Making sure there will be a next generation to tell the story of how hard we fought to survive will demand sacrifice. And sometimes, the price this life demands we pay is terrible. More than we think we can face and still stay on our feet.

"But we don't get to say *no*. We were not born to have that privilege. When the impossible is asked of you, don't think the darkness that's swallowing you is all there will ever be. There is hope beyond the horrors we face. We might not live to see the beautiful day we are giving everything we are to create, but we have to have faith that we are fighting for something worthwhile. We're fighting for the human race. My name is Lanni, and I believe humanity is worth saving."

I froze for a moment. Or maybe the whole room froze. I don't really know.

"Is she done?" the camera man whispered.

"Yeah, I'm done." I dipped my chin and stepped all the way back to lean against the door.

"You didn't say anything about Project Progeny or the pairing process." Leigh scrolled on her tablet. "You should have mentioned the new discreet copulation options as well."

"No one cares what I have to say about Project Progeny." I wiped the gloss from my mouth with the back of my hand. "As far as everyone in the Arc Domes is concerned, I'm just a whore who likes to dick hop. You wanted me to say something that would get my peers to go along with the project. I did my best. If they don't want to fight to save the human race, asking them to fuck each other in the woods isn't going to help."

"Lanni," Leigh gasped.

"I don't know how else to convince people! Can I please go?" I looked to Holbeck. "I just want to see my sister and sleep. I'll spy on whoever you want, just let me take Mari home."

Holbeck looked down at her hands.

"If you want me to be more convincing, write me a speech. Or bring Gideon up here, and I'll stand here and smile while he talks. Bring Walsh up here, and I'll lie down on your desk and let him screw me." I stepped toward Holbeck. "You asked me to speak from the heart, and this is all I have. I don't want to be a parent. I don't want to be paired so I can have a baby at seventeen. The thought of bringing a life into this screwed up world is terrifying and makes me feel completely incapable. But doing whatever it takes to make the world better for Mari, that I can manage. I'm sorry if I've disappointed you. I'm just a kid."

"I'm not disappointed, Lanni." Holbeck went to sit behind her desk. "You were actually far more convincing than I'd hoped, even if you did miss all the talking points. The guards will take you down to your sister."

"Thank you, ma'am." Genuine tears pooled in my eyes.

"I would say my guards could escort you home, but under the circumstances, that's a risk I am unwilling to take." Holbeck began working on her computer screens, her face passive, like it was all a normal day for her.

"I understand." I stepped sideways, making room for the guards to open the door. "And I can keep Mari at home with me, Director Holbeck?"

"I will personally ensure that no one in the Arcadia Domes bothers you or Mari," Holbeck said. "It's better if she stays with you. We all need a reminder of exactly what we're protecting."

"Thank you, ma'am." I looked at the screens one final time.

The smoke around the Plains Domes had thickened, stealing the glimmer of the sunlight from the glass. But the solid black stripe through the center of the River Domes screen was perfect, without anything to hint at an empire beginning to crumble.

"Thank you for seeing me, ma'am." I pressed my lips into a careful smile. "I hope I've made a difference by coming here today."

CHAPTER THIRTY-SEVEN

They had Mari waiting for me just inside the door to the Arc Domes' atrium.

She charged me, leapt into my arms, and clung to me, sobbing into my shoulder.

"I'm right here, Mar." I pressed my cheek to her hair, and my insides stopped shaking in fear. "I promised I'd get you back."

"We need to lock this area down." One of the Incorporation shits stepped toward the atrium door.

All the gray-clad guards raised their weapons, aiming for the door, like they were expecting a horde of blood-starved vampires to charge them.

"Are they still searching for the killer?" I settled Mari onto my hip. I couldn't bring myself to let go of her.

"We've received no orders concerning the end of the search." The guard pressed his wrist then his palm to the door scanner.

"Is somebody going to attack us?" Mari whispered in my ear.

"I won't let anybody hurt you," I said.

Mari squirmed her way out of my arms. "I won't let anybody hurt you, either." She stood in front of me as the door slid open, like she was ready to take on every demon Hell had to offer.

Seven Dome Guard waited in the atrium. Four had their weapons pointed toward the open space. Three aimed their guns at Mari and me.

I took Mari's shoulders, shifting her behind my back as we walked toward the kep. "Let's get you home, Mar."

With a swish, the door to Incorporation Headquarters slid shut behind us.

For one, tiny moment, it felt like I'd been abandoned. Dropped into a cage of snakes and had the door locked shut behind me.

At least these kep don't swim in a waterfall.

None of the Dome Guard said anything as I led Mari down the center path and toward the stairs.

Another group of guards blocked the steps.

I clung to Mari's hand, terrified they'd try and rip her away from me.

But they just parted and silently let me pass.

"This feels scary," Mari whispered as we went down the stairs.

"Director Holbeck promised I could keep you with me," I whispered back. "She said she wouldn't let anyone interfere. She probably gave the guards orders not to stop us."

"Well, they don't seem happy about it."

A new group of guards blocked the stairs on every level, their total silence as they let us pass becoming more nerve-racking each time.

"Is everybody else still in the bunkers?" Mari asked the guards stationed at the steps leading up into Bloom Dome.

None of the guards answered.

She stepped right in front of the shortest of the guards and glared up at him. "Are we safe to go home, or do we have to go back to the bunker?"

He looked down at her but said nothing.

She raised her foot like she was going to stomp on him.

"Don't, Mar." I lifted her away from the guard. "If we were

supposed to go back to the bunkers, someone would have yelled at us by now."

"So they're just letting two students go home while there's a murderer on the loose." Mari tried to dart around me. "What did the Incorporation say to you?"

"We'll be okay." I gripped her shoulders, keeping her behind me. "Let's just get home and get some rest."

"I'm scared of the murderer." Mari dissolved into sobs. "What if the person who killed those Incorporation Guard wants to kill you? What if the Dome Guard are sending us home because the murderer is waiting for us in our room?" She crumpled to the floor in a puddle of tears.

"I won't let anybody hurt you." I knelt beside her. I couldn't tell if she was giving a show for the guards or if she was genuinely afraid.

Little girls shouldn't be this good at lying.

"But they killed those Incorporation Guard. And the Incorporation keeps making you take pictures and read their speeches. And they don't let you decide what you want to say. And, and—" Her words became indistinguishable in her sobbing.

"Come on." I hauled Mari off the floor and lifted her onto my hip. "You're exhausted. Let's get you fed and put you to bed."

"But the killer!" Mari wailed.

"This dome has been cleared," the shortest Dome Guard said. "We're making sure it stays that way."

"And the silence from everybody we've passed," I asked. "Is that a security measure, too?"

"Orders from the Incorporation." Another guard shifted position to clearly be looking specifically at Mari. "Guards are not permitted to converse with each other outside of coordinating the search until further notice. Lanni Roberts is a member of the guard training program"

"But how would the Incorporation even know?" I asked.

The guard kept his gaze fixed on Mari as he raised his arm, holding up the black band around his wrist.

"Say thank you to the guards, Mari." I carried her past the guards. "They're doing so much to keep our dome safe."

"Thank you for keeping my sister safe." Mari spoke into my tear-soaked shoulder.

Her ribs stopped shaking with her tears as soon as we'd gotten up the stairs and onto the path home. "Lanni, I'm scared for real," she whispered. "Not just because of the killer. Because of the Incorporation. If they can make the guards be quiet—"

"I know." My arms ached from her weight, but I carried her all the way back to our room.

Her bed was still missing, so after I'd made her eat an apple, I put her to sleep in my bed.

It only took a minute for her to pass out. Once I was sure she'd fallen asleep, I sat on the floor where her bed had been.

I'd sunk beyond the edge of exhaustion. I wanted to curl up beside her and fade into the black that clawed at my brain. But I couldn't get myself to stop watching her.

Miranda wouldn't be pleased I'd gotten Mari back so quickly. Captain Tate and the rest of the Council would be pissed.

She belongs with me. It doesn't matter what the kep think.

Voices came from the hall. Not the sharp tones of guards. The sleepy voices of people who'd been trapped in a bunker for almost a full day.

It took me a moment to realize why their calm return wove panic through the haze of my fatigue.

Walsh.

They don't know. They haven't caught him. If they tried to catch him, he'd have taken a dozen guards out with him and every alarm in this Hell would be going off.

I gripped my hands together, trying to force myself to wake up enough to think.

"Shit." I made myself stand.

A tiny tap came from the window.

I dove for the kitchen drawer, grabbing a knife before I even looked toward the sound.

Walsh stood outside, pressing his palm to the glass. He stepped back, beckoning me toward him.

I watched Mari breathing, making sure she hadn't woken up before going Walsh. He stayed silent as I pushed the window open.

He backed farther away, making room for me to climb outside before beckoning me again.

He didn't have a band on his wrist, and I hadn't been forced to wear one, either. But if Holbeck was listening in through anyone's tablet, I had to believe mine would be at the top of her spying agenda.

I glanced to Mari one more time before climbing through the window. I slid it shut and flipped the lock with my knife.

Walsh took my hand, leading me into the trees.

He didn't take me to the place we'd hidden before. I wondered if he was afraid the guards had found our tiny fort and set up a way to spy on us there.

He didn't stop until we were deep enough into the trees I couldn't see the housing units around us. But there was no willow to sit beneath or low bushes to sneak behind. The place Walsh stopped didn't look like anywhere two people would want to meet.

He pulled me close to him, pressing his forehead to mine. We stayed that way for a while.

The heat of his hands against my back made me want to collapse into a useless ball of fear and exhaustion. I leaned against his shoulder, letting him hold me so tight I couldn't have fallen, even if my legs had given out.

I could trust Walsh that far. He'd hold the broken pieces of me together if I needed a moment to be weak and afraid.

It may sound strange, but the ability to really feel the fear I'd been trying so hard to fight was a relief.

"Is it done?" Walsh whispered in my ear.

Done seemed like too easy a word for the end of a mission hundreds of people had died to protect.

"Yeah." I eased away from him, making myself stand on my own. "It's done."

I'd finished Walsh's mission. Now, as soon as Holbeck was dead, he would leave. I wouldn't have anyone to lean on.

Not Jaime. Not Alec. Not Gideon.

Not Walsh.

"They've locked down the entrance to Incorporation Head-quarters," I said. "But if I can come up with a good enough photo-op, I think I can get Holbeck to come down here."

"I don't have time to wait." Walsh took my hands.

"But you have to. We had a deal. I plant the disk, you take care of Holbeck"

"And I'll keep my end of the bargain if that's still what you want."

"Of course that's what I want." I tried to pull away, but he held on tighter. "That's why I risked my ass going up there."

"Killing Holbeck might not make things any better for you or Mari."

"It's the best plan I have."

"The best plan is for you and Mari to come with me."

I yanked back hard enough he finally let go.

"It's time for me to leave. Either I can kill Holbeck, or I can take you and Mari with me. I can get you out of the domes. You can be free." Walsh reached for my hand. "I'm asking you to trust me, Lanni. Come with me. Please."

I don't know why I took the hand of the monster who'd offered to save me from paradise.

I wish the Incorporation had recorded that moment. They could have watched the decision that changed everything over and over as they tried to figure out how their plan for the perfect apocalypse got so royally fucked.

Lanni's journey concludes in Ash of Ages.

HEART OF SMOKE BOOK FOUR
ASH OF AGES
MEGAN O'RUSSELL

Nola escaped the River Domes.

Read on for a sample of *Girl of Glass*. Entire series available in eBook, paperback, and audiobook.

CHAPTER ONE

Nola dug her fingers into the warm dirt. Around her, the greenhouse smelled of damp earth, mist, and fresh, clean air.

Carefully, she took the tiny seed and placed it at the bottom of the hole her finger had made.

Thump.

Soon the seed would take root. A sprout would break through to the surface.

Thump, bang.

Then the green stem would grow until bean pods sprouted.

Bang, thump!

The food would be harvested and brought to their tables. All of the families would be fed.

"Ahhhhh!" the voice came from the other side of the glass. Nola knew she shouldn't look, but she couldn't ignore the sounds any longer.

It was a woman this time, her skin gray with angry, red patches dotting her face. She slammed her fists into the glass, leaving smears of red behind. The woman didn't seem to care as she banged her bloody hands into the glass over and over.

"Magnolia."

Nola jumped as Mrs. Pearson placed a hand on her shoulder.

"Don't pay her any mind," Mrs. Pearson said. "She can't get through the glass."

"But she's bleeding." Nola pushed the words past the knot in her throat.

The woman bashed her head against the glass.

"She needs help," Nola said. The woman stared right at her.

Mrs. Pearson took Nola's shoulders and turned her back to her plant tray. "That woman is beyond your help, Magnolia. Paying her any attention will only make it worse. There is nothing you can do."

Nola felt eyes staring at her. Not just the woman on the other side of the glass. The rest of the class was staring at her now, too.

Bang. Thump.

Families. The food she planted would feed the families.

Bang.

Pop.

Nola spun back to the glass. Two guards were outside now. One held his gun high. A thin spike protruded from the woman's neck. Her eyelids fluttered for a moment before she slid down the glass, leaving a streak of blood behind her.

"See," Mrs. Pearson said, smoothing Nola's hair, "they'll take her where she can't hurt herself or any of us ever again."

Nola nodded, turning back to the tray of dirt. Make a hole, plant the seed, grow the food. But the streaks of blood were burned into her mind.

The setting sun gave the greenhouse an orange-red gleam when the chime finally sounded.

"Students," Mrs. Pearson called over the sounds of her class packing up for the evening, "remember, tomorrow is Charity Day. Please dress and prepare accordingly. Anyone who doesn't come ready to leave the domes will be sent home, and their grades will be docked."

"Thank you, Mrs. Pearson," the students chorused as they drifted down into the hall.

"Magnolia."

Nola pretended she hadn't heard Mrs. Pearson call her name as she slipped in front of the group leaving the greenhouse. She didn't want to be asked if she was all right or told the sick woman would be cared for. And she didn't want to see if the glass had already been wiped clean.

Lights flickered on, sensing the group heading down the steps. Hooks lined the hallway, awaiting the gardening uniforms. Nola pulled off her rubber boots and unzipped her brown and green jumpsuit, straightening her sweater before shrugging out of the dirt-covered uniform. The rest of the class chatted as they changed—plans for the evening, talk of tomorrow's trip into the city. Nola beat the rest of them to the sink to scrub her hands. The harsh smell of the soap stung her nose, and the steaming water turned her hands red. But in a minute, the only sign of her time in the greenhouses that remained was a bit of dirt on the long brown braid that hung over her shoulder.

"Nola." Jeremy Ridgeway took his place next to Nola at the sinks, shaking the dirt from his light brown hair like a dog. It would have been funny if Nola had been in the mood to laugh. "Are you ready for tomorrow?"

"Sure. It's our duty to help the less fortunate." She sounded like a parrot, repeating what their teachers said every time Charity Day came around. Nola turned to walk away.

Jeremy stopped her, taking her hand.

"Are you okay?" Wrinkles formed on his forehead, and concern filled his deep brown eyes.

"Of course." Nola forced herself to smile.

"Do you want to come over tonight?" Jeremy asked, still holding her hand. "I mean"—his cheeks flushed—"my sister and my dad are off-duty tonight, and she hasn't seen you in a while."

"I've got to get home. My mom leaves tomorrow. But tell your dad and Gentry I said hi." Nola pulled her hand away and half-ran down the hall. More lights flickered on as she sped down the corridor. She made herself breathe, fighting her guilt at running away from Jeremy. She liked being in the greenhouses better than the tunnels that dug down into the earth. There might only be a few feet of dirt on top of her, but knowing it was there pressed an impossible weight on her lungs.

The hum of the air-filtration system calmly buzzed overhead. The solar panels aboveground generated power so she could breathe down here. She pictured the schematics in her head. Lots of vents. Great big vents. The air would be filtered, cleaned and purified, and the big vents would bring oxygen down to her.

Blue paint on the wall read *Bright Dome* above an arrow pointing to a corridor on the left. Nola ran faster, knowing soon she would be aboveground. In a minute she was sprinting up the steps. She took a deep, gulping breath. The air in the tunnels might be the same as the air in the domes, but it felt so different.

The sun had set, leaving only the bright lights of the city across the river and the faint twinkle of the other domes to peer through the glass. Nola squinted at the far side of Bright Dome. The other homestead domes glowed gently, but if she tried, she could almost make out a few stars. At least that's what she told herself. It might only have been wishful thinking.

Tall trees reached almost to the roof of Bright Dome. Grass and wildflowers coated the ground around the stone footpaths that led from house to house. Nola followed the path through the buildings to the far side of the dome. Twelve families shared Bright Dome, each of them lucky enough to have been granted independent housing units.

The trees in the dome hung heavy with crisp, green leaves. The flowers had begun to close their petals for the night. A squirrel darted past Nola's feet.

"A little late getting home, buddy." Nola's pulse slowed with each step closer to home.

The birds were all flying back to their nests. Bright Dome had been assigned robins and blue jays this cycle. The birds and the squirrels shared their home to be kept safe from contamination. The domes provided them all protection from the toxic air and tainted water.

The lights were on in Nola's house as she swung open the door.

"Hey, Mom," Nola called.

"Mmmhmm." The sound came from her mother's office in the back of the kitchen.

"How was your day?" Nola pulled the pot of steaming vegetables from the stove, knowing they would be overdone without having to lift the lid.

"Fine," her mother said, running her fingers through her shoulder-length, chestnut hair, which had been graying quickly of late. "We've been running samples in the lab all day."

"You'll figure it out." Nola didn't ask what the problem in the lab was. Her mother, Lenora Kent, was one of the heads of the botanical preservation group. It was their job to decide what plants from the outside needed to be preserved and how to take care of those plants once they were safely inside the domes. Whatever her mother was working on was for the good of them all. Beyond that it was all vague answers about classified projects.

Nola pulled bowls down from the cabinet, dishing out steamed beans and broccoli, adding spices to make the food taste like something real.

Nola pushed the bowl in front of her mother. Only when she put the spoon in Lenora's hand did her mother seem to notice Nola was still in the room.

"How was your day, sweetie?" Lenora looked up at her daughter.

Nola's mind flashed to the woman. Pounding on the glass, shattering the serenity of the greenhouse.

"It was fine." Nola smiled. "Don't forget to pack for the conference. It'll be colder at Green Leaf, so pack your sweaters."

"Of course." Lenora nodded, but she was already looking back at the charts on her computer screen.

Nola carried her dinner up the narrow stairs to the second floor. She crept into her mother's room and found the duffel bag under her bed. Nola pulled clothes out of the tiny closet. They were lucky. The residents of the domes hadn't been forced into uniforms outside of work and school. Yet. That would come when there was no one left on the outside to work in manufacturing.

When she had counted out enough blouses and slacks for her mother's week-long trip, Nola moved the suitcase to the head of the bed, where her mother would have to see it if she went to sleep that night. A picture in a carved wood frame sat on the nightstand. Six faces beamed out of the photo. A ten-year-old version of herself sat in a tree above her mother and father. Kieran sat on the branch next to her, and below him were his parents.

Nola touched her father's face, wishing the photo was larger so she could properly see his bright blue eyes that had matched her own. But her father was dead, killed in the same riot as Kieran's mother. And now Kieran and his father had been banished from the domes. The photo blurred as tears pooled in Nola's eyes.

She slid the picture into the top of her mother's bag. Lenora would need a bit of home during the Green Leaf Conference—even if their family had broken.

Nola snuck across the tiny landing at the top of the stairs and into her room. She climbed straight into bed, leaving her dinner forgotten on her desk. She pushed her face into her pillow, hoping sleep would come before the face of the woman desperate to get through the glass.

Order Girl of Glass *to continue the story.*

ESCAPE INTO ADVENTURE

Thank you for reading *Eye of Stone*. If you enjoyed the book, please consider leaving a review to help other readers find Lanni's story.

As always, thanks for reading,

Megan O'Russell

Never miss a moment of the danger or romance.

Join the Megan O'Russell mailing list to stay up to date on all the action by visiting https://www.meganorussell.com/book-signup.

ABOUT THE AUTHOR

Megan O'Russell is the author of several Young Adult series that invite readers to escape into worlds of adventure. From *Girl of Glass*, which blends dystopian darkness with the heart-pounding danger of vampires, to *Ena of Ilbrea*, which draws readers into an epic world of magic and assassins.

With the *Girl of Glass* series, *The Tethering* series, *The Chronicles of Maggie Trent*, *The Tale of Bryant Adams*, the *Ena of Ilbrea* series, and several more projects planned, there are always exciting new books on the horizon. To be the first to hear about new releases, free short stories, and giveaways, sign up for Megan's newsletter by visiting the following:

https://www.meganorussell.com/book-signup.

Originally from Upstate New York, Megan is a professional musical theatre performer whose work has taken her across North America. Her chronic wanderlust has led her from Alaska to Thailand and many places in between. Wanting to travel has fostered Megan's love of books that allow her to visit countless new worlds from her favorite reading nook. Megan is also a lyricist and playwright. Information on her theatrical works can be found at RussellCompositions.com.

She would be thrilled to chat with you on Facebook or Twitter

@MeganORussell, elated if you'd visit her website MeganORussell.com, and over the moon if you'd like the pictures of her adventures on Instagram @ORussellMegan.

ALSO BY MEGAN O'RUSSELL

The Girl of Glass Series

Girl of Glass

Boy of Blood

Night of Never

Son of Sun

The Tale of Bryant Adams

How I Magically Messed Up My Life in Four Freakin' Days

Seven Things Not to Do When Everyone's Trying to Kill You

Three Simple Steps to Wizarding Domination

Five Spellbinding Laws of International Larceny

The Tethering Series

The Tethering

The Siren's Realm

The Dragon Unbound

The Blood Heir

The Chronicles of Maggie Trent

The Girl Without Magic

The Girl Locked With Gold

The Girl Cloaked in Shadow

Ena of Ilbrea

Wrath and Wing

Ember and Stone

Mountain and Ash

Ice and Sky

Feather and Flame

.

Guilds of Ilbrea

Inker and Crown

Myth and Storm

Viper and Steel

The Heart of Smoke Series

Heart of Smoke

Soul of Glass

Eye of Stone

Ash of Ages